I0674992

CAST
ADRIFT

T. S. ARTHUR

1st WORLD
LIBRARY
Literary Society

Cast Adrift

T. S. Arthur

© 1st World Library, 2009
PO Box 2211
Fairfield, IA 52556
www.1stworldlibrary.com
First Edition

LCCN: 2009923500

Softcover ISBN: 978-1-4218-8886-6
Hardcover ISBN: 978-1-4218-8985-6
eBook ISBN: 978-1-4218-8787-6

Purchase *"Cast Adrift"*
as a traditional bound book at:
www.1stWorldLibrary.com/purchase.asp?ISBN=978-1-4218-8886-6

1st World Library is a literary, educational organization
dedicated to:

- Creating a free internet library of downloadable ebooks

- Hosting writing competitions and offering book publishing
scholarships.

Interested in more 1st World Library books? contact:
literacy@1stworldlibrary.com
Check us out at: www.1stworldlibrary.com

1st World Library Literary Society

Giving Back to the World

"If you want to work on the core problem, it's early school literacy."

- James Barksdale, former CEO of Netscape

"No skill is more crucial to the future of a child, or to a democratic and prosperous society, than literacy."

- Los Angeles Times

"Literacy... means far more than learning how to read and write... The aim is to transmit... knowledge and promote social participation."

- UNESCO

"Literacy is not a luxury, it is a right and a responsibility. If our world is to meet the challenges of the twenty-first century we must harness the energy and creativity of all our citizens."

- President Bill Clinton

"Parents should be encouraged to read to their children, and teachers should be equipped with all available techniques for teaching literacy, so the varying needs and capacities of individual kids can be taken into account."

- Hugh Mackay

TO THE READER

IN this romance of real life, in which the truth is stranger than the fiction, I have lifted only in part the veil that hides the victims of intemperance and other terrible vices—after they have fallen to the lower deeps of degradation to be found in our large cities, where the vile and degraded herd together more like wild beasts than men and women—and told the story of sorrow, suffering, crime and debasement as they really exist in Christian America with all the earnestness and power that in me lies.

Strange and sad and terrible as are some of the scenes from which I hare drawn this veil, I have not told the half of what exists. My book, apart from the thread of fiction that runs through its pages, is but a series of photographs from real life, and is less a work of the imagination than a record of facts.

If it stirs the hearts of American readers profoundly, and so awakens the people to a sense of their duty; if it helps to inaugurate more earnest and radical modes of reform for a state of society of which a distinguished author has said, "There is not a country throughout the earth on which it would not bring a curse; there is no religion upon the earth that it would not deny; there is no people upon the earth it would not put to shame;"—then will not my work be in vain.

Sitting in our comfortable homes with well-fed, well-clothed and happy-hearted children about us—children who have our tenderest care, whose cry of pain from a pin-prick or a fall on the carpeted floor hurts us like a blow—how few of us know or care anything about the homes in which some other children dwell, or of the hard and cruel battle for life they are doomed to fight from the very beginning!

To get out from these comfortable homes and from the midst of tenderly cared-for little ones, and stand face to face with squalor and hunger, with suffering, debasement and crime, to look upon the starved faces of children and hear their helpless cries, is what scarcely one in a thousand will do. It is too much for our sensibilities. And so we stand aloof, and the sorrow, and suffering, the debasement, the wrong and the crime, go on, and because we heed it not we vainly imagine that no responsibility lies at our door; and yet there is no man or woman who is not, according to the measure of his or her influence, responsible for the human debasement and suffering I have portrayed.

The task I set for myself has not been a pleasant one. It has hurt my sensibilities and sickened my heart many times as I stood face to face with the sad and awful degradation that exists in certain regions of our larger cities; and now that my work is done, I take a deep breath of relief. The result is in your hands, good citizen, Christian reader, earnest philanthropist! If it stirs your heart in the reading as it stirred mine in the writing, it will not die fruitless.

THE AUTHOR.

CONTENTS

Edith's slow return to intelligence—"There's something I can't understand, mother"—"Where is my baby?"—"What of George?"—No longer a child, but a broken hearted woman—The divorce

CHAPTER IV

Sympathy between father and daughter—Interest in public charities—A dreadful sight—A sick babe in the arms of a half-drunken woman—"Is there no law to meet such cases?"—"The poor baby has no vote!"—Edith seeks for the grave of her child, but cannot find it—She questions her mother, who baffles her curiosity—Mrs. Bray's visit—Interview between Mrs. Dinneford and Mrs. Bray—"The baby isn't living?"—"Yes; I saw it day before yesterday in the arms of a beggar-woman"—Edith's suspicions aroused—Determined to discover the fate of her child—Visits the doctor—"Your baby is in heaven"—"Would to God it were so, for I saw a baby in hell not long ago!"

CHAPTER V

Mrs. Dinneford visits Mrs. Bray—"The woman to whom you gave that baby was here yesterday"—The woman must be put out of the way—Exit Mrs. Dinneford, enter Pinky Swett—"You know your fate—New Orleans and the yellow fever"—"All I want of you is to keep track of the baby"—Division of the spoils—Lucky dreams—Consultation of the dream-book for lucky figures—Sam McFaddon and his backer, who "drives in the Park and wears a two thousand dollar diamond pin"—The fate of a baby begged with—The baby must not die—The lottery-policies

CHAPTER VI

Rottenness at the heart of a great city—Pinky Swett's attempted rescue of a child from cruel beating—The fight—Pinky's arrest—Appearance of the "queen"—Pinky's release at her command—The queen's home—The screams of children being beaten—The rescue of "Flanagan's Nell"—Death the great rescuer—"They don't look after things in here as they do outside—Everybody's got the screws on, and things must break sometimes, but it isn't called murder— The coroner understands it all"

Pinky Swett at the mercy of the crowd in the street—Taken to the nearest station-house—Mrs. Dinneford visits Mrs. Bray again—Fresh alarms—"She's got you in her power"— "Money is of no account"—The knock at the door—Mrs. Dinneford in hiding—The visitor gone—Mrs. Bray reports the woman insatiable in her demands—Must have two hundred dollars by sundown—No way of escape except through police interference—"People who deal with the devil generally have the devil to pay"—Suspicion—A mistake—Sound of feet upon the stairs—Mrs. Dinneford again in hiding—Enter Pinky Swett—Pinky disposed of— Mrs. Dinneford again released—Mrs. Bray's strategy—"Let us be friends still, Mrs. Bray"—Mrs. Dinneford's deprecation and humiliation—Mrs. Bray's triumph

Mrs. Bray receives a package containing two hundred dollars—"Poor baby! I must see better to its comfort"— Pinky meets a young girl from the country—The "Ladies' Restaurant"—Fried oysters and sangaree—The "bindery" girl—"My head feels strangely"—Through the back alley— The ten-cent lodging house—Robbery—A second robbery—A veil drawn—A wild prolonged cry of a woman—The policeman listens only for a moment, and then passes on—Foul play—"In all our large cities are savages more cruel and brutal in their instincts than the Comanches"—Who is responsible?

Valuation of the spoils—The receiver—The "policy-shop" and its customers—A victim of the lottery mania

the Briar street mission for assistance in her attempt—Mr. Paulding persuades her that it is best not to see the child, and promises that he himself will look after it—Returns home—Her father remonstrates with her, finally promises to help her

Mr. Dinneford sets out for the mission-house—An incident on the way—Encounters Mr. Paulding—Mr. Paulding makes his report—"The vicious mark their offspring with unmistakable signs of moral depravity; this baby has signs of a better origin"—A profitable conversation—"I think you had better act promptly"

Mr. Dinneford with a policeman goes in quest of the baby—The baby is gone—Inquiries—Mr. Dinneford resolves to persevere—Cause of the baby's disappearance—Pinky Swett's curiosity—Change of baby's nurse—Baby's improved condition—Baby's first experience of motherly tenderness—Baby's first smile—"Such beautiful eyes"—Pinky Swett visits the St. John mission-school— Edith is not there

Mr. Dinneford's return, and Edith's disappointment—"It is somebody's baby, and it may be mine"—An unsuspected listener—Mrs. Dinneford acts promptly—Conference between Mrs. Dinneford and Mrs. Hoyt, *alias* Bray—The child must be got out of the way—"If it will not starve, it must drown"—Mrs. Dinneford sees an acquaintance as she leaves Mrs. Hoyt's, and endeavors to escape his observation—A new danger and disgrace awaiting her

hurt the good" The malignant ulcer in the body politic of our city—The breeding-places of epidemics and malignant diseases—Little Italian street musicians—The existence of slavery in our midst—Facts in regard to it

Edith's continued interest in the children of the poor—Christmas dinner at the mission-house—Edith perceives Andy, and feels a strange attraction toward him—Andy's disappearance after dinner—Pinky Swett has been seen dragging him away—Lost sight of

Christmas dinner at Mr. Dinneford's—The dropped letter—It is missed—A scene of wild excitement—Mrs. Dinneford's sudden death—Edith reads the letter—A revelation—"Innocent!"—Edith is called to her mother—"Dead, and better so!"—Granger's innocence established—An agony of affection—No longer Granger's wife

Edith's sickness—Meeting of Mrs. Bray and Pinky Swett—A trial of sharpness, in which neither gains the advantage—Mr. Dinneford receives a call from a lady—The lady, who is Mrs. Bray, offers information—Mr. Dinneford surprises her into admitting an important fact—Mrs. Bray offers to produce the child for a price—Mr. Dinneford consents to pay the price on certain stipulations—Mrs. Bray departs, promising to come again

Granger's pardon procured—How he receives his pardon—Mrs. Bray tries to trace Pinky home—Loses sight of her in the street—Mrs. Bray interviews a shop-woman—Pinky's destination—The child is gone

CHAPTER I

A BABY had come, but he was not welcome. Could anything be sadder?

The young mother lay with her white face to the wall, still as death. A woman opened the chamber door noiselessly and came in, the faint rustle of her garments disturbing the quiet air.

A quick, eager turning of the head, a look half anxious, half fearful, and then the almost breathless question,

"Where is my baby?"

"Never mind about the baby," was answered, almost coldly; "he's well enough. I'm more concerned about you."

"Have you sent word to George?"

"George can't see you. I've said that before."

"Oh, mother! I must see my husband."

"Husband!" The tone of bitter contempt with which the word was uttered struck the daughter like a blow. She had partly risen in her excitement, but now fell back with a low moan, shutting her eyes and turning her face away. Even as she did so, a young man stepped back from the door of the elegant house in which she lay with a baffled, disappointed air. He looked pale and wretched.

"Edith!" Two hours afterward the doctor stood over the young mother, and called her name. She did not move nor reply. He laid his hand on her cheek, and almost started, then bent down and looked at her intently for a moment or two. She had fever. A serious expression came into his face, and there was cause.

The sweet rest and heavenly joy of maternity had been denied to his young patient. The new-born babe had not been suffered to lie even for one blissful moment on her bosom. Hard-hearted family pride and cruel worldliness had robbed her of the delight with which God ever seeks to dower young motherhood, and now the overtaxed body and brain had given way.

For many weeks the frail young creature struggled with delirium—struggled and overcame.

"Where is my baby?"

The first thought of returning consciousness was of her baby.

A woman who sat in a distant part of the chamber started up and crossed to the bed. She was past middle life, of medium stature, with small, clearly cut features and cold blue eyes. Her mouth was full, but very firm. Self-poise was visible even in her surprised movements. She bent over the bed and looked into Edith's wistful eyes.

"Where is my baby, mother?" Mrs. Dinneford put her fingers lightly on Edith's lips.

T. S. Arthur

"You must be very quiet," she said, in a low, even voice. "The doctor forbids all excitement. You have been extremely ill."

"Can't I see my baby, mother? It won't hurt me to see my baby."

"Not now. The doctor—"

Edith half arose in bed, a look of doubt and fear coming into her face.

"I want my baby, mother," she said, interrupting her.

A hard, resolute expression came into the cold blue eyes of Mrs. Dinneford. She put her hand firmly against Edith and pressed her back upon the pillow.

"You have been very ill for nearly two months," she said, softening her voice. "No one thought you could live. Thank God! the crisis is over, but not the danger."

"Two months! Oh, mother!"

The slight flush that had come into Edith's wan face faded out, and the pallor it had hidden for a few moments became deeper. She shut her eyes and lay very still, but it was plain from the expression of her face that thought was busy.

"Not two whole months, mother?" she said, at length, in doubtful tones. "Oh no! it cannot be."

"It is just as I have said, Edith; and now, my dear child, as you value your life, keep quiet; all excitement is dangerous."

But repression was impossible. To Edith's consciousness

there was no lapse of time. It seemed scarcely an hour since the birth of her baby and its removal from her sight. The inflowing tide of mother-love, the pressure and yearning sweetness of which she had begun to feel when she first called for the baby they had not permitted to rest, even for an instant, on her bosom, was now flooding her heart. Two months! If that were so, what of the baby? To be submissive was impossible.

Starting up half wildly, a vague terror in her face, she cried, piteously,

"Oh, mother, bring me my baby. I shall die if you do not!"

"Your baby is in heaven," said Mrs. Dinneford, softening her voice to a tone of tender regret.

Edith caught her breath, grew very white, and then, with a low, wailing cry that sent a shiver through Mrs. Dinneford's heart, fell back, to all appearance dead.

The mother did not call for help, but sat by the bedside of her daughter, and waited for the issue of this new struggle between life and death. There was no visible excitement, but her mouth was closely set and her cold blue eyes fixed in a kind of vacant stare.

Edith was Mrs. Dinneford's only child, and she had loved her with the strong, selfish love of a worldly and ambitious woman. In her own marriage she had not consulted her heart. Mr. Dinneford's social position and wealth were to her far more than his personal endowments. She would have rejected him without a quicker pulse-beat if these had been all he had to offer. He was disappointed, she was not. Strong, self-asserting, yet politic, Mrs Dinneford managed her good husband about as she pleased in all external matters, and left

T. S. Arthur

him to the free enjoyment of his personal tastes, preferences and friendships. The house they lived in, the furniture it contained, the style and equipage assumed by the family, were all of her choice, Mr. Dinneford giving merely a half-constrained or half-indifferent consent. He had learned, by painful and sometimes. humiliating experience, that any contest with Mrs. Helen Dinneford upon which he might enter was sure to end in his defeat.

He was a man of fine moral and intellectual qualities. His wealth gave him leisure, and his tastes, feelings and habits of thought drew him into the society of some of the best men in the city where he lived—best in the true meaning of that word. In all enlightened social reform movements you would be sure of finding Mr. Howard Dinneford. He was an active and efficient member in many boards of public charity, and highly esteemed in them all for his enlightened philanthropy and sound judgment. Everywhere but at home he was strong and influential; there he was weak, submissive and of little account. He had long ago accepted the situation, making a virtue of necessity. A different man—one of stronger will and a more imperious spirit—would have held his own, even though it wrought bitterness and sorrow. But Mr. Dinneford's aversion to strife, and gentleness toward every one, held him away from conflict, and so his home was at least tranquil.

Mrs. Dinneford had her own way, and so long as her husband made no strong opposition to that way all was peaceful.

For Edith, their only child, who was more like her father than her mother, Mr. Dinneford had the tenderest regard. The well-springs of love, choked up so soon after his marriage, were opened freely toward his daughter, and he lived in her a new, sweet and satisfying life. The mother was often jealous of her husband's demonstrative tenderness for Edith. A yearning instinct of womanhood, long repressed by worldliness and a mean social ambition, made her crave at times the love she had cast away, and then her cup of life was very bitter. But fear of Mr. Dinneford's influence over Edith was stronger than any jealousy of his love. She had high views for her daughter. In her own marriage she had set aside all considerations but those of social rank. She had made it a stepping-stone to a higher place in society than the one to which she was born. Still, above them stood many millionnaire families, living in palace-homes, and through her daughter she meant to rise into one of them. It mattered not for the personal quality of the scion of the house; he might be as coarse and common as his father before him, or weak, mean, selfish, and debased by sensual indulgence. This was of little account. To lift Edith to the higher social level was the all in all of Mrs. Dinneford's ambition.

But Mr. Dinneford taught Edith a nobler life-lesson than this, gave her better views of wedlock, pictured for her loving heart the bliss of a true marriage, sighing often as he did so, but unconsciously, at the lost fruition of his own sweet hopes. He was careful to do this only when alone with Edith, guarding his speech when Mrs. Dinneford was present. He had faith in true principles, and with these he sought to guard her life. He knew that she would be pushed forward into society, and knew but too well that one so pure and lovely in mind as well as person would become a centre of attraction, and that he, standing on the outside as it were, would have no power to save her from the saddest of all fates if she were passive and her mother resolute. Her safety must lie in herself.

Edith was brought out early. Mrs. Dinneford could not wait. At seventeen she was thrust into society, set up for sale to the highest bidder, her condition nearer that of a Circassian than a Christian maiden, with her mother as slave-dealer.

So it was and so, it is. You may see the thing every day. But it did not come out according to Mrs. Dinneford's programme. There was a highest bidder; but when he came for his slave, she was not to be found.

Well, the story is trite and brief—the old sad story. Among her suitors was a young man named Granger, and to him Edith gave her heart. But the mother rejected him with anger and scorn. He was not rich, though belonging to a family of high character, and so fell far below her requirements. Under a pressure that almost drove the girl to despair, she gave her consent to a marriage that looked more terrible than death. A month before the time fixed for, its consummation, she barred the contract by a secret union with Granger.

Edith knew her mother's character too well to hope for any reconciliation, so far as Mr. Granger was concerned. Coming in as he had done between her and the consummation of her highest ambition, she could never feel toward him anything but the most bitter hatred; and so, after remaining at home for about a week after her secret marriage, she wrote this brief letter to her mother and went away:

"My DEAR MOTHER: I do not love Spencer Wray, and would rather die than marry him, and so I have made the marriage to which my heart has never consented, an impossibility. You have left me no other alternative but this. I am the wife of George Granger, and go to cast my lot with his.

"Your loving daughter,

"EDITH."

To her father she wrote:

"My DEAR, DEAR FATHER: If I bring sorrow to your

good and loving heart by what I have done, I know that it will be tempered with joy at my escape from a union with one from whom my soul has ever turned with irrepressible dislike. Oh, my father, you can understand, if mother cannot, into what a desperate strait I have been brought. I am a deer hunted to the edge of a dizzy chasm, and I leap for life over the dark abyss, praying for strength to reach the farther edge. If I fail in the wild effort, I can only meet destruction; and I would rather be bruised to death on the jagged rocks than trust myself to the hounds and hunters. I write passionately —you will hardly recognize your quiet child; but the repressed instincts of my nature are strong, and peril and despair have broken their bonds. I did not consult you about the step I have taken, because I dared not trust you with my secret. You would have tried to hold me back from the perilous leap, fondly hoping for some other way of escape. I had resolved on putting an impassable gulf between me and danger, if I died in the attempt. I have taken the leap, and may God care for me!

"I have laid up in my heart of hearts, dearest of fathers, the precious life-truths that so often fell from your lips. Not a word that you ever said about the sacredness of marriage has been forgotten. I believe with you that it is a little less than crime to marry when no love exists—that she who does so, sells her heart's birthright for some mess of pottage, sinks down from the pure level of noble womanhood, and traffics away her person, is henceforth meaner in quality if not really vile.

"And so, my father, to save myself from such a depth of degradation and misery, I take my destiny into my own hands. I have grown very strong in my convictions and purposes in the last four weeks. My sight has become suddenly clear. I am older by many years.

"As for George Granger, all I can now say is that I love him, and believe him to be worthy of my love. I am willing to trust him, and am ready to share his lot, however humble.

"Still hold me in your heart, my precious father, as I hold you in mine.

"EDITH."

Mr. Dinneford read this letter twice. It took him some time, his eyes were so full of tears. In view of her approaching marriage with Spencer Wray, his heart had felt very heavy. It was something lighter now. Young Granger was not the man he would have chosen for Edith, but he liked him far better than he did the other, and felt that his child was safe now.

He went to his wife's room, and found her with Edith's letter crushed in her hand. She was sitting motionless, her face pale and rigid, her eyes fixed and stony and her lips tight against her teeth. She did not seem to notice his presence until he put his hand upon her, which he did without speaking. At this she started up and looked at him with a kind of fierce intentness.

"Are you a party to this frightful things?" she demanded.

Mr. Dinneford weakly handed her the letter he had received from Edith. She read it through in half the time it had taken his tear-dimmed eyes to make out the touching sentences. After she had done so, she stood for a few moments as if surprised or baffled. Then she sat down, dropping her head, and remained for a long time without speaking.

"The bitter fruit, Mr. Dinneford," she said, at last, in a voice so strange and hard that it seemed to his ears as if another had spoken. All passion had died out of it.

He waited, but she added nothing more. After a long silence she waved her hand slightly, and without looking at her husband, said,

"I would rather be alone."

Mr. Dinneford took Edith's letter from the floor, where it had dropped from his wife's hand, and withdrew from her presence. She arose quickly as he did so, crossed the room and silently turned the key, locking herself in. Then her manner changed; she moved about the room in a half-aimless, half-conscious way, as though some purpose was beginning to take shape in her mind. Her motions had an easy, cat-like grace, in contrast with their immobility a little while before. Gradually her step became quicker, while ripples of feeling began to pass over her face, which was fast losing its pallor. Gleams of light began shooting from her eyes, that were so dull and stony when her husband found her with Edith's letter crushed in her grasp. Her hands opened and shut upon themselves nervously. This went on, the excitement of her forming purpose, whatever it was, steadily increasing, until she swept about the room like a fury, talking to herself and gesticulating as one half insane from the impelling force of an evil passion.

"Baffled, but not defeated." The excitement had died out. She spoke these words aloud, and with a bitter satisfaction in her voice, then sat down, resting her face in her hands, and remaining for a long time in deep thought.

When she met her husband, an hour afterward, there was a veil over her face, and he tried in vain to look beneath it. She was greatly changed; her countenance had a new expression —something he had never seen there before. For years she had been growing away from him; now she seemed like one removed to a great distance—to have become almost stranger. He felt half afraid of her. She did not speak of Edith, but remained cold, silent and absorbed.

Mrs. Dinneford gave no sign of what was in her heart for many weeks. The feeling of distance and strangeness perceived by her husband went on increasing, until a vague feeling of mystery and fear began to oppress him. Several times he had spoken of Edith, but his wife made no response, nor could he read in her veiled face the secret purposes she was hiding from him.

No wonder that Mr. Dinneford was greatly surprised and overjoyed, on coming home one day, to meet his daughter, to feel her arms about his neck, and to hold her tearful face on his bosom.

"And I'm not going away again, father dear," she said as she kissed him fondly. "Mother has sent for me, and George is to come. Oh, we shall be so happy, so happy!"

And father and daughter cried together, like two happy children, in very excess of gladness. They had met alone, but Mrs. Dinneford came in, her presence falling on them like a cold shadow.

"Two great babies," she said, a covert sneer in her chilling voice.

The joy went slowly out of their faces, though not out of their hearts. There it nestled, and warmed the renewing blood. But a vague, questioning fear began to creep in, a sense of insecurity, a dread of hidden danger. The daughter did not fully trust her mother, nor the husband his wife.

CHAPTER II

THE reception of young Granger was as cordial as Mrs. Dinneford chose to make it. She wanted to get near enough to study his character thoroughly, to discover its weaknesses and defects, not its better qualities, so that she might do for him the evil work that was in her heart. She hated him with a bitter hatred, and there is nothing so subtle and tireless and unrelenting as the hatred of a bad woman.

She found him weak and unwary. His kindly nature, his high sense of honor, his upright purpose, his loving devotion to Edith, were nothing in her eyes. She spurned them in her thoughts, she trampled them under her feet with scorn. But she studied his defects, and soon knew every weak point in his character. She drew him out to speak of himself, of his aims and prospects, of his friends and associates, until she understood him altogether. Then she laid her plans for his destruction.

Granger was holding a clerkship at the time of his marriage, but was anxious to get a start for himself. He had some acquaintance with a man named Lloyd Freeling, and often spoke of him in connection with business. Freeling had a store on one of the best streets, and, as represented by himself, a fine run of trade, but wanted more capital. One day he said to Granger,

"If I could find the right man with ten thousand dollars, I would take him in. We could double this business in a year."

Granger repeated the remark at home, Mrs. Dinneford listened, laid it up in her thought, and on the next day called at the store of Mr. Freeling to see what manner of man he was.

Her first impression was favorable—she liked him. On a second visit she likes him better. She was not aware that Freeling knew her; in this he had something of the advantage. A third time she dropped in, asking to see certain goods and buying a small bill, as before. This time she drew Mr. Freeling into conversation about business, and put some questions the meaning of which he understood quite as well as she did.

A woman like Mrs. Dinneford can read character almost as easily as she can read a printed page, particularly a weak or bad character. She knew perfectly, before the close of this brief interview, that Freeling was a man without principle, false and unscrupulous, and that if Granger were associated with him in business, he could, if he chose, not only involve him in transactions of a dishonest nature, but throw upon him the odium and the consequences.

"Do you think," she said to Granger, not long afterward, "that your friend, Mr. Freeling, would like to have you for a partner in business?"

The question surprised and excited him.

"I know it," he returned; "he has said so more than once."

"How much capital would he require?"

"Ten thousand dollars."

"A large sum to risk."

"Yes; but I do not think there will be any risk. The business is well established."

"What do you know about Mr. Freeling?"

"Not a great deal; but if I am any judge of character, he is fair and honorable."

Mrs. Dinneford turned her head that Granger might not see the expression of her face.

"You had better talk with Mr. Dinneford," she said.

But Mr. Dinneford did not favor it. He had seen too many young men go into business and fail.

So the matter was dropped for a little while. But Mrs. Dinneford had set her heart on the young man's destruction, and no better way of accomplishing the work presented itself than this. He must be involved in some way to hurt his good name, to blast his reputation and drive him to ruin. Weak, trusting and pliable, a specious villain in whom he had confidence might easily get him involved in transactions that were criminal under the law. She would be willing to sacrifice twice ten thousand dollars to accomplish this result.

Neither Mr. Dinneford nor Edith favored the business connection with Freeling, and said all they could against it. In weak natures we often find great pertinacity. Granger had this quality. He had set his mind on the copartnership, and saw in it a high road to fortune, and no argument of Mr. Dinneford, nor opposition of Edith, had power to change his views, or to hold him back from the arrangement favored by Mrs. Dinneford, and made possible by the capital she almost compelled her husband to supply.

In due time the change from clerk to merchant was made, and the new connection announced, under the title of "FREELING & GRANGER."

Clear seeing as evil may be in its schemes for hurting others, it is always blind to the consequent exactions upon itself; it strikes fiercely and desperately, not calculating the force of a rebound. So eager was Mrs. Dinneford to compass the ruin of Granger that she stepped beyond the limit of common prudence, and sought private interviews with Freeling, both before and after the completion of the partnership arrangement. These took place in the parlor of a fashionable hotel, where the gentleman and lady seemed to meet accidentally, and without attracting attention.

Mrs. Dinneford was very confidential in these interviews not concealing her aversion to Granger. He had come into the family, she said, as an unwelcome intruder; but now that he was there, they had to make the best of him. Not in spoken words did Mrs. Dinneford convey to Freeling the bitter hatred that was in her heart, nor in spoken words let him know that she desired the young man's utter ruin, but he understood it all before the close of their first private interview. Freeling was exceedingly deferential in the beginning and guarded in his speech. He knew by the quick intuitions of his nature that Mrs. Dinneford cherished an evil purpose, and had chosen him as the agent for its accomplishment. She was rich, and occupied a high social position, and his ready conclusion was that, be the service what it might, he could make it pay. To get such a woman in his power was worth an effort.

One morning—it was a few months after the date of the copartnership—Mrs. Dinneford received a note from Freeling. It said, briefly,

"At the usual place, 12 M. to-day. Important." There was no signature.

The sharp knitting of her brows and the nervous crumpling of the note in her hand showed that she was not pleased at the summons. She had come already to know her partner in evil too well. At 12 M. she was in the hotel parlor. Freeling was already there. They met in external cordiality, but it was very evident from the manner of Mrs. Dinneford, that she felt herself in the man's power, and had learned to be afraid of him.

"It will be impossible to get through to-morrow," he said, in a kind of imperative voice, that was half a threat, "unless we have two thousand dollars."

"I cannot ask Mr. Dinneford for anything more," Mrs. Dinneford replied; "we have already furnished ten thousand dollars beyond the original investment."

"But it is all safe enough—that is, if we do not break down just here for lack of so small a sum."

Mrs. Dinneford gave a start.

"Break down!" She repeated the words in a husky, voice, with a paling face. "What do you mean?"

"Only that in consequence of having in store a large stock of unsalable goods bought by your indiscreet son-in-law, who knows no more about business than a child, we are in a temporary strait."

T. S. Arthur

"Why did you trust him to buy?" asked Mrs. Dinneford.

"I didn't trust him. He bought without consulting me," was replied, almost rudely.

"Will two thousand be the end of this thing?"

"I think so."

"You only think so?"

"I am sure of it."

"Very well; I will see what can be done. But all this must have an end, Mr. Freeling. We cannot supply any more money. You must look elsewhere if you have further need. Mr. Dinneford is getting very much annoyed and worried. You surely have other resources."

"I have drawn to the utmost on all my resources," said the man, coldly.

Mrs. Dinneford remained silent for a good while, her eyes upon the floor. Freeling watched her face intently, trying to read what was in her thoughts. At last she said, in a suggestive tone,

"There are many ways of getting money known to business-men—a little risky some of them, perhaps, but desperate cases require desperate expedients. You understand me?"

Freeling took a little time to consider before replying.

"Yes," he said, at length, speaking slowly, as one careful of his words. "But all expedients are 'risky,' as you say—some of them very risky. It takes a long, cool head to manage them safely."

"I don't know a longer or cooler head than yours," returned Mrs. Dinneford, a faint smile playing about her lips.

"Thank you for the compliment," said Freeling, his lips reflecting the smile on hers.

"You must think of some expedient." Mrs. Dinneford's manner grew impressive. She spoke with emphasis and deliberation. "Beyond the sum of two thousand dollars, which I will get for you by to-morrow, I shall not advance a single penny. You may set that down as sure. If you are not sharp enough and strong enough, with the advantage you possess, to hold your own, then you must go under; as for me, I have done all that I can or will."

Freeling saw that she was wholly in earnest, and understood what she meant by "desperate expedients." Granger was to be ruined, and she was growing impatient of delay. He had no desire to hurt the young man—he rather liked him. Up to this time he had been content with what he could draw out of Mrs. Dinneford. There was no risk in this sort of business. Moreover, he enjoyed his interviews and confidences with the elegant lady, and of late the power he seemed to be gaining over her; this power he regarded as capital laid up for another use, and at another time.

But it was plain that he had reached the end of his present financial policy, and must decide whether to adopt the new one suggested by Mrs. Dinneford or make a failure, and so get rid of his partner. The question he had to settle with himself was whether he could make more by a failure than by using Granger a while longer, and then throwing him overboard, disgraced and ruined. Selfish and unscrupulous as he was, Freeling hesitated to do this. And besides, the

T. S. Arthur

"desperate expedients" he would have to adopt in the new line of policy were fraught with peril to all who took part in them. He might fall into the snare set for another—might involve himself so deeply as not to find a way of escape.

"To-morrow we will talk this matter over," he said in reply to Mrs. Dinneford's last remark; "in the mean time I will examine the ground thoroughly and see how it looks."

"Don't hesitate to make any use you can of Granger," suggested the lady. "He has done his part toward getting things tangled, and must help to untangle them."

"All right, ma'am."

And they separated, Mrs. Dinneford reaching the street by one door of the hotel, and Freeling by another.

On the following day they met again, Mrs. Dinneford bringing the two thousand dollars.

"And now what next?" she asked, after handing over the money and taking the receipt of "Freeling & Granger." Her eyes had a hard glitter, and her face was almost stern in its expression. "How are you going to raise money and keep afloat?"

"Only some desperate expedient is left me now," answered Freeling, though not in the tone of a man who felt himself at bay. It was said with a wicked kind of levity.

Mrs. Dinneford looked at him keenly. She was beginning to mistrust the man. They gazed into each other's faces in silence for some moments, each trying to read what was in the other's thought. At length Freeling said,

"There is one thing more that you will have to do, Mrs. Dinneford."

"What?" she asked.

"Get your husband to draw two or three notes in Mr. Granger's favor. They should not be for less than five hundred or a thousand dollars each. The dates must be short —not over thirty or sixty days."

"It can't be done," was the emphatic answer.

"It must be done," replied Freeling; "they need not be for the business. You can manage the matter if you will; your daughter wants an India shawl, or a set of diamonds, or a new carriage—anything you choose. Mr. Dinneford hasn't the ready cash, but we can throw his notes into bank and get the money; don't you see?"

But Mrs. Dinneford didn't see.

"I don't mean," said Freeling, "that we are to use the money. Let the shawl, or the diamond, or the what-not, be bought and paid for. We get the discounts for your use, not ours."

"All very well," answered Mrs. Dinneford; "but how is that going to help you?"

"Leave that to me. You get the notes," said Freeling.

"Never walk blindfold, Mr. Freeling," replied the lady, drawing herself up, with a dignified air. "We ought to understand each other by this time. I must see beyond the mere use of these notes."

Freeling shut his mouth tightly and knit his heavy brows.

Mrs. Dinneford watched him, closely.

"It's a desperate expedient," he said, at length.

"All well as far as that is concerned; but if I am to have a hand in it, I must know all about it," she replied, firmly. "As I said just now, I never walk blindfold."

Freeling leaned close to Mrs. Dinneford, and uttered a few sentences in a low tone, speaking rapidly. The color went and came in her face, but she sat motionless, and so continued for some time after he had ceased speaking.

"You will get the notes?" Freeling put the question as one who has little doubt of the answer.

"I will get them," replied Mrs. Dinneford.

"When?"

"It will take time."

"We cannot wait long. If the thing is done at all, it must be done quickly. 'Strike while the iron is hot' is the best of all maxims."

"There shall be no needless delay on my part. You may trust me for that," was answered.

Within a week Mrs. Dinneford brought two notes, drawn by her husband in favor of George Granger—one for five hundred and the other for one thousand dollars. The time was short—thirty and sixty days. On this occasion she came to the store and asked for her son-in-law. The meeting between her and Freeling was reserved and formal. She expressed regret for the trouble she was giving the firm in procuring a discount for her use, and said that if she could reciprocate the favor in any way she would be happy to do so.

"The notes are drawn to your order," remarked Freeling as soon as the lady had retired. Granger endorsed them, and was about handing them to his partner, when the latter said:

"Put our name on them while you are about it." And the young man wrote also the endorsement of the firm.

After this, Mr. Freeling put the bank business into Granger's hands. Nearly all checks were drawn and all business paper endorsed by the younger partner, who became the financier of the concern, and had the management of all negotiations for money in and out of bank.

One morning, shortly after the first of Mr. Dinneford's notes was paid, Granger saw his mother-in-law come into the store. Freeling was at the counter. They talked together for some time, and then Mrs. Dinneford went out.

On the next day Granger saw Mrs. Dinneford in the store again. After she had gone away, Freeling came back, and laying a note-of-hand on his partner's desk, said, in a pleased, confidential way.

"Look at that, my friend."

Granger read the face of the note with a start of surprise. It was drawn to his order, for three thousand dollars, and bore the signature of Howard Dinneford.

"A thing that is worth having is worth asking for," said Freeling. "We obliged your mother-in-law, and now she has returned the favor. It didn't come very easily, she said, and your father-in-law isn't feeling rather comfortable about it; so

T. S. Arthur

she doesn't care about your speaking of it at home."

Granger was confounded.

"I can't understand it," he said.

"You can understand that we have the note, and that it has come in the nick of time," returned Freeling.

"Yes, I can see all that."

"Well, don't look a gift-horse in the mouth, but spring into the saddle and take a ride. Your mother-in-law is a trump. If she will, she will, you may depend on't."

Freeling was unusually excited. Granger looked the note over and over in a way that seemed to annoy his partner, who said, presently, with a shade of ill-nature in his voice,

"What's the matter? Isn't the signature all right?"

"That's right enough," returned the young man, "after looking at it closely. "But I can't understand it."

"You will when you see the proceeds passed to our accounted in bank—ha! ha!"

Granger looked up at his partner quickly, the laugh had so strange a sound, but saw nothing new in his face.

In about a month Freeling had in his possession another note, signed by Mr. Dinneford and drawn to the order of George Granger. This one was for five thousand dollars. He handed it to his partner soon after the latter had observed Mrs. Dinneford in the store.

A little over six weeks from this time Mrs. Dinneford was in the store again. After she had gone away, Freeling handed Granger three more notes drawn by Mr. Dinneford to his order, amounting in all to fifteen thousand dollars. They were at short dates.

Granger took these notes without any remark, and was about putting them in his desk, when Freeling said,

"I think you had better offer one in the People's Bank and another in the Fourth National. They discount to-morrow."

"Our line is full in both of these banks," replied Granger.

"That may or may not be. Paper like this is not often thrown out. Call on the president of the Fourth National and the cashier of the People's Bank. Say that we particularly want the money, and would like them to see that the notes go through. Star & Giltedge can easily place the other."

Granger's manner did not altogether please his partner. The notes lay before him on his desk, and he looked at them in a kind of dazed way.

"What's the matter?" asked Freeling, rather sharply.

"Nothing," was the quiet answer.

"You saw Mrs. Dinneford in the store just now. I told her last week that I should claim another favor at her hands. She tried to beg off, but I pushed the matter hard. It must end here, she says. Mr. Dinneford won't go any farther."

"I should think not," replied Granger. "I wouldn't if I were he. The wonder to me is that he has gone so far. What about the renewal of these notes?"

T. S. Arthur

"Oh, that is all arranged," returned Freeling, a little hurriedly. Granger looked at him for some moments. He was not satisfied.

"See that they go in bank," said Freeling, in a positive way.

Granger took up his pen in an abstracted manner and endorsed the notes, after which he laid them in his bank-book. An important customer coming in at the moment, Freeling went forward to see him. After Granger was left alone, he took the notes from his bank-book and examined them with great care. Suspicion was aroused. He felt sure that something was wrong. A good many things in Freeling's conduct of late had seemed strange. After thinking for a while, he determined to take the notes at once to Mr. Dinneford and ask him if all was right. As soon as his mind had reached this conclusion he hurried through the work he had on hand, and then putting his bank-book in his pocket, left the store.

On that very morning Mr. Dinneford received notice that he had a note for three thousand dollars falling due at one of the banks. He went immediately and asked to see the note. When it was shown to him, he was observed to become very pale, but he left the desk of the note-clerk without any remark, and returned home. He met his wife at the door, just coming in.

"What's the matter?" she asked, seeing how pale he was. "Not sick, I hope?"

"Worse than sick," he replied as they passed into the house together. "George has been forging my name."

"Impossible!" exclaimed Mrs. Dinneford.

"I wish it were," replied Mr. Dinneford, sadly; "but, alas! it is too true. I have just returned from the Fourth National Bank. They have a note for three thousand dollars, bearing my signature. It is drawn to the order of George Granger, and endorsed by him. The note is a forgery."

Mrs. Dinneford became almost wild with excitement. Her fair face grew purple. Her eyes shone with a fierce light.

"Have you had him arrested?" she asked.

"Oh no, no, no!" Mr. Dinneford answered. "For poor Edith's sake, if for nothing else, this dreadful business must be kept secret. I will take up the note when due, and the public need be none the wiser."

"If," said Mrs. Dinneford, "he has forged your name once, he has, in all probability, done it again and again. No, no; the thing can't be hushed up, and it must not be. Is he less a thief and a robber because he is our son-in-law? My daughter the wife of a forger! Great heavens! has it come to this Mr. Dinneford?" she added, after a pause, and with intense bitterness and rejection in her voice. "The die is cast! Never again, if I can prevent it, shall that scoundrel cross our threshold. Let the law have its course. It is a crime to conceal crime."

"It will kill our poor child!" answered Mr. Dinneford in a broken voice.

"Death is better than the degradation of living with a criminal," replied his wife. "I say it solemnly, and I mean it; the die is cast! Come what will, George Granger stands now and for ever on the outside! Go at once and give information to the bank officers. If you do not, I will."

With a heavy heart Mr. Dinneford returned to the bank and

T. S. Arthur

informed the president that the note in question was a forgery. He had been gone from home a little over half an hour, when Granger, who had come to ask him about the three notes given him that morning by Freeling, put his key in the door, and found, a little to his surprise, that the latch was down. He rang the bell, and in a few moments the servant appeared. Granger was about passing in, when the man said, respectfully but firmly, as he held the door partly closed,

"My orders are not to let you come in."

"Who gave you those orders?" demanded Granger, turning white.

"Mrs. Dinneford."

"I wish to see Mr. Dinneford, and I must see him immediately."

"Mr. Dinneford is not at home," answered the servant.

"Shut that door instantly!"

It was the voice of Mrs. Dinneford, speaking from within. Granger heard it; in the next moment the door was shut in his face.

The young man hardly knew how he got back to the store. On his arrival he found himself under arrest, charged with forgery, and with fresh evidence of the crime on his person in the three notes received that morning from his partner, who denied all knowledge of their existence, and appeared as a witness against him at the hearing before a magistrate. Granger was held to bail to answer the charge at the next term of court.

It would have been impossible to keep all this from Edith, even if there had been a purpose to do so. Mrs. Dinneford chose to break the dreadful news at her own time and in her own way. The shock was fearful. On the night that followed her baby was born.

T. S. Arthur

CHAPTER III

"*IT* is a splendid boy," said the nurse as she came in with the new-born baby in her arms, "and perfect as a bit of sculpture. Just look at that hand."

"Faugh!" ejaculated Mrs. Dinneford, to whom this was addressed. Her countenance expressed disgust. She turned her head away. "Hide the thing from my sight!" she added, angrily. "Cover it up! smother it if you will!"

"You are still determined?" said the nurse.

"Determined, Mrs. Bray; I am not the woman to look back when I have once resolved. You know me." Mrs. Dinneford said this passionately.

The two women were silent for a little while. Mrs. Bray, the nurse, kept her face partly turned from Mrs. Dinneford. She was a short, dry, wiry little woman, with French features, a sallow complexion and very black eyes.

The doctor looked in. Mrs. Dinneford went quickly to the door, and putting her hand on his arm, pressed him back, going out into the entry with him and closing the door behind them. They talked for a short time very earnestly.

"The whole thing is wrong," said the doctor as he turned to go, "and I will not be answerable for the consequences."

"No one will require them at your hand, Doctor Radcliffe," replied Mrs. Dinneford. "Do the best you can for Edith. As for the rest, know nothing, say nothing. You understand."

Doctor Burt Radcliffe had a large practice among rich and fashionable people. He had learned to be very considerate of their weaknesses, peculiarities and moral obliquities. His business was to doctor them when sick, to humor them when they only thought themselves sick, and to get the largest possible fees for his, services. A great deal came under his observation that he did not care to see, and of which he saw as little as possible. From policy he had learned to be reticent. He held family secrets enough to make, in the hands of a skillful writer, more than a dozen romances of the saddest and most exciting character.

Mrs. Dinneford knew him thoroughly, and just how far to trust him. "Know nothing, say nothing" was a good maxim in the case, and so she divulged only the fact that the baby was to be cast adrift. His weak remonstrance might as well not have been spoken, and he knew it.

While this brief interview was in progress, Nurse Bray sat with the baby on her lap. She had taken the soft little hands into her own; and evil and cruel though she was, an impulse of tenderness flowed into her heart from the angels who were present with the innocent child. It grew lovely in her eyes. Its helplessness stirred in her a latent instinct of protection. "No no, it must not be," she was saying to herself, when the door opened and Mrs. Dinneford came back.

Mrs. Bray did not lift her head, but sat looking down at the baby and toying with its hands.

T. S. Arthur

"Pshaw!" ejaculated Mrs. Dinneford, in angry disgust, as she noticed this manifestation of interest. "Bundle the thing up and throw into that basket. Is the woman down stairs?"

"Yes," replied Mrs. Bray as she slowly drew a light blanket over the baby.

"Very well. Put it in the basket, and let her take it away."

"She is not a good woman," said the nurse, whose heart was failing her at the last moment.

"She may be the devil for all I care," returned Mrs. Dinneford.

Mrs. Bray did as she was ordered, but with an evident reluctance that irritated Mrs. Dinneford.

"Go now and bring up the woman," she said, sharply.

The woman was brought. She was past the prime of life, and had an evil face. You read in it the record of bad passions indulged and the signs of a cruel nature. She was poorly clad, and her garments unclean.

"You will take this child?" said Mrs. Dinneford abruptly, as the woman came into her presence.

"I have agreed to do so," she replied, looking toward Mrs. Bray.

"She is to have fifty dollars," said the nurse.

"And that is to be the last of it!" Mrs. Dinneford's face was pale, and she spoke in a hard, husky voice.

Opening her purse, she took from it a small roll of bills, and as she held out the money said, slowly and with a hard emphasis,

"You understand the terms. I do not know you—not even your name. I don't wish to know you. For this consideration you take the child away. That is the end of it between you and me. The child is your own as much as if he were born to you, and you can do with him as you please. And now go." Mrs. Dinneford waved her hand.

"His name?" queried the woman.

"He has no name!" Mrs. Dinneford stamped her foot in angry impatience.

The woman stooped down, and taking up the basket, tucked the covering that had been laid over the baby close about its head, so that no one could see what she carried, and went off without uttering another word.

It was some moments before either Mrs. Dinneford or the nurse spoke. Mrs. Bray was first to break silence.

"All this means a great deal more than you have counted on," she said, in a voice that betrayed some little feeling. "To throw a tender baby out like that is a hard thing. I am afraid—"

"There, there! no more of that," returned Mrs. Dinneford, impatiently. "It's ugly work, I own, but it had to be done— like cutting off a diseased limb. He will die, of course, and the sooner it is over, the better for him and every one else."

"He will have a hard struggle for life, poor little thing!" said the nurse. "I would rather see him dead."

T. S. Arthur

Mrs. Dinneford, now that this wicked and cruel deed was done, felt ill at ease. She pushed the subject away, and tried to bury it out of sight as we bury the dead, but did not find the task an easy one.

What followed the birth and removal of Edith's baby up to the time of her return to reason after long struggle for life, has already been told. Her demand to have her baby—"Oh, mother, bring me my baby! I shall die if you do not!" and the answer, "Your baby is in heaven!"—sent the feeble life-currents back again upon her heart. There was another long period of oblivion, out of which she came very slowly, her mind almost as much a blank as the mind of a child.

She had to learn again the names of things, and to be taught their use. It was touching to see the untiring devotion of her father, and the pleasure he took in every new evidence of mental growth. He went over the alphabet with her, letter by letter, many times each day, encouraging her and holding her thought down to the unintelligible signs with a patient tenderness sad yet beautiful to see; and when she began to combine letters into words, and at last to put words together, his delight was unbounded.

Very slowly went on the new process of mental growth, and it was months before thought began to reach out beyond the little world that lay just around her.

Meanwhile, Edith's husband had been brought to trial for forgery, convicted and sentenced to the State's prison for a term of years. His partner came forward as the chief witness, swearing that he had believed the notes genuine, the firm having several times had the use of Mr. Dinneford's paper, drawn to the order of Granger.

Ere the day of trial came the poor young man was nearly

broken-hearted. Public disgrace like this, added to the terrible private wrongs he was suffering, was more than he had the moral strength to bear. Utterly repudiated by his wife's family, and not even permitted to see Edith, he only knew that she was very ill. Of the birth of his baby he had but a vague intimation. A rumor was abroad that it had died, but he could learn nothing certain. In his distress and uncertainty he called on Dr. Radcliffe, who replied to his questions with a cold evasion. "It was put out to nurse," said the doctor, "and that is all I know about it." Beyond this he would say nothing.

Granger was not taken to the State's prison after his sentence, but to an insane asylum. Reason gave way under the terrible ordeal through which he had been made to pass.

"Mother," said Edith, one day, in a tone that caused Mrs. Dinneford's heart to leap. She was reading a child's simple story-book, and looked up as she spoke. Her eyes were wide open and full of questions.

"What, my dear?" asked Mrs. Dinneford, repressing her feelings and trying to keep her voice calm.

"There's something I can't understand, mother." She looked down at herself, then about the room. Her manner was becoming nervous.

"What can't you understand?"

Edith shut her hands over her eyes and remained very still. When she removed them, and her mother looked into her face the childlike sweetness and content were all gone, and a conscious woman was before her. The transformation was as sudden as it was marvelous.

T. S. Arthur

Both remained silent for the space of nearly a minute. Mrs. Dinneford knew not what to say, and waited for some sign from her daughter.

"Where is my baby, mother?" Edith said this in a low, tremulous whisper, leaning forward as she spoke, repressed and eager.

"Have you forgotten?" asked Mrs. Dinneford, with regained composure.

"Forgotten what?"

"You were very ill after your baby was born; no one thought you could live; you were ill for a long time. And the baby—"

"What of the baby, mother?" asked Edith, beginning to tremble violently. Her mother, perceiving her agitation, held back the word that was on her lips.

"What of the baby, mother?" Edith repeated the question.

"It died," said Mrs. Dinneford, turning partly away. She could not look at her child and utter this cruel falsehood.

"Dead! Oh, mother, don't say that! The baby can't be dead!"

A swift flash of suspicion came into her eyes.

"I have said it, my child," was the almost stern response of Mrs. Dinneford. "The baby is dead."

A weight seemed to fall on Edith. She bent forward, crouching down until her elbows rested on her knees and her hands supported her head. Thus she sat, rocking her body with a slight motion. Mrs. Dinneford watched her without speaking.

"And what of George?" asked Edith, checking her nervous movement at last.

Her mother did not reply. Edith waited a moment, and then lifted herself erect.

"What of George?" she demanded.

"My poor child!" exclaimed Mrs. Dinneford, with a gush of genuine pity, putting her arms about Edith and drawing her head against her bosom. "It is more than you have strength to bear."

"You must tell me," the daughter said, disengaging herself. "I have asked for my husband."

"Hush! You must not utter that word again;" and Mrs. Dinneford put her fingers on Edith's lips. "The wretched man you once called by that name is a disgraced criminal. It is better that you know the worst."

When Mr. Dinneford came home, instead of the quiet, happy child he had left in the morning, he found a sad, almost broken-hearted woman, refusing to be comforted. The wonder was that under the shock of this terrible awakening, reason had not been again and hopelessly dethroned.

After a period of intense suffering, pain seemed to deaden sensibility. She grew calm and passive. And now Mrs. Dinneford set herself to the completion of the work she had begun. She had compassed the ruin of Granger in order to make a divorce possible; she had cast the baby adrift that no sign of the social disgrace might remain as an impediment to her first ambition. She would yet see her daughter in the position to which she had from the beginning resolved to lift her, cost what it might. But the task was not to be an easy one.

T. S. Arthur

After a period of intense suffering, as we have said, Edith grew calm and passive. But she was never at ease with her mother, and seemed to be afraid of her. To her father she was tender and confiding. Mrs. Dinneford soon saw that if Edith's consent to a divorce from her husband was to be obtained, it must come through her father's influence; for if she but hinted at the subject, it was met with a flash of almost indignant rejection. So her first work was to bring her husband over to her side. This was not difficult, for Mr. Dinneford felt the disgrace of having for a son-in-law a condemned criminal, who was only saved from the State's prison by insanity. An insane criminal was not worthy to hold the relation of husband to his pure and lovely child.

After a feeble opposition to her father's arguments and persuasions, Edith yielded her consent. An application for a divorce was made, and speedily granted.

CHAPTER IV

OUT of this furnace Edith came with a new and purer spirit. She had been thrust in a shrinking and frightened girl; she came out a woman in mental stature, in feeling and self-consciousness.

The river of her life, which had cut for itself a deeper channel, lay now so far down that it was out of the sight of common observation. Even her mother failed to apprehend its drift and strength. Her father knew her better. To her mother she was reserved and distant; to her father, warm and confiding. With the former she would sit for hours without speaking unless addressed; with the latter she was pleased and social, and grew to be interested in what interested him. As mentioned, Mr. Dinneford was a man of wealth and leisure, and active in many public charities. He had come to be much concerned for the neglected and cast-off children of poor and vicious parents, thousands upon thousands of whom were going to hopeless ruin, unthought of and uncared for by Church or State, and their condition often formed the subject of his conversation as well at home as elsewhere.

Mrs. Dinneford had no sympathy with her husband in this direction. A dirty, vicious child was an offence to her, not an object of pity, and she felt more like, spurning it with her foot than touching it with her hand. But it was not so with

T. S. Arthur

Edith; she listened to her father, and became deeply interested in the poor, suffering, neglected little ones whose sad condition he could so vividly portray, for the public duties of charity to which he was giving a large part of his time made him familiar with much that was sad and terrible in human suffering and degradation.

One day Edith said to her father,

"I saw a sight this morning that made me sick. It has haunted me ever since. Oh, it was dreadful!"

"What was it?" asked Mr. Dinneford.

"A sick baby in the arms of a half-drunken woman. It made me shiver to look at its poor little face, wasted by hunger and sickness and purple with cold. The woman sat at the street corner begging, and the people went by, no one seeming to care for the helpless, starving baby in her arms. I saw a police-officer almost touch the woman as he passed. Why did he not arrest her?"

"That was not his business," replied Mr. Dinneford. "So long as she did not disturb the peace, the officer had nothing to do with her."

"Who, then, has?"

"Nobody."

"Why, father!" exclaimed Edith. "Nobody?"

"The woman was engaged in business. She was a beggar, and the sick, half-starved baby was her capital in trade," replied Mr. Dinneford. "That policeman had no more authority to arrest her than he had to arrest the organ-man or the peanut-vender."

"But somebody should see after a poor baby like that. Is there no law to meet such cases?"

"The poor baby has no vote," replied Mr. Dinneford, "and law-makers don't concern themselves much about that sort of constituency; and even if they did, the executors of law would be found indifferent. They are much more careful to protect those whose business it is to make drunken beggars like the one you saw, who, if men, can vote and give them place and power. The poor baby is far beneath their consideration."

"But not of Him," said Edith, with eyes full of tears, "who took little children in his arms and blessed them, and said, Suffer them to come unto me and forbid them not, for of such is the kingdom of heaven."

"Our law-makers are not, I fear, of his kingdom," answered Mr. Dinneford, gravely, "but of the kingdom of this world."

A little while after, Edith, who had remained silent and thoughtful, said, with a tremor in her voice,

"Father, did you see my baby?"

Mr. Dinneford started at so unexpected a question, surprised and disturbed. He did not reply, and Edith put the question again.

"No, my dear," he answered, with a hesitation of manner that was almost painful.

After looking into his face steadily for some moments, Edith dropped her eyes to the floor, and there was a constrained

T. S. Arthur

silence between them for a good while.

"You never saw it?" she queried, again lifting her eyes to her father's face. Her own was much paler than when she first put the question.

"Never."

"Why?" asked Edith.

She waited for a little while, and then said,

"Why don't you answer me, father?"

"It was never brought to me."

"Oh, father!"

"You were very ill, and a nurse was procured immediately."

"I was not too sick to see my baby," said Edith, with white, quivering lips. "If they had laid it in my bosom as soon as it was born, I would never have been so ill, and the baby would not have died. If—if—"

She held back what she was about saying, shutting her lips tightly. Her face remained very pale and strangely agitated. Nothing more was then said.

A day or two afterward, Edith asked her mother, with an abruptness that sent the color to her face, "Where was my baby buried?"

"In our lot at Fairview," was replied, after a moment's pause.

Edith said no more, but on that very day, regardless of a

heavy rain that was falling, went out to the cemetery alone and searched in the family lot for the little mound that covered her baby—searched, but did not find it. She came back so changed in appearance that when her mother saw her she exclaimed,

"Why, Edith! Are you sick?"

"I have been looking for my baby's grave and cannot find it," she answered. "There is something wrong, mother. What was done with my baby? I must know." And she caught her mother's wrists with both of her hands in a tight grip, and sent searching glances down through her eyes.

"Your baby is dead," returned Mrs. Dinneford, speaking slowly and with a hard deliberation. "As for its grave—well, if you will drag up the miserable past, know that in my anger at your wretched *mesalliance* I rejected even the dead body of your miserable husband's child, and would not even suffer it to lie in our family ground. You know how bitterly I was disappointed, and I am not one of the kind that forgets or forgives easily. I may have been wrong, but it is too late now, and the past may as well be covered out of sight."

"Where, then, was my baby buried?" asked Edith, with a calm resolution of manner that was not to be denied.

"I do not know. I did not care at the time, and never asked."

"Who can tell me?"

"I don't know."

"Who took my baby to nurse?"

"I have forgotten the woman's name. All I know is that she is

T. S. Arthur

dead. When the child died, I sent her money, and told her to bury it decently."

"Where did she live?"

"I never knew precisely. Somewhere down town."

"Who brought her here? who recommended her?" said Edith, pushing her inquiries rapidly.

"I have forgotten that also," replied Mrs. Dinneford, maintaining her coldness of manner.

"My nurse, I presume," said Edith. "I have a faint recollection of her—a dark little woman with black eyes whom I had never seen before. What was her name?"

"Bodine," answered Mrs. Dinneford, without a moment's hesitation.

"Where does she live?"

"She went to Havana with a Cuban lady several months ago."

"Do you know the lady's name?"

"It was Casteline, I think."

Edith questioned no further. The mother and daughter were still sitting together, both deeply absorbed in thought, when a servant opened the door and said to Mrs. Dinneford,

"A lady wishes to see you."

"Didn't she give you her card?"

"No ma'am."

"Nor send up her name?"

"No, ma'am."

"Go down and ask her name."

The servant left the room. On returning, she said,

"Her name is Mrs. Bray."

Mrs. Dinneford turned her face quickly, but not in time to prevent Edith from seeing by its expression that she knew her visitor, and that her call was felt to be an unwelcome one. She went from the room without speaking. On entering the parlor, Mrs. Dinneford said, in a low, hurried voice,

"I don't want you to come here, Mrs. Bray. If you wish to see me send me word, and I will call on you, but you must on no account come here."

"Why? Is anything wrong?"

"Yes."

"What?"

"Edith isn't satisfied about the baby, has been out to Fairview looking for its grave, wants to know who her nurse was."

"What did you tell her?"

"I said that your name was Mrs. Bodine, and that you had gone to Cuba."

T. S. Arthur

"Do you think she would know me?"

"Can't tell; wouldn't like to run the risk of her seeing you here. Pull down your veil. There! close. She said, a little while ago, that she had a faint recollection of you as a dark little woman with black eyes whom she had never seen before."

"Indeed!" and Mrs. Bray gathered her veil close about her face.

"The baby isn't living?" Mrs. Dinneford asked the question in a whisper.

"Yes."

"Oh, it can't be! Are you sure?"

"Yes; I saw it day before yesterday."

"You did! Where?"

"On the street, in the arms of a beggar-woman."

"You are deceiving me!" Mrs. Dinneford spoke with a throb of anger in her voice.

"As I live, no! Poor little thing! half starved and half frozen. It 'most made me sick."

"It's impossible! You could not know that it was Edith's baby."

"I do know," replied Mrs. Bray, in a voice that left no doubt on Mrs. Dinneford's mind.

"Was the woman the same to whom we gave the baby?"

"No; she got rid of it in less than a month."

"What did she do with it?"

"Sold it for five dollars, after she had spent all the money she received from you in drink and lottery-policies."

"Sold it for five dollars!"

"Yes, to two beggar-women, who use it every day, one in the morning and the other in the afternoon, and get drunk on the money they receive, lying all night in some miserable den."

Mrs. Dinneford gave a little shiver.

"What becomes of the baby when they are not using it?" she asked.

"They pay a woman a dollar a week to take care of it at night."

"Do you know where this woman lives?"

"Yes."

"Were you ever there?"

"Yes."

"What kind of a place is it?"

"Worse than a dog-kennel."

"What does all this mean?" demanded Mrs. Dinneford, with

T. S. Arthur

repressed excitement. "Why have you so kept on the track of this baby, when you knew I wished it lost sight of?"

"I had my own reasons," replied Mrs. Bray. "One doesn't know what may come of an affair like this, and it's safe to keep well up with it."

Mrs. Dinneford bit her lips till the blood almost came through. A faint rustle of garments in the hall caused her to start. An expression of alarm crossed her face.

"Go now," she said, hurriedly, to her visitor; "I will call and see you this afternoon."

Mrs. Bray quietly arose, saying, as she did so, "I shall expect you," and went away.

There was a menace in her tone as she said, "I shall expect you," that did not escape the ears of Mrs. Dinneford.

Edith was in the hall, at some distance from the parlor door. Mrs. Bray had to pass her as she went out. Edith looked at her intently.

"Who is that woman?" she asked, confronting her mother, after the visitor was gone.

"If you ask the question in a proper manner, I shall have no objection to answer," said Mrs. Dinneford, with a dignified and slightly offended air; "but my daughter is assuming rather, too much."

"Mrs. Bray, the servant said."

"No, Mrs. Gray."

"I understood her to say Mrs. Bray."

"I can't help what you understood." The mother spoke with some asperity of manner. "She calls herself Gray, but you can have it anything you please; it won't change her identity."

"What did she want?"

"To see me."

"I know." Edith was turning away with an expression on her face that Mrs. Dinneford did not like, so she said,

"She is in trouble, and wants me to help her, if you must know. She used to be a dressmaker, and worked for me before you were born; she got married, and then her troubles began. Now she is a widow with a house full of little children, and not half bread enough to feed them. I've helped her a number of times already, but I'm getting tired of it; she must look somewhere else, and I told her so."

Edith turned from her mother with an unsatisfied manner, and went up stairs. Mrs. Dinneford was surprised, not long afterward, to meet her at her chamber door, dressed to go out. This was something unusual.

"Where are you going?" she asked, not concealing her surprise.

"I have a little errand out," Edith replied.

This was not satisfactory to her mother. She asked other questions, but Edith gave only evasive answers.

On leaving the house, Edith walked quickly, like one in

earnest about something; her veil was closely drawn. Only a few blocks from where she lived was the office of Dr. Radcliffe. Hither she directed her steps.

"Why, Edith, child!" exclaimed the doctor, not concealing the surprise he felt at seeing her. "Nobody sick, I hope?"

"No one," she answered.

There was a momentary pause; then Edith said, abruptly,

"Doctor, what became of my baby?"

"It died," answered Doctor Radcliffe, but not without betraying some confusion. The question had fallen upon him too suddenly.

"Did you see it after it was dead?" She spoke in a firm voice, looking him steadily in the face.

"No," he replied, after a slight hesitation.

"Then how do you know that it died?" Edith asked.

"I had your mother's word for it," said the doctor.

"What was done with my baby after it was born?"

"It was given out to nurse."

"With your consent?"

"I did not advise it. Your mother had her own views in the case. It was something over which I had no control."

"And you never saw it after it was taken away?"

"Never."

"And do not really know whether it be dead or living?"

"Oh, it's dead, of course, my child. There is no doubt of that," said the doctor, with sudden earnestness of manner.

"Have you any evidence of the fact?"

"My dear, dear child," answered the doctor, with much feeling, "it is all wrong. Why go back over this unhappy ground? why torture yourself for nothing? Your baby died long ago, and is in heaven."

"Would God I could believe it!" she exclaimed, in strong agitation. "If it were so, why is not the evidence set before me? I question my mother; I ask for the nurse who was with me when my baby was born, and for the nurse to whom it was given afterward, and am told that they are dead or out of the country. I ask for my baby's grave, but it cannot be found. I have searched for it where my mother told me it was, but the grave is not there. Why all this hiding and mystery? Doctor, you said that my baby was in heaven, and I answered, 'Would God it were so!' for I saw a baby in hell not long ago!"

The doctor was scared. He feared that Edith was losing her mind, she looked and spoke so wildly.

"A puny, half-starved, half-frozen little thing, in the arms of a drunken beggar," she added. "And, doctor, an awful thought has haunted me ever since."

"Hush, hush!" said the doctor, who saw what was in her mind. "You must not indulge such morbid fancies."

"It is that I may not indulge them that I have come to you. I want certainty, Dr. Radcliffe. Somebody knows all about my baby. Who was my nurse?"

"I never saw her before the night of your baby's birth, and have never seen her since. Your mother procured her."

"Did you hear her name?"

"No."

"And so you cannot help me at all?" said Edith, in a disappointed voice.

"I cannot, my poor child," answered the doctor.

All the flush and excitement died out of Edith's face. When she arose to go, she was pale and haggard, like one exhausted by pain, and her steps uneven, like the steps of an invalid walking for the first time. Dr. Radcliffe went with her in silence to the door.

"Oh, doctor," said Edith, in a choking voice, as she lingered a moment on the steps, "can't you bring out of this frightful mystery something for my heart to rest upon? I want the truth. Oh, doctor, in pity help me to find the truth!"

"I am powerless to help you," the doctor replied. "Your only hope lies in your mother. She knows all about it; I do not."

And he turned and left her standing at the door. Slowly she descended the steps, drawing her veil as she did so about her face, and walked away more like one in a dream than conscious of the tide of life setting so strongly all about her.

CHAPTER V

MEANTIME, obeying the unwelcome summons, Mrs. Dinneford had gone to see Mrs. Bray. She found her in a small third-story room in the lower part of the city, over a mile away from her own residence. The meeting between the two women was not over-gracious, but in keeping with their relations to each other. Mrs. Dinneford was half angry and impatient; Mrs. Bray cool and self-possessed.

"And now what is it you have to say?" asked the former, almost as soon as she had entered.

"The woman to whom you gave that baby was here yesterday."

A frightened expression came into Mrs. Dinneford's face. Mrs. Bray watched her keenly as, with lips slightly apart, she waited for what more was to come.

"Unfortunately, she met me just as I was at my own door, and so found out my residence," continued Mrs. Bray. "I was in hopes I should never see her again. We shall have trouble, I'm afraid."

"In what way?"

T. S. Arthur

"A bad woman who has you in her power can trouble you in many ways," answered Mrs. Bray.

"She did not know my name—you assured me of that. It was one of the stipulations."

"She does know, and your daughter's name also. And she knows where the baby is. She's deeper than I supposed. It's never safe to trust such people; they have no honor."

Fear sent all the color out of Mrs. Dinneford's face.

"What does she want?"

"Money."

"She was paid liberally."

"That has nothing to do with it. These people have no honor, as I said; they will get all they can."

"How much does she want?"

"A hundred dollars; and it won't end there, I'm thinking. If she is refused, she will go to your house; she gave me that alternative—would have gone yesterday, if good luck had not thrown her in my way. I promised to call on you and see what could be done."

Mrs. Dinneford actually groaned in her fear and distress.

"Would you like to see her yourself?" coolly asked Mrs. Bray.

"Oh dear! no, no!" and the lady put up her hands in dismay.

"It might be best," said her wily companion.

"No, no, no! I will have nothing to do with her! You must keep her away from me," replied Mrs. Dinneford, with increasing agitation.

"I cannot keep her away without satisfying her demands. If you were to see her yourself, you would know just what her demands were. If you do not see her, you will only have my word for it, and I am left open to misapprehension, if not worse. I don't like to be placed in such a position."

And Mrs. Bray put on a dignified, half-injured manner.

"It's a wretched business in every way," she added, "and I'm sorry that I ever had anything to do with it. It's something dreadful, as I told you at the time, to cast a helpless baby adrift in such a way. Poor little soul! I shall never feel right about it."

"That's neither here nor there;" and Mrs. Dinneford waved her hand impatiently. "The thing now in hand is to deal with this woman."

"Yes, that's it—and as I said just now, I would rather have you deal with her yourself; you may be able to do it better than I can."

"It's no use to talk, Mrs. Bray. I will not see the woman."

"Very well; you must be your own judge in the case."

"Can't you bind her up to something, or get her out of the city? I'd pay almost anything to have her a thousand miles away. See if you can't induce her to go to New Orleans. I'll pay her passage, and give her a hundred dollars besides, if she'll go."

Mrs. Bray smiled a faint, sinister smile:

"If you could get her off there, it would be the end of her. She'd never stand the fever."

"Then get her off, cost what it may," said Mrs. Dinneford.

"She will be here in less than half an hour." Mrs. Bray looked at the face of a small cheap clock that stood on the mantel.

"She will?" Mrs. Dinneford became uneasy, and arose from her chair.

"Yes; what shall I say to her?"

"Manage her the best you can. Here are thirty dollars—all the money I have with me. Give her that, and promise more if necessary. I will see you again."

"When?" asked Mrs. Bray.

"At any time you desire."

"Then you had better come to-morrow morning. I shall not go out."

"I will be here at eleven o'clock. Induce her if possible to leave the city—to go South, so that she may never come back."

"The best I can shall be done," replied Mrs. Bray as she folded the bank-bills she had received from Mrs. Dinneford in a fond, tender sort of way and put them into her pocket.

Mrs. Dinneford retired, saying as she did so,

"I will be here in the morning."

An instant change came over the shallow face of the wiry little woman as the form of Mrs. Dinneford vanished through the door. A veil seemed to fall away from it. All its virtuous sobriety was gone, and a smile of evil satisfaction curved about her lips and danced in her keen black eyes. She stood still, listening to the retiring steps of her visitor, until she heard the street door shut. Then, with a quick, cat-like step, she crossed to the opposite side of the room, and pushed open a door that led to an adjoining chamber. A woman came forward to meet her. This woman was taller and stouter than Mrs. Bray, and had a soft, sensual face, but a resolute mouth, the under jaw slightly protruding. Her eyes were small and close together, and had that peculiar wily and alert expression you sometimes see, making you think of a serpent's eyes. She was dressed in common finery and adorned by cheap jewelry.

"What do you think of that, Pinky Swett?" exclaimed Mrs. Bray, in a voice of exultation. "Got her all right, haven't I?"

"Well, you have!" answered the woman, shaking all over with unrestrained laughter. "The fattest pigeon I've happened to see for a month of Sundays. Is she very rich?"

"Her husband is, and that's all the same. And now, Pinky"— Mrs. Bray assumed a mock gravity of tone and manner— "you know your fate—New Orleans and the yellow fever. You must pack right off. Passage free and a hundred dollars for funeral expenses. Nice wet graves down there—keep off the fire;" and she gave a low chuckle.

"Oh yes; all settled. When does the next steamer sail?" and

Pinky almost screamed with merriment. She had been drinking.

"H-u-s-h! h-u-s-h! None of that here, Pinky. The people down stairs are good Methodists, and think me a saint."

"You a saint? Oh dear!" and she shook with repressed enjoyment.

After this the two women grew serious, and put their heads together for business.

"Who is this woman, Fan? What's her name, and where does she live?" asked Pinky Swett.

"That's my secret, Pinky," replied Mrs. Bray, "and I can't let it go; it wouldn't be safe. You get a little off the handle sometimes, and don't know what you say—might let the cat out of the bag. Sally Long took the baby away, and she died two months ago; so I'm the only one now in the secret. All I want of you is to keep track of the baby. Here is a five-dollar bill; I can't trust you with more at a time. I know your weakness, Pinky;" and she touched her under the chin in a familiar, patronizing way.

Pinky wasn't satisfied with this, and growled a little, just showing her teeth like an unquiet dog.

"Give me ten," she said; "the woman gave you thirty. I heard her say so. And she's going to bring you seventy to-morrow."

"You'll only waste it, Pinky," remonstrated Mrs. Bray. "It will all be gone before morning."

"Fan," said the woman, leaning toward Mrs. Bray and speaking in a low, confidential tone, "I dreamed of a cow last night, and that's good luck, you know. Tom Oaks made a splendid hit last Saturday—drew twenty dollars—and Sue Minty got ten. They're all buzzing about it down in our street, and going to Sam McFaddon's office in a stream."

"Do they have good luck at Sam McFaddon's?" asked Mrs. Bray, with considerable interest in her manner.

"It's the luckiest place that I know. Never dreamed of a cow or a hen that I didn't make a hit, and I dreamed of a cow last night. She was giving such a splendid pail of milk, full to the brim, just as old Spot and Brindle used to give. You remember our Spot and Brindle, Fan?"

"Oh yes." There was a falling inflection in Mrs. Bray's voice, as if the reference had sent her thoughts away back to other and more innocent days.

The two women sat silent for some moments after that; and when Pinky spoke, which she did first, it was in lower and softer tones:

"I don't like to think much about them old times, Fan; do you? I might have done better. But it's no use grizzling about it now. What's done's done, and can't be helped. Water doesn't run up hill again after it's once run down. I've got going, and can't stop, you see. There's nothing to catch at that won't break as soon as you touch it. So I mean to be jolly as I move along."

"Laughing is better than crying at any time," returned Mrs. Bray; "here are five more;" and she handed Pinky Swett another bank-bill. "I'm going to try my luck. Put half a dollar on ten different rows, and we'll go shares on what is drawn. I dreamed the other night that I saw a flock of sheep, and that's good luck, isn't it?"

Pinky thrust her hand into her pocket and drew out a worn and soiled dream-book.

"A flock of sheep; let me see;" and she commenced turning over the leaves. "Sheep; here it is: 'To see them is a sign of sorrow—11, 20, 40, 48. To be surrounded by many sheep denotes good luck—2, 11, 55.' That's your row; put down 2, 11, 55. We'll try that. Next put down 41 11, 44—that's the lucky row when you dream of a cow."

As Pinky leaned toward her friend she dropped her parasol.

"That's for luck, maybe," she said, with a brightening face. "Let's see what it says about a parasol;" and she turned over her dream-book.

"For a maiden to dream she loses her parasol shows that her sweetheart is false and will never marry her—5, 51, 56."

"But you didn't dream about a parasol, Pinky."

"That's no matter; it's just as good as a dream. 5, 51, 56 is the row. Put that down for the second, Fan."

As Mrs. Bray was writing out these numbers the clock on the mantel struck five.

"8, 12, 60," said Pinky, turning to the clock; "that's the clock row."

And Mrs. Bray put down these figures also.

"That's three rows," said Pinky, "and we want ten." She arose, as she spoke, and going to the front window, looked down upon the street.

"There's an organ-grinder; it's the first thing I saw;" and she came back fingering the leaves of her dream-book. "Put down 40, 50, 26."

Mrs. Bray wrote the numbers on her slip of paper.

"It's November; let's find the November row." Pinky consulted her book again. "Signifies you will have trouble through life—7, 9, 63. That's true as preaching; I was born in November, and I've had it all trouble. How many rows does that make?"

"Five."

"Then we will cut cards for the rest;" and Pinky drew a soiled pack from her pocket, shuffled the cards and let her friends cut them.

"Ten of diamonds;" she referred to the dream-book. "10, 13, 31; put that down."

The cards were shuffled and cut again.

"Six of clubs—6, 35, 39."

Again they were cut and shuffled. This time the knave of clubs was turned up.

"That's 17, 19, 28," said Pinky, reading from her book.

The next cut gave the ace of clubs, and the policy numbers were 18, 63, 75.

"Once more, and the ten rows will be full;" and the cards were cut again.

"Five of hearts—5, 12, 60;" and the ten rows were complete.

"There's luck there, Fan; sure to make a hit," said Pinky, with almost childish confidence, as she gazed at the ten rows of figures. 'One of 'em can't help coming out right, and that would be fifty dollars—twenty-five for me and twenty-five for you; two rows would give a hundred dollars, and the whole ten a thousand. Think of that, Fan! five hundred dollars apiece."

"It would break Sam McFaddon, I'm afraid," remarked Mrs. Bray.

"Sam's got nothing to do with it," returned Pinky.

"He hasn't?"

"No."

"Who has, then?"

"His backer."

"What's that?"

"Oh, I found it all out—I know how it's done. Sam's got a backer—a man that puts up the money. Sam only sells for his backer. When there's a hit, the backer pays."

"Who's Sam's backer, as you call him?"

"Couldn't get him to tell; tried him hard, but he was close as an oyster. Drives in the Park and wears a two thousand dollar diamond pin; he let that out. So he's good for the hits. Sam always puts the money down, fair and square."

"Very well; you get the policy, and do it right off, Pinky, or the money'll slip through your fingers."

"All right," answered Pinky as she folded the slip of paper containing the lucky rows. "Never you fear. I'll be at Sam McFaddon's in ten minutes after I leave here."

"And be sure," said Mrs. Bray, "to look after the baby to-night, and see that it doesn't perish with cold; the air's getting sharp."

"It ought to have something warmer than cotton rags on its poor little body," returned Pinky. "Can't you get it some flannel? It will die if you don't."

"I sent it a warm petticoat last week," said Mrs. Bray.

"You did?"

"Yes; I bought one at a Jew shop, and had it sent to the woman."

"Was it a nice warm one?"

"Yes."

Pinky drew a sigh. "I saw the poor baby last night; hadn't anything on but dirty cotton rags. It was lying asleep in a cold cellar on a little heap of straw. The woman had given it something, I guess, by the way it slept. The petticoat had gone, most likely, to Sam McFaddon's. She spends every-thing she can lay her hands on in policies and whisky."

"She's paid a dollar a week for taking care of the baby at night and on Sundays," said Mrs. Bray.

"It wouldn't help the baby any if she got ten dollars," returned Pinky. "It ought to be taken away from her."

"But who's to do that? Sally Long sold it to the two beggar women, and they board it out. I have no right to interfere; they own the baby, and can do as they please with it."

"It could be got to the almshouse," said Pinky; "it would be a thousand times better off."

"It mustn't go to the almshouse," replied Mrs. Bray; "I might lose track of it, and that would never do."

"You'll lose track of it for good and all before long, if you don't get it out of them women's bands. No baby can hold out being begged with long; it's too hard on the little things. For you know how it is, Fan; they must keep 'em half starved and as sick as they will bear without dying right off, so as to make 'em look pitiful. You can't do much at begging with a fat, hearty-looking baby."

"What's to be done about it?" asked Mrs. Bray. "I don't want that baby to die."

"Would its mother know it if she saw it?" asked Pinky.

"No; for she never set eyes on it."

"Then, if it dies, get another baby, and keep track of that. You can steal one from a drunken mother any night in the week. I'll do it for you. One baby is as good as another."

"It will be safer to have the real one," replied Mrs. Bray. "And now, Pinky that you have put this thing into my head, I guess I'll commission you to get the baby away from that woman."

"All right!"

"But what are we to do with it? I can't have it here."

"Of course you can't. But that's easily managed, if your're willing to pay for it."

"Pay for it?"

"Yes; if it isn't begged with, and made to pay its way and earn something into the bargain, it's got to be a dead weight on somebody. So you see how it is, Fan. Now, if you'll take a fool's advice, you'll let 'it go to the almshouse, or let it alone to die and get out of its misery as soon as possible. You can find another baby that will do just as well, if you should ever need one."

"How much would it cost, do you think, to have it boarded with some one who wouldn't abuse it? She might beg with it herself, or hire it out two or three times a week. I guess it would stand that."

"Beggars don't belong to the merciful kind," answered Pinky; "there's no trusting any of them. A baby in their hands is never safe. I've seen 'em brought in at night more dead than alive, and tossed on a dirty rag-heap to die before morning. I'm always glad when they're out of their misery, poor things! The fact is, Fan, if you expect that baby to live, you've got to take it clean out of the hands of beggars."

"What could I get it boarded for outright?" asked Mrs. Bray.

"For 'most anything, 'cording to how it's done. But why not, while you're about it, bleed the old lady, its grandmother, a little deeper, and take a few drops for the baby?"

"Guess you're kind o' right about that, Fan; anyhow, we'll make a start on it. You find another place for the brat."

"Greed; when shall I do it?"

"The sooner, the better. It might die of cold any night in that horrible den. Ugh!"

"I've been in worse places. Bedlow street is full of them, and so is Briar street and Dirty alley. You don't know anything about it."

"Maybe not, and maybe I don't care to know. At present I want to settle about this baby. You'll find another place for it?"

"Yes."

"And then steal it from the woman who has it now?"

"Yes; no trouble in the world. She's drunk every night," answered Pinky Swett, rising to go.

"You'll see me to-morrow?" said Mrs. Bray.

"Oh yes."

"And you won't forget about the policies?"

"Not I. We shall make a grand hit, or I'm a fool. Day-day!" Pinky waved her hand gayly, and then retired.

CHAPTER VI

A COLD wet drizzling rain was beginning to fall when Pinky Swett emerged from the house. Twilight was gathering drearily. She drew her thin shawl closely, and shivered as the east wind struck her with a chill.

At hurried walk of five or ten minutes brought her to a part of the town as little known to its citizens generally as if it were in the centre of Africa—a part of the town where vice, crime, drunkenness and beggary herd together in the closest and most shameless contact; where men and women, living in all foulness, and more like wild beasts than human beings, prey greedily upon each other, hurting, depraving and marring God's image in all over whom they can get power or influenced—*a very hell upon the earth!*—at part of the town where theft and robbery and murder are plotted, and from which prisons and almshouses draw their chief population.

That such a herding together, almost in the centre of a great Christian city, of the utterly vicious and degraded, should be permitted, when every day's police and criminal records give warning of its cost and danger, is a marvel and a reproach. Almost every other house, in portions of this locality, is a dram-shop, where the vilest liquors are sold. Policy-offices, doing business in direct violation of law, are in every street and block, their work of plunder and demoralization going

T. S. Arthur

on with open doors and under the very eyes of the police. Every one of them is known to these officers. But arrest is useless. A hidden and malign influence, more potent than justice, has power to protect the traffic and hold the guilty offenders harmless. Conviction is rarely, if ever, reached.

The poor wretches, depraved and plundered through drink and policy-gambling, are driven into crime. They rob and steal and debase themselves for money with which to buy rum and policies, and sooner or later the prison or death removes the greater number of them from their vile companions. But drifting toward this fatal locality under the attraction of affinity, or lured thither by harpies in search of new supplies of human victims to repair the frightful waste perpetually made, the region keeps up its dense population, and the work of destroying human souls goes on. It is an awful thing to contemplate. Thousands of men and women, boys and girls, once innocent as the babes upon whom Christ laid his hand in blessing, are drawn into this whirlpool of evil every year, and few come out except by the way of prison or death.

It was toward this locality that Pinky Swett directed her feet, after parting with Mrs. Bray. Darkness was beginning to settle down as she turned off from one of the most populous streets, crowded at the time by citizens on their way to quiet and comfortable homes, few if any of whom had ever turned aside to look upon and get knowledge of the world or crime and wretchedness so near at hand, but girdled in and concealed from common observation.

Down a narrow street she turned from the great thorough-fare, walking with quick steps, and shivering a little as the penetrating east wind sent a chill of dampness through the thin shawl she drew closer and closer about her shoulders. Nothing could be in stronger contrast than the rows of handsome dwellings and stores that lined the streets through which she had just passed, and the forlorn, rickety, unsightly and tumble-down houses amid which she now found herself.

Pinky had gone only a little way when the sharp cries of a child cut the air suddenly, the shrill, angry voice of a woman and the rapid fall of lashes mingled with the cries. The child begged for mercy in tones of agony, but the loud voice, uttering curses and imprecations, and the cruel blows, ceased not. Pinky stopped and shivered. She felt the pain of these blows, in her quickly-aroused sympathy, almost as much as if they had been falling on her own person. Opposite to where she had paused was a one-story frame house, or enclosed shed, as unsightly without as a pig-pen, and almost as filthy within. It contained two small rooms with very low ceilings. The only things in these rooms that could be called furniture were an old bench, two chairs from which the backs had been broken, a tin cup black with smoke and dirt, two or three tin pans in the same condition, some broken crockery and an iron skillet. Pinky stood still for a moment, shivering, as we have said. She knew what the blows and the curses and the cries of pain meant; she had heard them before. A depraved and drunken woman and a child ten years old, who might or might not be her daughter, lived there. The child was sent out every day to beg or steal, and if she failed to bring home a certain sum of money, was cruelly beaten by the woman. Almost every day the poor child was cut with lashes, often on the bare flesh; almost every day her shrieks rang out from the miserable hovel. But there was no one to interfere, no one to save her from the smarting blows, no one to care what she suffered.

Pinky Swett could stand it no longer. She had often noticed the ragged child, with her pale, starved face and large, wistful eyes, passing in and out of this miserable woman's den, sometimes going to the liquor-shops and sometimes to

T. S. Arthur

the nearest policy-office to spend for her mother, if such the woman really was, the money she had gained by begging.

With a sudden impulse, as a deep wail and a more piteous cry for mercy smote upon her ears, Pinky sprang across the street and into the hovel. The sight that met her eyes left no hesitation in her mind. Holding up with one strong arm the naked body of the poor child—she had drawn the clothes over her head—the infuriated woman was raining down blows from a short piece of rattan upon the quivering flesh, already covered with welts and bruises.

"Devil!" cried Pinky as she rushed upon this fiend in human shape and snatched the little girl from her arm. "Do you want to kill the child?"

She might almost as well have assaulted a tigress.

The woman was larger, stronger, more desperate and more thoroughly given over to evil passions than she. To thwart her in anything was to rouse her into a fury. A moment she stood in surprise and bewilderment; in the next, and ere Pinky had time to put herself on guard, she had sprung upon her with a passionate cry that sounded more like that of a wild beast than anything human. Clutching her by the throat with one hand, and with the other tearing the child from her grasp, she threw the frightened little thing across the room.

"Devil, ha!" screamed the woman; "devil!" and she tightened her grasp on Pinky's throat, at the same time striking her in the face with her clenched fist.

Like a war-horse that snuffs the battle afar off and rushes to the conflict, so rushed the inhabitants of that foul neighborhood to the spot from whence had come to their ears the familiar and not unwelcome sound of strife. Even before

Pinky had time to shake off her assailant, the door of the hovel was darkened by a screen of eager faces. And such faces! How little of God's image remained in them to tell of their divine origination!—bloated and scarred, ashen pale and wasted, hollow-eyed and red-eyed, disease looking out from all, yet all lighted up with the keenest interest and expectancy.

Outside, the crowd swelled with a marvelous rapidity. Every cellar and room and garret, every little alley and hidden rookery, "hawk's nest" and "wren's nest," poured out its unseemly denizens, white and black, old and young, male and female, the child of three years old, keen, alert and self-protective, running to see the "row" side by side with the toothless crone of seventy; or most likely passing her on the way. Thieves, beggars, pick-pockets, vile women, rag-pickers and the like, with the harpies who prey upon them, all were there to enjoy the show.

Within, a desperate fight was going on between Pinky Swett and the woman from whose hands she had attempted to rescue the child—a fight in which Pinky was getting the worst of it. One garment after another was torn from her person, until little more than a single one remained.

"Here's the police! look out!" was cried at this juncture.

"Who cares for the police? Let 'em come," boldly retorted the woman. "I haven't done nothing; it's her that's come in drunk and got up a row."

Pushing the crowd aside, a policeman entered the hovel.

"Here she is!" cried the woman, pointing toward Pinky, from whom she had sprung back the moment she heard the word police. "She came in here drunk and got up a row. I'm a decent woman, as don't meddle with nobody. But she's awful when she gets drunk. Just look at her—been tearing her clothes off!"

At this there was a shout of merriment from the crowd who had witnessed the fight.

"Good for old Sal! she's one of 'em! Can't get ahead of old Sal, drunk or sober!" and like expressions were shouted by one and another.

Poor Pinky, nearly stripped of her clothing, and with a great bruise swelling under one of her eyes, bewildered and frightened at the aspect of things around her, could make no acceptable defence.

"She ran over and pitched into Sal, so she did! I saw her! She made the fight, she did!" testified one of the crowd; and acting on this testimony and his own judgment of the case, the policeman said roughly, as he laid his hand on Pinky.

"Pick up your duds and come along."

Pinky lifted her torn garments from the dirty floor and gathered them about her person as best she could, the crowd jeering all the time. A pin here and there, furnished by some of the women, enabled her to get them into a sort of shape and adjustment. Then she tried to explain the affair to the policeman, but he would not listen.

"Come!" he said, sternly.

"What are you going to do with me?" she asked, not moving from where she stood.

"Lock you up," replied the policeman. "So come along."

"What's the matter here?" demanded a tall, strongly-built woman, pressing forward. She spoke with a foreign accent, and in a tone of command. The motley crowd, above whom she towered, gave way for her as she approached. Everything about the woman showed her to be superior in mind and moral force to the unsightly wretches about her. She had the fair skin, blue eyes and light hair of her nation. Her features were strong, but not masculine. You saw in them no trace of coarse sensuality or vicious indulgence.

"Here's Norah! here's the queen!" shouted a voice from the crowd.

"What's the matter here?" asked the woman as she gained an entrance to the hovel.

"Going to lock up Pinky Swett," said a ragged little girl who had forced her way in.

"What for?" demanded the woman, speaking with the air of one in authority.

"'Cause she wouldn't let old Sal beat Kit half to death," answered the child.

"Ho! Sal's a devil and Pinky's a fool to meddle with her." Then turning to the policeman, who still had his hand on the girl, she said,

"What're you goin' to do, John?"

"Goin' to lock her up. She's drunk an' bin a-fightin'."

"You're not goin' to do any such thing."

"I'm not drunk, and it's a lie if anybody says so," broke in

T. S. Arthur

Pinky. "I tried to keep this devil from beating the life out of poor little Kit, and she pitched into me and tore my clothes off. That's what's the matter."

The policeman quietly removed his hand from Pinky's shoulder, and glanced toward the woman named Sal, and stood as if waiting orders.

"Better lock *her* up," said the "queen," as she had been called. Sal snarled like a fretted wild beast.

"It's awful, the way she beats poor Kit," chimed in the little girl who had before spoken against her. "If I was Kit, I'd run away, so I would."

"I'll wring your neck off," growled Sal, in a fierce undertone, making a dash toward the girl, and swearing frightfully. But the child shrank to the side of the policeman.

"If you lay a finger on Kit to-night," said the queen, "I'll have her taken away, and you locked up into the the bargain."

Sal responded with another snarl.

"Come." The queen moved toward the door. Pinky followed, the policeman offering no resistance. A few minutes later, and the miserable crowd of depraved human beings had been absorbed again into cellar and garret, hovel and rookery, to take up the thread of their evil and sensual lives, and to plot wickedness, and to prey upon and deprave each other—to dwell as to their inner and real lives among infernals, to be in hell as to their spirits, while their bodies yet remained upon the earth.

Pinky and her rescuer passed down the street for a short distance until they came to another that was still narrower.

On each side dim lights shone from the houses, and made some revelation of what was going on within. Here liquor was sold, and there policies. Here was a junk-shop, and there an eating-saloon where for six cents you could make a meal out of the cullings from beggars' baskets. Not very tempting to an ordinary appetite was the display inside, nor agreeable to the nostrils the odors that filled the atmosphere. But hunger like the swines', that was not over-nice, satisfied itself amid these disgusting conglomerations, and kept off starvation.

Along this wretched street, with scarcely an apology for a sidewalk, moved Pinky and the queen, until they reached a small two-story frame house that presented a different aspect from the wretched tenements amid which it stood. It was clean upon the outside, and had, as contrasted with its neighbors, an air of superiority. This was the queen's residence. Inside, all was plain and homely, but clean and in order.

The excitement into which Pinky had been thrown was nearly over by this time.

"You've done me a good turn, Norah," she said as the door closed upon them, "and I'll not soon forget you."

"Ugh!" ejaculated Norah as she looked into Pinky's bruised face; "Sal's hit you square in the eye; it'll be black as y'r boot by morning. I'll get some cold water."

A basin of cold water was brought, and Pinky held a wet cloth to the swollen spot for a long time, hoping thereby not only to reduce the swelling, but to prevent discoloration.

"Y'r a fool to meddle with Sal," said Norah as she set the basin of water before Pinky.

T. S. Arthur

"Why don't you meddle with her? Why do you let her beat poor little Kit the way she does?" demanded Pinky.

Norah shrugged her shoulders, and answered with no more feeling in her voice than if she had been speaking of inanimate things:

"She's got to keep Kit up to her work."

"Up to her work!"

"Yes; that's just it. Kit's lazy and cheats—buys cakes and candies; and Sal has to come down on her; it's the way, you know. If Sal didn't come down sharp on her all the while, Kit wouldn't bring her ten cents a day. They all have to do it—so much a day or a lickin'; and a little lickin' isn't any use—got to 'most kill some of 'em. We're used to it in here. Hark!"

The screams of a child in pain rang out wildly, the sounds coming from across the narrow street. Quick, hard strokes of a lash were heard at the same time. Pinky turned a little pale.

"Only Mother Quig," said Norah, with an indifferent air; "she has to do it 'most every night—no getting along any other way with Tom. It beats all how much he can stand."

"Oh, Norah, won't she never stop?" cried Pinky, starting up. "I can't bear it a minute longer."

"Shut y'r ears. You've got to," answered the woman, with some impatience in her voice. "Tom has to be kept to his work as well as the rest of 'em. Half the fuss he's making is put on, anyhow; he doesn't mind a beating any more than a horse. I know his hollers. There's Flanagan's Nell getting it now," added Norah as the cries and entreaties of another child were heard. She drew herself up and listened, a slight shade of concern drifting across her face.

A long, agonizing wail shivered through the air.

"Nell's Sick, and can't do her work." The woman rose as she spoke. "I saw her goin' off to-day, and told Flanagan she'd better keep her at home."

Saying this, Norah went out quickly, Pinky following. With head erect and mouth set firmly, the queen strode across the street and a little way down the pavement, to the entrance of a cellar, from which the cries and sounds of whipping came. Down the five or six rotten and broken steps she plunged, Pinky close after her.

"Stop!" shouted Norah, in a tone of command.

Instantly the blows ceased, and the cries were hushed.

"You'll be hanged for murder if you don't take care," said Norah. "What's Nell been doin'?"

"Doin', the slut!" ejaculated the woman, a short, bloated, revolting creature, with scarcely anything human in her face. "Doin', did ye say? It's nothin' she's been doin', the lazy, trapsing huzzy! Who's that intrudin' herself in here?" she added fiercely, as she saw Pinky, making at the same time a movement toward the girl. "Get out o' here, or I'll spile y'r pictur'!"

"Keep quiet, will you?" said Norah, putting her hand on the woman and pushing her back as easily as if she had been a child. "Now come here, Nell, and let me look at you."

Out of the far corner of the cellar into which Flanagan had thrown her when she heard Norah's voice, and into the small circle of light made by a single tallow candle, there crept slowly the figure of a child literally clothed in rags. Norah reached out her hand to her as she came up—there was a scared look on her pinched face—and drew her close to the light.

"Gracious! your hand's like an ice-ball!" exclaimed Norah.

Pinky looked at the child, and grew faint at heart. She had large hazel eyes, that gleamed with a singular lustre out of the suffering, grimed and wasted little face, so pale and sad and pitiful that the sight of it was enough to draw tears from any but the brutal and hardened.

"Are you sick?" asked Norah.

"No, she's not sick; she's only shamming," growled Flanagan.

"You shut up!" retorted Norah. "I wasn't speaking to you." Then she repeated her question:

"Are you sick, Nell?"

"Yes."

"Whcre?"

"I don't know."

Norah laid her hand on the child's head:

"Does it hurt here?"

"Oh yes! It hurts so I can't see good," answered Nell.

"It's all a lie! I know her; she's shamming."

"Oh no, Norah!" cried the child, a sudden hope blending with the fear in her voice. "I ain't shamming at all. I fell down ever so many times in the street, and 'most got run over. Oh dear! oh dear!" and she clung to the woman with a gesture of despair piteous to see.

"I don't believe you are, Nell," said Norah, kindly. Then, to the woman, "Now mind, Flanagan, Nell's sick; d'ye hear?"

The woman only uttered a defiant growl.

"She's not to be licked again to-night." Norah spoke as one having authority.

"I wish ye'd be mindin' y'r own business, and not come interfarin' wid me. She's my gal, and I've a right to lick her if I plaze."

"Maybe she is and maybe she isn't," retorted Norah.

"Who says she isn't my gal?" screamed the woman, firing up at this and reaching out for Nell, who shrunk closer to Norah.

"Maybe she is and maybe she isn't," said the queen, quietly repeating her last sentence; "and I think maybe she isn't. So take care and mind what I say. Nell isn't to be licked any more to-night."

"Oh, Norah," sobbed the child, in a husky, choking voice, "take me, won't you? She'll pinch me, and she'll hit my head on the wall, and she'll choke me and knock me. Oh, Norah, Norah!"

Pinky could stand this no longer. Catching up the bundle of rags in her arms, she sprang out of the cellar and ran across the street to the queen's house, Norah and Flanagan coming quickly after her. At the door, through which Pinky had passed, Norah paused, and turning to the infuriated Irish woman, said, sternly,

"Go back! I won't have you in here; and if you make a row, I'll tell John to lock you up."

"I want my Nell," said the woman, her manner changing. There was a shade of alarm in her voice.

"You can't have her to-night; so that's settled. And if there's any row, you'll be locked up." Saying which, Norah went in and shut the door, leaving Flanagan on the outside.

The bundle of dirty rags with the wasted body of a child inside, the body scarcely heavier than the rags, was laid by Pinky in the corner of a settee, and the unsightly mass shrunk together like something inanimate.

"I thought you'd had enough with old Sal," said Norah, in a tone of reproof, as she came in.

"Couldn't help it," replied Pinky. "I'm bad enough, but I can't stand to see a child abused like that—no, not if I die for it."

Norah crossed to the settee and spoke to Nell. But there was no answer, nor did the bundle of rags stir.

"Nell! Nell!" She called to deaf ears. Then she put her hand on the child and raised one of the arms. It dropped away limp as a withered stalk, showing the ashen white face across which it had lain.

The two women manifested no excitement. The child had fainted or was dead—which, they did not know. Norah straightened out the wasted little form and turned up the face.

The eyes were shut, the mouth closed, the pinched features rigid, as if still giving expression to pain, but there was no mistaking the sign that life had gone out of them. It might be for a brief season, it might be for ever.

A little water was thrown into the child's face. Its only effect was to streak the grimy skin.

"Poor little thing!" said Pinky. "I hope she's dead."

"They're tough. They don't die easy," returned Norah.

"She isn't one of the tough kind."

"Maybe not. They say Flanagan stole her when she was a little thing, just toddling."

"Don't let's do anything to try to bring her to," said Pinky.

Norah stood for some moment's with an irresolute air, then bent over the child and examined her more carefully. She could feel no pulse beat, nor any motion of the heart,

"I don't want the coroner here," she said, in a tone of annoyance. "Take her back to Flanagan; it's her work, and she must stand by it."

"Is she really dead?" asked Pinky.

"Looks like it, and serves Flanagan right. I've told her over and over that Nell wouldn't stand it long if she didn't ease up a little. Flesh isn't iron."

Again she examined the child carefully, but without the slightest sign of feeling.

T. S. Arthur

"It's all the same now who has her," she said, turning off from the settee. "Take her back to Flanagan."

But Pinky would not touch the child, nor could threat or persuasion lead her to do so. While they were contending, Flanagan, who had fired herself up with half a pint of whisky, came storming through the door in a blind rage and screaming out,

"Where's my Nell? I want my Nell!"

Catching sight of the child's inanimate form lying on the settee, she pounced down upon it like some foul bird and bore it off, cursing and striking the senseless clay in her insane fury.

Pinky, horrified at the dreadful sight, and not sure that the child was really dead, and so insensible to pain, made a movement to follow, but Norah caught her arm with a tight grip and held her back.

"Are you a fool?" said the queen, sternly. "Let Flanagan alone. Nell's out of her reach, and I'm glad of it."

"If I was only sure!" exclaimed Pinky.

"You may be. I know death—I've seen it often enough. They'll have the coroner over there in the morning. It's Flanagan's concern, not yours or mine, so keep out of it if you know when you're well off."

"I'll appear against her at the inquest," said Pinky.

"You'll do no such thing. Keep your tongue behind your teeth. It's time enough to show it when it's pulled out. Take my advice, and mind your own business. You'll have enough to do caring for your own head, without looking after other people's."

"I'm not one of that kind," answered Pinky, a little tartly; "and if there's any way to keep Flanagan from murdering another child, I'm going to find it out."

"You'll find out something else first," said Norah, with a slight curl of her lip.

"What?"

"The way to prison."

"Pshaw! I'm not afraid."

"You'd better be. If you appear against Flanagan, she'll have you caged before to-morrow night."

"How can she do it?"

"Swear against you before an alderman, and he'll send you down if it's only to get his fee. She knows her man."

"Suppose murder is proved against her?"

"Suppose!" Norah gave a little derisive laugh.

"They don't look after things in here as they do outside. Everybody's got the screws on, and things must break sometimes, but it isn't called murder. The coroner understands it all. He's used to seeing things break."

CHAPTER VII

FOR a short time the sounds of cruel exultation came over from Flanagan's; then all was still.

"Sal's put her mark on you," said Norah, looking steadily into Pinky's face, and laughing in a cold, half-amused way.

Pinky raised her hand to her swollen cheek. "Does it look very bad?" she asked.

"Spoils your beauty some."

"Will it get black?"

"Shouldn't wonder. But what can't be helped, can't. You'll mind your own business next time, and keep out of Sal's way. She's dangerous. What's the matter?"

"Got a sort of chill," replied the girl, who from nervous reaction was beginning to shiver.

"Oh, want something to warm you up." Norah brought out a bottle of spirits. Pinky poured a glass nearly half full, added some water, and then drank off the fiery mixture.

"None of your common stuff," said Norah, with a smile, as

Pinky smacked her lips. The girl drew her handkerchief from her pocket, and as she did so a piece of paper dropped on the floor.

"Oh, there it is!" she exclaimed, light flashing into her face. "Going to make a splendid hit. Just look at them rows."

Norah threw an indifferent glance on the paper.

"They're lucky, every one of them," said Pinky. "Going to put half a dollar on each row—sure to make a hit."

The queen gave one of her peculiar shrugs.

"Going to break Sam McFaddon," continued Pinky, her spirits rising under the influence of Norah's treat.

"Soft heads don't often break hard rocks," returned the woman, with a covert sneer.

"That's an insult!" cried Pinky, on whom the liquor she had just taken was beginning to have a marked effect, "and I won't stand an insult from you or anybody else."

"Well, I wouldn't if I was you," returned Norah, coolly. A hard expression began settling about her mouth.

"And I don't mean to. I'm as good as you are, any day!"

"You may be a great deal better, for all I care," answered Norah. "Only take my advice, and keep a civil tongue in your head." There was a threatening undertone in the woman's voice. She drew her tall person more erect, and shook herself like a wild beast aroused from inaction.

Pinky was too blind to see the change that had come so

T. S. Arthur

suddenly. A stinging retort fell from her lips. But the words had scarcely died on the air ere she found herself in the grip of vice-like hands. Resistance was of no more avail than if she had been a child. In what seemed but a moment of time she was pushed back through the door and dropped upon the pavement. Then the door shut, and she was alone on the outside—no, not alone, for scores of the denizens who huddle together in that foul region were abroad, and gathered around her as quickly as flies about a heap of offal, curious, insolent and aggressive. As she arose to her feet she found herself hemmed in by a jeering crowd.

"Ho! it's Pinky Swett!" cried a girl, pressing toward her. "Hi, Pinky! what's the matter? What's up?"

"Norah pitched her out! I saw it!" screamed a boy, one of the young thieves that harbored in the quarter.

"It's a lie!" Pinky answered back as she confronted the crowd.

At this moment another boy, who had come up behind Pinky, gave her dress so violent a jerk that she fell over backward on the pavement, striking her head on a stone and cutting it badly. She lay there, unable to rise, the crowd laughing with as much enjoyment as if witnessing a dog-fight.

"Give her a dose of mud!" shouted one of the boys; and almost as soon as the words were out of his mouth her face was covered with a paste of filthy dirt from the gutter. This, instead of exciting pity, only gave a keener zest to the show. The street rang with shouts and peals of merriment, bringing a new and larger crowd to see the fun. With them came one or two policemen.

Seeing that it was only a drunken woman, they pushed back the crowd and raised her to her feet. As they did so the blood streamed from the back of her head and stained her dress to the waist. She was taken to the nearest station-house.

At eleven o'clock on the next morning, punctual to the minute, came Mrs. Dinneford to the little third-story room in which she had met Mrs. Bray. She repeated her rap at the door before it was opened, and noticed that a key was turned in the lock.

"You have seen the woman?" she said as she took an offered seat, coming at once to the object of her visit.

"Yes."

"Well?"

"I gave her the money."

"Well?"

Mrs. Bray shook her head:

"Afraid I can't do much with her."

"Why?" an anxious expression coming into Mrs. Dinneford's face.

"These people suspect everybody; there is no honor nor truth in them, and they judge every one by themselves. She half accused me of getting a larger amount of money from you, and putting her off with the paltry sum of thirty dollars."

Mrs. Bray looked exceedingly hurt and annoyed.

T. S. Arthur

"Threatened," she went on, "to go to you herself—didn't want any go-betweens nor brokers. I expected to hear you say that she'd been at your house this morning."

"Good Gracious! no!" Mrs. Dinneford's face was almost distorted with alarm.

"It's the way with all these people," coolly remarked Mrs. Bray. "You're never safe with them."

"Did you hint at her leaving the city?—going to New Orleans, for instance?"

"Oh dear, no! She isn't to be managed in that way—is deeper and more set than I thought. The fact is, Mrs. Dinneford"—and Mrs. Bray lowered her voice and looked shocked and mysterious—"I'm beginning to suspect her as being connected with a gang."

"With a gang? What kind of a gang?" Mrs. Dinneford turned slightly pale.

"A gang of thieves. She isn't the right thing; I found that out long ago. You remember what I said when you gave her the child. I told you that she was not a good woman, and that it was a cruel thing to put a helpless, new-born baby into her hands."

"Never mind about that." Mrs. Dinneford waved her hand impatiently. "The baby's out of her hands, so far as that is concerned. A gang of thieves!"

"Yes, I'm 'most sure of it. Goes to people's houses on one excuse and another, and finds out where the silver is kept and how to get in. You don't know half the wickedness that's going on. So you see it's no use trying to get her away."

Mrs. Bray was watching the face of her visitor with covert scrutiny, gauging, as she did so, by its weak alarms, the measure of her power over her.

"Dreadful! dreadful!" ejaculated Mrs. Dinneford, with dismay.

"It's bad enough," said Mrs. Bray, "and I don't see the end of it. She's got you in her power, and no mistake, and she isn't one of the kind to give up so splendid an advantage. I'm only surprised that she's kept away so long."

"What's to be done about it?" asked Mrs. Dinneford, her alarm and distress increasing.

"Ah! that's more than I can tell," coolly returned Mrs. Bray. "One thing is certain—I don't want to have anything more to do with her. It isn't safe to let her come here. You'll have to manage her yourself."

"No, no, no, Mrs. Bray! You mustn't desert me!" answered Mrs. Dinneford, her face growing pallid with fear. "Money is of no account. I'll pay 'most anything, reasonable or unreasonable, to have her kept away."

And she drew out her pocket-book while speaking. At this moment there came two distinct raps on the door. It had been locked after Mrs. Dinneford's entrance. Mrs. Bray started and changed countenance, turning her face quickly from observation. But she was self-possessed in an instant. Rising, she said in a whisper,

"Go silently into the next room, and remain perfectly still. I believe that's the woman now. I'll manage her as best I can."

Almost as quick as thought, Mrs. Dinneford vanished

T. S. Arthur

through a door that led into an adjoining room, and closing it noiselessly, turned a key that stood in the lock, then sat down, trembling with nervous alarm. The room in which she found herself was small, and overlooked the street; it was scantily furnished as a bed-room. In one corner, partly hid by a curtain that hung from a hoop fastened to the wall, was an old wooden chest, such as are used by sailors. Under the bed, and pushed as far back as possible, was another of the same kind. The air of the room was close, and she noticed the stale smell of a cigar.

A murmur of voices from the room she had left so hastily soon reached her ears; but though she listened intently, standing close to the door, she was not able to distinguish a word. Once or twice she was sure that she heard the sound of a man's voice. It was nearly a quarter of an hour by her watch—it seemed two hours—before Mrs. Bray's visitor or visitors retired; then there came a light rap on the door. She opened it, and stood face to face again with the dark-eyed little woman.

"You kept me here a long time," said Mrs. Dinneford, with ill-concealed impatience.

"No longer than I could help," replied Mrs. Bray. "Affairs of this kind are not settled in a minute."

"Then it was that miserable woman?"

"Yes."

"Well, what did you make out of her?"

"Not much; she's too greedy. The taste of blood has sharpened her appetite."

"What does she want?"

"She wants two hundred dollars paid into her hand to-day, and says that if the money isn't here by sundown, you'll have a visit from her in less than an hour afterward."

"Will that be the end of it?"

A sinister smile curved Mrs. Bray's lips slightly.

"More than I can say," she answered.

"Two hundred dollars?"

"Yes. She put the amount higher, but I told her she'd better not go for too big a slice or she might get nothing—that there was such a thing as setting the police after her. She laughed at this in such a wicked, sneering way that I felt my flesh creep, and said she knew the police, and some of their masters, too, and wasn't afraid of them. She's a dreadful woman;" and Mrs. Bray shivered in a very natural manner.

"If I thought this would be the last of it!" said Mrs. Dinneford as she moved about the room in a disturbed way, and with an anxious look on her face.

"Perhaps," suggested her companion, "it would be best for you to grapple with this thing at the outset—to take our vampire by the throat and strangle her at once. The knife is the only remedy for some forms of disease. If left to grow and prey upon the body, they gradually suck away its life and destroy it in the end."

"If I only knew how to do it," replied Mrs. Dinneford. "If I could only get her in my power, I'd make short works of her." Her eyes flashed with a cruel light.

"It might be done."

"How?"

"Mr. Dinneford knows the chief of police."

The light went out of Mrs. Dinneford's eyes:

"It can't be done in that way, and you know it as well as I do."

Mrs. Dinneford turned upon Mrs. Bray sharply, and with a gleam of suspicion in her face.

"I don't know any other way, unless you go to the chief yourself," replied Mrs. Bray, coolly. "There is no protection in cases like this except through the law. Without police interference, you are wholly in this woman's power."

Mrs. Dinneford grew very pale.

"It is always dangerous," went on Mrs. Bray, "to have anything to do with people of this class. A woman who for hire will take a new-born baby and sell it to a beggar-woman will not stop at anything. It is very unfortunate that you are mixed up with her."

"I'm indebted to you for the trouble," replied. Mrs. Dinneford, with considerable asperity of manner. "You ought to have known something about the woman before employing her in a delicate affair of this kind."

"Saints don't hire themselves to put away new-born babies," retorted Mrs. Bray, with an ugly gurgle in her throat. "I told you at the time that she was a bad woman, and have not forgotten your answer."

"What did I answer?"

"That she might be the devil for all you cared!"

"You are mistaken."

"No; I repeat your very words. They surprised and shocked me at the time, and I have not forgotten them. People who deal with the devil usually have the devil to pay; and your case, it seems, is not to be an exception."

Mrs. Bray had assumed an air of entire equality with her visitor.

A long silence followed, during which Mrs. Dinneford walked the floor with the quick, restless motions of a caged animal.

"How long do you think two hundred dollars will satisfy her?" she asked, at length, pausing and turning to her companion.

"It is impossible for me to say," was answered; "not long, unless you can manage to frighten her off; you must threaten hard."

Another silence followed.

"I did not expect to be called on for so large a sum," Mrs. Dinneford said at length, in a husky voice, taking out her pocket-book as she spoke. "I have only a hundred dollars with me. Give her that, and put her off until to-morrow."

"I will do the best I can with her," replied Mrs. Bray, reaching out her hand for the money, "but I think it will be safer for you to let me have the balance to-day. She will, most likely, take it into her head that I have received the whole sum from you, and think I am trying to cheat her. In that case she will be as good as her word, and come down on you."

"Mrs. Bray!" exclaimed Mrs. Dinneford, suspicion blazing from her eyes. "Mrs. Bray!"—and she turned upon her and caught her by the arms with a fierce grip—"as I live, you are deceiving me. There is no woman but yourself. You are the vampire!"

She held the unresisting little woman in her vigorous grasp for some moments, gazing at her in stern and angry accusation.

Mrs. Bray stood very quit and with scarcely a change of countenance until this outburst of passion had subsided. She was still holding the money she had taken from Mrs. Dinneford. As the latter released her she extended her hand, saying, in a low resolute voice, in which not the faintest thrill of anger could be detected,

"Take your money." She waited for a moment, and then let the little roll of bank-bills fall at Mrs. Dinneford's feet and turned away.

Mrs. Dinneford had made a mistake, and she saw it—saw that she was now more than ever in the power of this woman, whether she was true or false. If false, more fatally in her power.

At this dead-lock in the interview between these women there came a diversion. The sound of feet was heard on the stairs, then a hurrying along the narrow passage; a hand was on the door, but the key had been prudently turned on the inside.

With a quick motion, Mrs. Bray waved her hand toward the adjoining chamber. Mrs. Dinneford did not hesitate, but glided in noiselessly, shutting and locking the door behind her.

"Pinky Swett!" exclaimed Mrs. Bray, in a low voice, putting her finger to her lips, as she admitted her visitor, at the same time giving a warning glance toward the other room. Eyeing her from head to foot, she added, "Well, you are an object!"

Pinky had drawn aside a close veil, exhibiting a bruised and swollen face. A dark band lay under one of her eyes, and there was a cut with red, angry margins on the cheek.

"You are an object," repeated Mrs. Bray as Pinky moved forward into the room.

"Well, I am, and no mistake," answered Pinky, with a light laugh. She had been drinking enough to overcome the depression and discomfort of her feelings consequent on the hard usage she had received and a night in one of the city station-houses. "Who's in there?"

Mrs. Bray's finger went again to her lips. "No matter," was replied. "You must go away until the coast is clear. Come back in half an hour."

And she hurried Pinky out of the door, locking it as the girl retired. When Mrs. Dinneford came out of the room into which he had gone so hastily, the roll of bank-notes still lay upon the floor. Mrs. Bray had prudently slipped them into her pocket before admitting Pinky, but as soon as she was alone had thrown them down again.

The face of Mrs. Dinneford was pale, and exhibited no ordinary signs of discomfiture and anxiety.

T. S. Arthur

"Who was that?" she asked.

"A friend," replied Mrs. Bray, in a cold, self-possessed manner.

A few moments of embarrassed silence followed. Mrs. Bray crossed the room, touching with her foot the bank-bills, as if they were of no account to her.

"I am half beside myself," said Mrs. Dinneford.

Mrs. Bray made no response, did not even turn toward her visitor.

"I spoke hastily."

"A vampire!" Mrs. Bray swept round upon her fiercely. "A blood-sucker!" and she ground her teeth in well-feigned passion.

Mrs. Dinneford sat down trembling.

"Take your money and go," said Mrs. Bray, and she lifted the bills from the floor and tossed them into her visitor's lap. "I am served right. It was evil work, and good never comes of evil."

But Mrs. Dinneford did not stir. To go away at enmity with this woman was, so far as she could see, to meet exposure and unutterable disgrace. Anything but that.

"I shall leave this money, trusting still to your good offices," she said, at length, rising. Her manner was much subdued. "I spoke hastily, in a sort of blind desperation. We should not weigh too carefully the words that are extorted by pain or fear. In less than an hour I will send you a hundred dollars more."

Mrs. Dinneford laid the bank-bills on a table, and then moved to the door, but she dared not leave in this uncertainty. Looking back, she said, with an appealing humility of voice and manner foreign to her character,

"Let us be friends still, Mrs. Bray; we shall gain nothing by being enemies. I can serve you, and you can serve me. My suspicions were ill founded. I felt wild and desperate, and hardly knew what I was saying."

She stood anxiously regarding the little dark-eyed woman, who did not respond by word or movement.

Taking her hand from the door she was about opening, Mrs. Dinneford came back into the room, and stood close to Mrs. Bray:

"Shall I send you the money?"

"You can do as you please," was replied, with chilling indifference.

"Are you implacable?"

"I am not used to suspicion, much less denunciation and assault. A vampire! Do you know what that means?"

"It meant, as used by me, only madness. I did not know what I was saying. It was a cry of pain—nothing more. Consider how I stand, how much I have at stake, in what a wretched affair I have become involved. It is all new to me, and I am bewildered and at fault. Do not desert me in this crisis. I must have some one to stand between me and this woman; and if you step aside, to whom can I go?"

Mrs. Bray relented just a little. Mrs. Dinneford pleaded and

T. S. Arthur

humiliated herself, and drifted farther into the toils of her confederate.

"You are not rich, Mrs. Bray," she said, at parting, "independent in spirit as you are. I shall add a hundred dollars for your own use; and if ever you stand in need, you will know where to find an unfailing friend."

Mrs. Bray put up her hands, and replied, "No, no, no; don't think of such a thing. I am not mercenary. I never serve a friend for money."

But Mrs. Dinneford heard the "yes" which flushed into the voice that said "no." She was not deceived.

A rapid change passed over Mrs. Bray on the instant her visitor left the room. Her first act was to lock the door; her next, to take the roll of bank-bills from the table and put it into her pocket. Over her face a gleam of evil satisfaction had swept.

"Got you all right now, my lady!" fell with a chuckle from her lips. "A vampire, ha!" The chuckle was changed for a kind of hiss. "Well, have it so. There is rich blood in your veins, and it will be no fault of mine if I do not fatten upon it. As for pity, you shall have as much of it as you gave to that helpless baby. Saints don't work in this kind of business, and I'm not a saint."

And she chuckled and hissed and muttered to herself, with many signs of evil satisfaction.

CHAPTER VIII

FOR an hour Mrs. Bray waited the reappearance of Pinky Swett, but the girl did not come back. At the end of this time a package which had been left at the door was brought to her room. It came from Mrs. Dinneford, and contained two hundred dollars. A note that accompanied the package read as follows:

"Forgive my little fault of temper. It is your interest to be my friend. The woman must not, on any account, be suffered to come near me."

Of course there was no signature. Mrs. Bray's countenance was radiant as she fingered the money.

"Good luck for me, but bad for the baby," she said, in a low, pleased murmur, talking to herself. "Poor baby! I must see better to its comfort. It deserves to be looked after. I wonder why Pinky doesn't come?"

Mrs. Bray listened, but no sound of feet from the stairs or entries, no opening or shutting of doors, broke the silence that reigned through the house.

"Pinky's getting too low down—drinks too much; can't count on her any more." Mrs. Bray went on talking to herself. "No rest; no quiet; never satisfied; for ever knocking round, and for ever getting the worst of it. She was a real nice girl once, and I always liked her. But she doesn't take any care of herself."

As Pinky went out, an hour before, she met a fresh-looking girl, not over seventeen, and evidently from the country. She was standing on the pavement, not far from the house in which Mrs. Bray lived, and had a traveling-bag in her hand. Her perplexed face and uncertain manner attracted Pinky's attention.

"Are you looking for anybody?" she asked.

"I'm trying to find a Mrs. Bray," the girl answered. "I'm a stranger from the country."

"Oh, you are?" said Pinky, drawing her veil more tightly so that her disfigured face could not be seen.

"Yes I'm from L—."

"Indeed? I used to know some people there."

"Then you've been in L—?" said the girl, with a pleased, trustful manner, as of one who had met a friend at the right time.

"Yes, I've visited there."

"Indeed? Who did you know in L—?"

"Are you acquainted with the Cartwrights?"

"I know of them. They are among our first people," returned the girl.

"I spent a week in their family a few years ago, and had a very pleasant time," said Pinky.

"Oh, I'm glad to know that," remarked the girl. "I'm a stranger here; and if I can't find Mrs. Bray, I don't see what I am to do. A lady from here who was staying at the hotel gave me at letter to Mrs. Bray. I was living at the hotel, but I didn't like it; it was too public. I told the lady that I wanted to learn a trade or get into a store, and she said the city was just the place for me, and that she would give me a letter to a particular friend, who would, on her recommendation, interest he self for me. It's somewhere along here that she lived, I'm sure;" and she took a letter from her pocket and examined the direction.

The girl was fresh and young and pretty, and had an artless, confiding manner. It was plain she knew little of the world, and nothing of its evils and dangers.

"Let me see;" and Pinky reached out her hand for the letter. She put it under her veil, and read,

"MRS. FANNY BRAY, "No. 631—street, "—

"By the hand of Miss Flora Bond."

"Flora Bond," said Pinky, in a kind, familiar tone.

"Yes, that is my name," replied the girl; "isn't this—street?"

"Yes; and there, is the number you are looking for."

"Oh, thank you! I'm so glad to find the place. I was beginning to feel scared."

"I will ring the bell for you," said Pinky, going to the door of

T. S. Arthur

No. 631. A servant answered the summons.

"Is Mrs. Bray at home?" inquired Pinky.

"I don't know," replied the servant, looking annoyed. "Her rooms are in the third story;" and she held the door wide open for them to enter. As they passed into the hall Pinky said to her companion,

"Just wait here a moment, and I will run up stairs and see if she is in."

The girl stood in the hall until Pinky came back.

"Not at home, I'm sorry to say."

"Oh dear! that's bad; what shall I do?" and the girl looked distressed.

"She'll be back soon, no doubt," said Pinky, in a light, assuring voice. "I'll go around with you a little and see things."

The girl looked down at her traveling-bag.

"Oh, that's nothing; I'll help you to carry it;" and Pinky took it from her hand.

"Couldn't we leave it here?" asked Flora.

"It might not be safe; servants are not always to be trusted, and Mrs. Bray's rooms are locked; we can easily carry it between us. I'm strong—got good country blood in my veins. You see I'm from the country as well as you; right glad we met. Don't know what you would have done."

And she drew the girl out, talking familiarly, as they went.

"Haven't had your dinner yet?"

"No; just arrived in the cars, and came right here."

"You must have something to eat, then. I know a nice place; often get dinner there when I'm out."

The girl did not feel wholly at ease. She had not yet been able to get sight of Pinky's closely-veiled features, and there was something in her voice that made her feel uncomfortable.

"I don't care for any dinner," she said; "I'm not hungry."

"Well, I am, then, so come. Do you like oysters?"

"Yes."

"Cook them splendidly. Best place in the city. And you'd like to get into a store or learn a trade?"

"Yes."

"What trade did you think of?"

"None in particular."

"How would you like to get into a book-bindery? I know two or three girls in binderies, and they can make from five to ten dollars a week. It's the nicest, cleanest work I know of."

"Oh, do you?" returned Flora, with newly-awakening interest.

T. S. Arthur

"Yes; we'll talk it all over while we're eating dinner. This way."

And Pinky turned the corner of a small street that led away from the more crowded thoroughfare along which they had been passing.

"It's a quiet and retired place, where only the nicest kind of people go," she added. "Many working-girls and girls in stores get their dinners there. We'll meet some of them, no doubt; and if any that I know should happen in, we might hear of a good place. Just the thing, isn't it? I'm right glad I met you."

They had gone halfway down the square, when Pinky stopped before the shop of a confectioner. In the window was a display of cakes, pies and candies, and a sign with the words, "LADIES' RESTAURANT."

"This is the place," she said, and opening the door, passed in, the young stranger following.

A sign of caution, unseen by Flora, was made to a girl who stood behind the counter. Then Pinky turned, saying,

"How will you have your oysters? stewed, fried, broiled or roasted?"

"I'm not particular—any way," replied Flora.

"I like them fried. Will you have them the same way?"

Flora nodded assent.

"Let them be fried, then. Come, we'll go up stairs. Anybody there?"

"Two or three only."

"Any girls from the bindery?"

"Yes; I think so."

"Oh. I'm glad of that! Want to see some of them. Come, Miss Bond."

And Pinky, after a whispered word to the attendant, led the way to a room up stairs in which were a number of small tables. At one of these were two girls eating, at another a girl sitting by herself, and at another a young man and a girl. As Pinky and her companion entered, the inmates of the room stared at them familiarly, and then winked and leered at each other. Flora did not observe this, but she felt a sudden oppression and fear. They sat down at a table not far from one of the windows. Flora looked for the veil to be removed, so that she might see the face of her new friend. But Pinky kept it closely down.

In about ten minutes the oysters were served. Accompanying them were two glasses of some kind of liquor. Floating on one of these was a small bit of cork. Pinky took this and handed the other to her companion, saying,

"Only a weak sangaree. It will refresh you after your fatigue; and I always like something with oysters, it helps to make them lay lighter on the stomach."

Meantime, one of the girls had crossed over and spoken to Pinky. After word or two, the latter said,

"Don't you work in a bindery, Miss Peter?"

"Yes," was answered, without hesitation.

T. S. Arthur

"I thought so. Let me introduce you to my friend, Miss Flora Bond. She's from the country, and wants to get into some good establishment. She talked about a store, but I think a bindery is better."

"A great deal better," was replied by Miss Peter. "I've tried them both, and wouldn't go back to a store again on any account. If I can serve your friend, I shall be most happy."

"Thank you!" returned Flora; "you are very kind."

"Not at all; I'm always glad when I can be of service to any one. You think you'd like to go into a bindery?"

"Yes. I've come to the city to get employment, and haven't much choice."

"There's no place like the city," remarked the other. "I'd die in the country—nothing going on. But you won't stagnate here. When did you arrive?"

"To-day."

"Have you friends here?"

"No. I brought a letter of introduction to a lady who resides in the city."

"What's her name?"

"Mrs. Bray."

Miss Peter turned her head so that Flora could not see her face. It was plain from its expression that she knew Mrs. Bray.

"Have you seen her yet?" she asked.

"No. She was out when I called. I'm going back in a little while."

The girl sat down, and went on talking while the others were eating. Pinky had emptied her glass of sangaree before she was half through with her oysters, and kept urging Flora to drink.

"Don't be afraid of it, dear," she said, in a kind, persuasive way; "there's hardly a thimbleful of wine in the whole glass. It will soothe your nerves, and make you feel ever so much better."

There was something in the taste of the sangaree that Flora did not like—a flavor that was not of wine. But urged repeatedly by her companion, whose empty glass gave her encouragement and confidence, she sipped and drank until she had taken the whole of it. By this time she was beginning to have a sense of fullness and confusion in the head, and to feel oppressed and uncomfortable. Her appetite suddenly left her, and she laid down her knife and fork and leaned her head upon her hand.

"What's the matter?" asked Pinky.

"Nothing," answered the girl; "only my head feels a little strangely. It will pass off in a moment."

"Riding in the cars, maybe," said Pinky. "I always feel bad after being in the cars; it kind of stirs me up."

Flora sat very quietly at the table, still resting her head upon her hands. Pinky and the girl who had joined them exchanged looks of intelligence. The former had drawn her

T. S. Arthur

veil partly aside, yet concealing as much as possible the bruises on her face.

"My! but you're battered!" exclaimed Miss Peter, in a whisper that was unheard by Flora.

Pinky only answered by a grimace. Then she said to Flora, with well-affected concern,

"I'm afraid you are ill, dear? How do you feel?"

"I don't know," answered the poor girl, in a voice that betrayed great anxiety, if not alarm. "It came over me all at once. I'm afraid that wine was too strong; I am not used to taking anything."

"Oh dear, no! it wasn't that. I drank a glass, and don't feel it any more than if it had been water."

"Let's go," said Flora, starting up. "Mrs. Bray must be home by this time."

"All right, if you feel well enough," returned Pinky, rising at the same time.

"Oh dear! how my head swims!" exclaimed Flora, putting both hands to her temples. She stood for a few moments in an uncertain attitude, then reached out in a blind, eager way.

Pinky drew quickly to her side, and put one arm about her waist.

"Come," she said, "the air is too close for you here;" and with the assistance of the girl who had joined them, she steadied Flora down stairs.

"Doctored a little too high," whispered Miss Peter, with her mouth close to Pinky's ear.

"All right," Pinky whispered back; "they know how to do it."

At the foot of the stairs Pinky said,

"You take her out through the yard, while I pay for the oysters. I'll be with you in a moment."

Poor Flora, was already too much confused by the drugged liquor she had taken to know what they were doing with her.

Hastily paying for the oysters and liquor, Pinky was on hand in a few moments. From the back door of the house they entered a small yard, and passed from this through a gate into a narrow private alley shut in on each side by a high fence. This alley ran for a considerable distance, and had many gates opening into it from yards, hovels and rear buildings, all of the most forlorn and wretched character. It terminated in a small street.

Along this alley Pinky and the girl she had met at the restaurant supported Flora, who was fast losing strength and consciousness. When halfway down, they held a brief consultation.

"It won't do," said Pinky, "to take her through to—street. She's too far gone, and the police will be down on us and carry her off."

"Norah's got some place in there," said the other, pointing to an old wooden building close by.

"I'm out with Norah," replied Pinky, "and don't mean to have anything more to do with her."

"Where's your room?"

"That isn't the go. Don't want her there. Pat Maley's cellar is just over yonder. We can get in from the alley."

"Pat's too greedy a devil. There wouldn't be anything left of her when he got through. No, no, Pinky; I'll have nothing to do with it if she's to go into Pat Maley's cellar."

"Not much to choose between 'em," answered Pinky. "But it won't do to parley here. We must get her in somewhere."

And she pushed open a gate as she spoke. It swung back on one hinge and struck the fence with a bang, disclosing a yard that beggared description in its disorder and filth. In the back part of this yard was a one-and-a-half-story frame building, without windows, looking more like an old chicken-house or pig-stye than a place for human beings to live in. The loft over the first story was reached by ladder on the outside. Above and below the hovel was laid off in kind of stalls or bunks furnished with straw. There were about twenty of these. It was a ten-cent lodging-house, filled nightly. If this wretched hut or stye—call it what you will—had been torn down, it would not have brought ten dollars as kindling-wood. Yet its owner, a gentleman (?) living handsomely up town, received for it the annual rent of two hundred and fifty dollars. Subletted at an average of two dollars a night, it gave an income of nearly seven hundred dollars a year. It was known as the "Hawk's Nest," and no bird of prey ever had a fouler nest than this.

As the gate banged on the fence a coarse, evil-looking man, wearing a dirty Scotch cap and a red shirt, pushed his head up from the cellar of the house that fronted on the street.

"What's wanted?" he asked, in a kind of growl, his upper lip twitching and drawing up at one side in a nervous way, letting his teeth appear.

"We want to get this girl in for a little while," said Pinky. "We'll take her away when she comes round. Is anybody in there?" and she pointed to the hovel.

The man shook his head.

"How much?" asked Pinky.

"Ten cents apiece;" and he held out his hand.

Pinky gave him thirty cents. He took a key from his pocket, and opened the door that led into the lower room. The stench that came out as the door swung back was dreadful. But poor Flora Bond was by this time so relaxed in every muscle, and so dead to outward things, that it was impossible to get her any farther. So they bore her into this horrible den, and laid her down in one of the stalls on a bed of loose straw. Inside, there was nothing but these stalls and straw—not a table or chair, or any article of furniture. They filled up nearly the entire room, leaving only a narrow passage between them. The only means of ventilation was by the door.

As soon as Pinky and her companion in this terrible wickedness were alone with their victim, they searched her pocket for the key of her traveling-bag. On finding it, Pinky was going to open it, when the other said,

"Never mind about that; we can examine her baggage in safer place. Let's go for the movables."

And saying this, she fell quickly to work on the person of Flora, slipping out the ear-rings first, then removing her breast-pin and finger-rings, while Pinky unbuttoned the new

T. S. Arthur

gaiter boots, and drew off both boots and stockings, leaving upon the damp straw the small, bare feet, pink and soft almost as a baby's.

It did not take these harpies five minutes to possess themselves of everything but the poor girl's dress and under-garments. Cloth oversack, pocket-book, collar, linen cuffs, hat, shoes and stockings—all these were taken.

"Hallo!" cried the keeper of this foul den as the two girls hurried out with the traveling-bag and a large bundle sooner than he had expected; and he came quickly forth from the cellar in which he lived like a cruel spider and tried to intercept them, but they glided through the gate and were out of his reach before he could get near. He could follow them only with obscene invectives and horrible oaths. Well he knew what had been done—that there had been a robbery in the "Hawk's Nest," and he not in to share the booty.

Growling like a savage dog, this wretch, in whom every instinct of humanity had long since died—this human beast, who looked on innocence and helplessness as a wolf looks upon a lamb—strode across the yard and entered the den. Lying in one of the stalls upon the foul, damp straw he found Flora Bond. Cruel beast that he was, even he felt himself held back as by an invisible hand, as he looked at the pure face of the insensible girl. Rarely had his eyes rested on a countenance so full of innocence. But the wolf has no pity for the lamb, nor the hawk for the dove. The instinct of his nature quickly asserted itself.

Avarice first. From the face his eyes turned to see what had been left by the two girls. An angry imprecation fell from his lips when he saw how little remained for him. But when he lifted Flora's head and unbound her hair, a gleam of pleasure came info his foul face. It was a full suit of rich chestnut brown, nearly three feet long, and fell in thick masses over her breast and shoulders. He caught it up eagerly, drew it through his great ugly hands, and gloated over it with something of a miser's pleasure as he counts his gold. Then taking a pair of scissors from his pocket, he ran them over the girl's head with the quickness and skill of a barber, cutting close down, that he might not lose even the sixteenth part of an inch of her rich tresses. An Indian scalping his victim could not have shown more eagerness. An Indian's wild pleasure was in his face as he lifted the heavy mass of brown hair and held it above his head. It was not a trophy— not a sign of conquest and triumph over an enemy—but simply plunder, and had a market value of fifteen or twenty dollars.

The dress was next examined; it was new, but not of a costly material. Removing this, the man went out with his portion of the spoils, and locked the door, leaving the half-clothed, unconscious girl lying on the damp, filthy straw, that swarmed with vermin. It was cold as well as damp, and the chill of a bleak November day began creeping into her warm blood. But the stupefying draught had been well compounded, and held her senses locked.

Of what followed we cannot write, and we shiver as we draw a veil over scenes that should make the heart of all Christendom ache—scenes that are repeated in thousands of instances year by year in our large cities, and no hand is stretched forth to succor and no arm to save. Under the very eyes of the courts and the churches things worse than we have described—worse than the reader can imagine—are done every day. The foul dens into which crime goes freely, and into which innocence is betrayed, are known to the police, and the evil work that is done is ever before them. From one victim to another their keepers pass unquestioned, and plunder, debauch, ruin and murder with an impunity

T. S. Arthur

frightful to contemplate. As was said by a distinguished author, speaking of a kindred social enormity, "There is not a country throughout the earth on which a state of things like this would not bring a curse. There is no religion upon earth that it would not deny; there is no people on earth that it would not put to shame."

And we are Christians!

No. Of what followed we cannot write. Those who were near the "Hawk's Nest" heard that evening, soon after nightfall, the single wild, prolonged cry of a woman. It was so full of terror and despair that even the hardened ears that heard it felt a sudden pain. But they were used to such things in that region, and no one took the trouble to learn what it meant. Even the policeman moving on his beat stood listening for only a moment, and then passed on.

Next day, in the local columns of a city paper, appeared the following:

"FOUL PLAY.—About eleven o'clock last night the body of a beautiful young girl, who could not have been over seventeen years of age, was discovered lying on the pavement in—street. No one knew how she came there. She was quite dead when found. There was nothing by which she could be identified. All her clothes but a single undergarment had been removed, and her hair cut off close to her head. There were marks of brutal violence on her person. The body was placed in charge of the coroner, who will investigate the matter."

On the day after, this paragraph appeared:

"SUSPICION OF FOUL PLAY.—The coroner's inquest elicited nothing in regard to the young girl mentioned yesterday as having been found dead and stripped of her clothing in—street. No one was able to identify her. A foul deed at which the heart shudders has been done; but the wretches by whom it was committed have been able to cover their tracks."

And that was the last of it. The whole nation gives a shudder of fear at the announcement of an Indian massacre and outrage. But in all our large cities are savages more cruel and brutal in their instincts than the Comanches, and they torture and outrage and murder a hundred poor victims for every one that is exposed to Indian brutality, and there comes no succor. Is it from ignorance of the fact? No, no, no! There is not a Judge on the bench, not a lawyer at the bar, not a legislator at the State capital, not a mayor or police-officer, not a minister who preaches the gospel of Christ, who came to seek and to save, not an intelligent citizen, but knows of all this.

What then? Who is responsible? The whole nation arouses itself at news of an Indian assault upon some defenseless frontier settlement, and the general government sends troops to succor and to punish. But who takes note of the worse than Indian massacres going on daily and nightly in the heart of our great cities? Who hunts down and punishes the human wolves in our midst whose mouths are red with the blood of innocence? Their deeds of cruelty outnumber every year a hundred—nay, a thousand—fold the deeds of our red savages. Their haunts are known, and their work is known. They lie in wait for the unwary, they gather in the price of human souls, none hindering, at our very church doors. Is no one responsible for all this? Is there no help? Is evil stronger than good, hell stronger than heaven? Have the churches nothing to do in this matter? Christ came to seek and to save that which was lost—came to the lowliest, the poorest and the vilest, to those over whom devils had gained power, and cast out the devils. Are those who call themselves by his name diligent in the work to which he put his blessed hands? Millions of dollars go yearly into magnificent churches, but how little to the work of saving and succoring the weak, the helpless, the betrayed, the outcast and the dying, who lie uncared for at the mercy of human fiends, and often so near to the temples of God that their agonized appeals for help are drowned by the organ and choir!

CHAPTER IX

THE two girls, on leaving the "Hawk's Nest" with their plunder, did not pass from the narrow private alley into the small street at its termination, but hurried along the way they had come, and re-entered the restaurant by means of the gate opening into the yard. Through the back door they gained a small, dark room, from which a narrow stairway led to the second and third stories of the rear building. They seemed to be entirely familiar with the place.

On reaching the third story, Pinky gave two quick raps and then a single rap on a closed door. No movement being heard within, she rapped again, reversing the order—that is, giving one distinct rap, and then two in quick succession. At this the door came slowly open, and the two girls passed in with their bundle of clothing and the traveling-bag.

The occupant of this room was a small, thin, well-dressed man, with cold, restless gray eyes and the air of one who was alert and suspicious. His hair was streaked with gray, as were also his full beard and moustache. A diamond pin of considerable value was in his shirt bosom. The room contained but few articles. There was a worn and faded carpet on the floor, a writing-table and two or three chairs, and a small bookcase with a few books, but no evidence whatever of business—not a box or bundle or article of merchandise was to be seen.

As the two girls entered he, shut the door noiselessly, and turned the key inside. Then his manner changed; his eyes lighted, and there was an expression of interest in his face. He looked toward the bag and bundle.

Pinky sat down upon the floor and hurriedly unlocked the traveling-bag. Thrusting in her hand, she drew out first a muslin nightgown and threw it down, then a light shawl, a new barege dress, a pair of slippers, collars, cuffs, ribbons and a variety of underclothing, and last of all a small Bible and a prayer-book. These latter she tossed from her with a low derisive laugh, which was echoed by her companion, Miss Peter.

The bundle was next opened, and the cloth sacque, the hat, the boots and stockings and the collar and cuffs thrown upon the floor with the contents of the bag.

"How much?" asked Pinky, glancing up at the man.

They were the first words that had been spoken. At this the man knit his brows in an earnest way, and looked business. He lifted each article from the floor, examined it carefully and seemed to be making a close estimate of its value. The traveling-bag was new, and had cost probably five dollars. The cloth sacque could not have been made for less than twelve dollars. A fair valuation of the whole would have been near forty dollars.

"How much?" repeated Pinky, an impatient quiver in her voice.

"Six dollars," replied the man.

"Six devils!" exclaimed Pinky, in a loud, angry voice.

"Six devils! you old swindler!" chimed in Miss Peter.

"You can take them away. Just as you like," returned the man, with cool indifference. "Perhaps the police will give you more. It's the best I can do."

"But see here, Jerkin," said Pinky: "that sacque is worth twice the money."

"Not to me. I haven't a store up town. I can't offer it for sale in the open market. Don't you understand?"

"Say ten dollars."

"Six."

"Here's a breast-pin and a pair of ear-rings," said Miss Peter; "we'll throw them in;" and she handed Jerkin, as he was called, the bits of jewelry she had taken from the person of Flora Bond. He looked at them almost contemptuously as he replied,

"Wouldn't give you a dollar for the set."

"Say eight dollars for the whole," urged Pinky.

"Six fifty, and not a cent more," answered Jerkin.

"Hand over, then, you old cormorant!" returned the girl, fretfully. "It's a shame to swindle us in this way."

The man took out his pocket-book and paid the money, giving half to each of the girls.

"It's just a swindle!" repeated Pinky. "You're an old hard-fisted money-grubber, and no better than a robber. Three dollars and a quarter for all that work! It doesn't pay for the trouble. We ought to have had ten apiece."

"You can make it ten or twenty, or maybe a hundred, if you will," said Jerkin, with a knowing twinkle in his eyes. He gave his thumb a little movement over his shoulder as he spoke.

"That's so!" exclaimed Pinky, her manner undergoing a change, and her face growing bright—at least as much of it as could brighten. "Look here, Nell," speaking to Miss Peter, and drawing a piece of paper from her pocket, "I've got ten rows here. Fanny Bray gave me five dollars to go a half on each row. Meant to have gone to Sam McFaddon's last night, but got into a muss with old Sal and Norah, and was locked up."

"They make ten hits up there to one at Sam McFaddon's," said Jerkin, again twitching his thumb over his shoulder. "It's the luckiest office I ever heard of. Two or three hits every day for a week past—got a lucky streak, somehow. If you go in anywhere, take my advice and go in there," lifting his hand and twitching his thumb upward and over his shoulder again.

The two girls passed from the room, and the door was shut and locked inside. No sooner had they done so than Jerkin made a new examination of the articles, and after satisfying himself as to their value proceeded to put them out of sight. Lifting aside a screen that covered the fireplace, he removed from the chimney back, just above the line of sight, a few loose bricks, and through the hole thus made thrust the articles he had bought, letting them drop into a fireplace on the other side.

On leaving the room of this professional receiver of stolen goods, Pinky and her friend descended to the second story, and by a door which had been cut through into the adjoining property passed to the rear building of the house next door. They found themselves on a landing, or little square hall, with a stairway passing down to the lower story and another leading to the room above. A number of persons were going up and coming down—a forlorn set, for the most part, of all sexes, ages and colors. Those who were going up appeared eager and hopeful, while those who were coming down looked disappointed, sorrowful, angry or desperate. There was a "policy shop" in one of the rooms above, and these were some of its miserable customers. It was the hour when the morning drawings of the lotteries were received at the office, or "shop," and the poor infatuated dupes who had bet on their favorite "rows" were crowding in to learn the result.

Poor old men and women in scant or wretched clothing, young girls with faces marred by evil, blotched and bloated creatures of both sexes, with little that was human in their countenances, except the bare features, boys and girls not yet in their teens, but old in vice and crime, and drunkards with shaking nerves,—all these were going up in hope and coming down in disappointment. Here and there was one of a different quality, a scantily-dressed woman with a thin, wasted face and hollow eyes, who had been fighting the wolf and keeping fast hold of her integrity, or a tender, innocent-looking girl, the messenger of a weak and shiftless mother, or a pale, bright-eyed boy whose much-worn but clean and well-kept garments gave sad evidence of a home out of which prop and stay had been removed. The strong and the weak, the pure and the defiled, were there. A poor washerwoman who in a moment of weakness has pawned the garments entrusted to her care, that she might venture upon a "row" of which she had dreamed, comes shrinking down with a pale, frightened face, and the bitterness of despair in her heart. She has lost. What then? She has no friend from whom she can borrow enough money to redeem the clothing, and if it is not taken home she may be arrested as a thief and sent to prison. She goes away, and temptation lies close at her feet. It is her extremity and the evil one's opportunity. So far she has kept herself pure, but the disgrace of a public prosecution and a sentence to prison are terrible things to contemplate. She is in peril of her soul. God help her!

Who is this dressed in rusty black garments and closely veiled, who comes up from the restaurant, one of the convenient and unsuspected entrances to this robber's den?—for a "policy-shop" is simply a robbery shop, and is so regarded by the law, which sets a penalty upon the "writer" and the "backer" as upon other criminals. But who is this veiled woman in faded mourning garments who comes gliding as noiselessly as a ghost out from one of the rooms of the restaurant, and along the narrow entry leading to the stair-way, now so thronged with visitors? Every day she comes and goes, no one seeing her face, and every day, with rare exceptions, her step is slower and her form visibly more shrunken when she goes out than when she comes in. She is a broken-down gentlewoman, the widow of an officer, who left her at his death a moderate fortune, and quite sufficient for the comfortable maintenance of herself and two nearly grown-up daughters. But she had lived at the South, and there acquired a taste for lottery gambling. During her husband's lifetime she wasted considerable money in lottery tickets, once or twice drawing small prizes, but like all lottery dupes spending a hundred dollars for one gained. The thing had become a sort of mania with her. She thought so much of prizes and drawn numbers through the day that she dreamed of them all night. She had a memorandum-book in which were all the combinations she had ever heard of as taking prizes. It contained page after page of lucky numbers and fancy "rows," and was oftener in her hand than any other book.

There being no public sale of lottery tickets in Northern cities, this weak and infatuated woman found out where some of the "policy-shops" were kept, and instead of buying tickets, as before, risked her money on numbers that might or might not come out of the wheel in lotteries said to be drawn in certain Southern States, but chiefly in Kentucky. The numbers rarely if ever came out. The chances were too remote. After her husband's death she began fretting over the smallness of her income. It was not sufficient to give her daughters the advantages she desired them to have, and she knew of but one way to increase it. That way was through the policy-shops. So she gave her whole mind to this business, with as much earnestness and self-absorption as a merchant gives himself to trade. She had a dream-book, gotten up especially for policy buyers, and consulted it as regularly as a merchant does his price-current or a broker the sales of stock. Every day she bet on some "row" or series of "rows," rarely venturing less than five dollars, and sometimes, when she felt more than usually confident, laying down a twenty-dollar bill, for the "hit" when made gave from fifty to two hundred dollars for each dollar put down, varying according to the nature of the combinations. So the more faith a policy buyer had in his "row," the larger the venture he would feel inclined to make.

Usually it went all one way with the infatuated lady. Day after day she ventured, and day after day she lost, until from hundreds the sums she was spending had aggregated themselves into thousands. She changed from one policy-shop to another, hoping for better luck. It was her business to find them out, and this she was able to do by questioning some of those whom she met at the shops. One of these was in a building on a principal street, the second story of which was occupied by a milliner. It was visited mostly by ladies, who could pass in from the street, no one suspecting their errand. Another was in the attic of a house in which were many offices and places of business, with people going in and coming out all the while, none but the initiated being in the secret; while another was to be found in the rear of a photograph gallery. Every day and often twice a day, as punctually as any man of business, did this lady make her calls at one and another of these policy-offices to get the drawings or make new ventures. At remote intervals she would make a "hit;" once she drew twenty dollars, and once fifty. But for these small gains she had paid thousands of dollars.

After a "hit" the betting on numbers would be bolder. Once she selected what was known as a "lucky row," and determined to double on it until it came out a prize. She began by putting down fifty cents. On the next day she put down a dollar upon the same combination, losing, of course, Two dollars were ventured on the next day; and so she went on doubling, until, in her desperate infatuation, she doubled for the ninth time, putting down two hundred and fifty-six dollars.

If successful now, she would draw over twenty-five thousand dollars. There was no sleep for the poor lady during the night that followed. She walked the floor of her chamber in a state of intense nervous excitement, sometimes in a condition of high hope and confidence and sometimes haunted by demons of despair. She sold five shares of stock on which she had been receiving an annual dividend of ten per cent., in order to get funds for this desperate gambling venture, in which over five hundred dollars had now been absorbed.

Pale and nervous, she made her appearance at the breakfast-table on the next morning, unable to take a mouthful of food. It was in vain that her anxious daughters urged her to eat.

A little after twelve o'clock she was at the policy-office. The drawn numbers for the morning were already in. Her combination was 4, 10, 40. With an eagerness that could not be repressed, she caught up the slip of paper containing the thirteen numbers out of seventy-five, which purported to have been drawn that morning somewhere in "Kentucky," and reported by telegraph—caught it up with hands that shook so violently that she could not read the figures. She had to lay the piece of paper down upon the little counter before which she stood, in order that it might be still, so that she could read her fate.

The first drawn number was 4. What a wild leap her heart gave! The next was 24; the next 8; the next 70; the next 41, and the next 39. Her heart grew almost still; the pressure as of a great hand was on her bosom. 10 came next. Two numbers of her row were out. A quiver of excitement ran through her frame. She caught up the paper, but it shook as before, so that she could not see the figures. Dashing it back upon the counter, and holding it down almost violently, she bent over, with eyes starting from their sockets, and read the line of figures to the end, then sank over upon the counter with a groan, and lay there half fainting and too weak to lift herself up. If the 40 had been there, she would have made a hit of twenty-five thousand dollars. But the 40 was not there, and this made all the difference.

"Once more," said the policy-dealer, in a tone of encourage-ment, as he bent over the miserable woman. Yesterday, 4 came out; to-day, 4, 10; tomorrow will be the lucky chance; 4, 10, 40 will surely be drawn. I never knew this order to fail. If it had been 10 first, and then 4, 10, or 10, 4, I would not advise you to go on. But 4, 10, 40 will be drawn to-morrow as sure as fate."

"What numbers did you say? 4, 10, 40?" asked an old man, ragged and bloated, who came shuffling in as the last remarks was made.

"Yes," answered the dealer. "This lady has been doubling, and as the chances go, her row is certain to make a hit to-morrow."

"Ha! What's the row? 4, 10, 40?"

"Yes."

The old man fumbled in his pocket, and brought out ten cents.

"I'll go that on the row. Give me a piece."

The dealer took a narrow slip of paper and wrote on it the date, the sum risked and the combination of figures, and handed it to the old man, saying,

"Come here to-morrow; and if the bottom of the world doesn't drop out, you'll find ten dollars waiting for you."

Two or three others were in by this time, eager to look over the list of drawn numbers and to make new bets.

"Glory!" cried one of them, a vile-looking young woman, and she commenced dancing about the room.

All was excitement now. "A hit! a hit!" was cried. "How much? how much?" and they gathered to the little counter and desk of the policy-dealer.

"1, 2, 3," cried the girl, dancing about and waving her little slip of paper over her head. "I knew it would come— dreamed of them numbers three nights hand running! Hand over the money, old chap! Fifteen dollars for fifteen cents!

That's the go!"

The policy-dealer took the girl's "piece," and after comparing it with the record of drawn numbers, said, in a pleased voice,

"All right! A hit, sure enough. You're in luck to-day."

The girl took the money, that was promptly paid down, and as she counted it over the dealer remarked,

"There's a doubling game going on, and it's to be up to-morrow, sure."

"What's the row?" inquired the girl.

"4, 10, 40," said the dealer.

"Then count me in;" and she laid down five dollars on the counter.

"Take my advice and go ten," urged the policy-dealer.

"No, thank you! shouldn't know what to do with more than five hundred dollars. I'll only go five dollars this time."

The "writer," as a policy-seller is called, took the money and gave the usual written slip of paper containing the selected numbers; loudly proclaiming her good luck, the girl then went away. She was an accomplice to whom a "piece" had been secretly given after the drawn numbers were in.

Of course this hit was the sensation of the day among the policy-buyers at that office, and brought in large gains.

The wretched woman who had just seen five hundred dollars vanish into nothing instead of becoming, as under the wand of an enchanter, a great heap of gold, listened in a kind of maze to what passed around her—listened and let the tempter get to her ear again. She went away, stooping in her gait as one bearing a heavy burden. Before an hour had passed hope had lifted her again into confidence. She had to make but one venture more to double on the risk of the day previous, and secure a fortune that would make both herself and daughters independent for life.

Another sale of good stocks, another gambling venture and another loss, swelling the aggregate in this wild and hopeless "doubling" experiment to over a thousand dollars.

But she was not cured. As regularly as a drunkard goes to the bar went she to the policy-shops, every day her fortune growing less. Poverty began to pinch. The house in which she lived with her daughters was sold, and the unhappy family shrunk into a single room in a third-rate boarding-house. But their income soon became insufficient to meet the weekly demand for board. Long before this the daughters had sought for something to do by which to earn a little money. Pride struggled hard with them, but necessity was stronger than pride.

We finish the story in a few words. In a moment of weakness, with want and hard work staring her in the face, one of the daughters married a man who broke her heart and buried her in less than two years. The other, a weak and sickly girl, got a situation as day governess in the family of an old friend of her father's, where she was kindly treated, but she lived only a short time after her sister's death.

And still there was no abatement of the mother's infatuation. She was more than half insane on the subject of policy gambling, and confident of yet retrieving her fortunes.

At the time Pinky Swett and her friend in evil saw her come gliding up from the restaurant in faded mourning garments and closely veiled, she was living alone in a small, meagrely furnished room, and cooking her own food.

Everything left to her at her husband's death was gone. She earned a dollar or two each week by making shirts and drawers for the slop-shops, spending every cent of this in policies. A few old friends who pitied her, but did not know of the vice in which she indulged, paid her rent and made occasional contributions for her support. All of these contributions, beyond the amount required for a very limited supply of food, went to the policy-shops. It was a mystery to her friends how she had managed to waste the handsome property left by her husband, but no one suspected the truth.

CHAPTER X

"*WHO'S* that, I wonder?" asked Nell Peter as the dark, close-veiled figure glided past them on the stairs.

"Oh, she's a policy-drunkard," answered Pinky, loud enough to be heard by the woman, who, as if surprised or alarmed, stopped and turned her head, her veil falling partly away, and disclosing features so pale and wasted that she looked more like a ghost than living flesh and blood. There was a strange gleam in her eyes. She paused only for an instant, but her steps were slower as she went on climbing the steep and narrow stairs that led to the policy-office.

"Good Gracious, Pinky! did you ever see such a face?" exclaimed Nell Peter. "It's a walking ghost, I should say, and no woman at all."

"Oh, I've seen lots of 'em," answered Pinky. "She's a policy-drunkard. Bad as drinking when it once gets hold of 'em. They tipple all the time, sell anything, beg, borrow, steal or starve themselves to get money to buy policies. She's one of 'em that's starving."

By this time they had reached the policy-office. It was in a small room on the third floor of the back building, yet as well known to the police of the district as if it had been on the front street. One of these public guardians soon after his appointment through political influence, and while some wholesome sense of duty and moral responsibility yet remained, caused the "writer" in this particular office to be arrested. He thought that he had done a good thing, and looked for approval and encouragement. But to his surprise and chagrin he found that he had blundered. The case got no farther than the alderman's. Just how it was managed he did not know, but it was managed, and the business of the office went on as before.

A little light came to him soon after, on meeting a prominent politician to whom he was chiefly indebted for his appointment. Said this individual, with a look of warning and a threat in his voice,

"See here, my good fellow; I'm told that you've been going out of your way and meddling with the policy-dealers. Take my advice, and mind your own business. If you don't. it will be all day with you. There isn't a man in town strong enough to fight this thing, so you'd better let it alone."

And he did let it alone. He had a wife and three little children, and couldn't afford to lose his place. So he minded his own business, and let it alone.

Pinky and her friend entered this small third-story back room. Behind a narrow, unpainted counter, having a desk at one end, stood a middle-aged man, with dark, restless eyes that rarely looked you in the face. He wore a thick but rather closely-cut beard and moustache. The police knew him very well; so did the criminal lawyers, when he happened to come in their way; so did the officials of two or three State prisons in which he had served out partial sentences. He was too valuable to political "rings" and associations antagonistic to moral and social well-being to be left idle in the cell of a penitentiary for the whole term of a commitment. Politicians have great influence, and governors are human.

On the walls of the room were pasted a few pictures cut from the illustrated papers, some of them portraits of leading politicians, and some of them portraits of noted pugilists and sporting-men. The picture of a certain judge, who had made himself obnoxious to the fraternity of criminals by his severe sentences, was turned upside down. There was neither table nor chair in the room.

The woman in black had passed in just before the girls, and was waiting her turn to examine the drawn numbers. She had not tasted food since the day before, having ventured her only dime on a policy, and was feeling strangely faint and bewildered. She did not have to wait long. It was the old story. Her combination had not come out, and she was starving. As she moved back toward the door she staggered a little. Pinky, who had become curious about her, noticed this, and watched her as she went out.

"It's about up with the old lady, I guess," she said to her companion, with an unfeeling laugh.

And she was right. On the next morning the poor old woman was found dead in her room, and those who prepared her for burial said that she was wasted to a skeleton. She had, in fact, starved herself in her infatuation, spending day after day in policies what she should have spent for food. Pinky's strange remark was but too true. She had become a policy-drunkard—a vice almost as disastrous in its effects as its kindred, vice, intemperance, though less brutalizing and less openly indulged.

"Where now?" was the question of Pinky's friend as they came down, after spending in policies all the money they had received from the sale of Flora Bond's clothing. "Any other game?"

"Yes."

"What?"

"Come along to my room, and I'll tell you."

"Round in Ewing street?"

"Yes. Great game up, if I can only get on the track."

"What is it?"

"There's a cast-off baby in Dirty Alley, and Fan Bray knows its mother, and she's rich."

"What?"

"Fan's getting lots of hush-money."

"Goody! but that is game!"

"Isn't it? The baby's owned by two beggar-women who board it in Dirty Alley. It's 'most starved and frozen to death, and Fan's awful 'fraid it may die. She wants me to steal it for her, so that she may have it better taken care of, and I was going to do it last night, when I got into a muss."

"Who's the woman that boards it?"

"She lives in a cellar, and is drunk every night. Can steal the brat easily enough; but if I can't find out who it belongs to, you see it will be trouble for nothing."

"No, I don't see any such thing," answered Nell Peter. "If you can't get hush-money out of its mother, you can bleed Fanny Bray."

"That's so, and I'm going to bleed her. The mother, you see, thinks the baby's dead. The proud old grandmother gave it away, as soon as was born, to a woman that Fan Bray found for her. Its mother was out of her head, and didn't know nothing. That woman sold the baby to the women who keep it to beg with. She's gone up the spout now, and nobody knows who the mother and grandmother are but Fan, and nobody knows where the baby is but me and Fan. She's bleeding the old lady, and promises to share with me if I keep track of the baby and see that it isn't killed or starved to death. But I don't trust her. She puts me off with fives and tens, when I'm sure she gets hundreds. Now, if we have the baby all to ourselves, and find out the mother and grand-mother, won't we have a splendid chance? I'll bet you on that."

"Won't we? Why, Pinky, this is a gold-mine!"

"Didn't I tell you there was great game up? I was just wanting some one to help me. Met you in the nick of time."

The two girls had now reached Pinky's room in Ewing street, where they continued in conference for a long time before settling their plans.

"Does Fan know where you live?" queried Nell Peter.

"Yes."

"Then you will have to change your quarters."

"Easily done. Doesn't take half a dozen furniture-cars to

move me."

"I know a room."

"Where?"

"It's a little too much out of the way, you'll think, maybe, but it's just the dandy for hiding in. You cart keep the brat there, and nobody—"

"Me keep the brat?" interrupted Pinky, with a derisive laugh. "That's a good one! I see myself turned baby-tender! Ha! ha! that's funny!"

"What do you expect to do with the child after you steal it?" asked Pinky's friend.

"I don't intend to nurse it or have it about me."

"What then?"

"Board if with some one who doesn't get drunk or buy policies."

"You'll hunt for a long time."

"Maybe, but I'll try. Anyhow, it can't be worse off than it is now. What I'm afraid of is that it will be out of its misery before we can get hold of it. The woman who is paid for keeping it at night doesn't give it any milk—just feeds it on bread soaked in water, and that is slow starvation. It's the way them that don't want to keep their babies get rid of them about here."

"The game's up if the baby dies," said Nell Peter, growing excited under this view of the case. "If it only gets bread soaked in water, it can't live. I've seen that done over and over again. They're starving a baby on bread and water now just over from my room, and it cries and frets and moans all the time it's awake, poor little wretch! I've been in hopes for a week that they'd give it an overdose of paregoric or something else."

"We must fix it to-night in some way," answered Pinky. "Where's the room you spoke of?"

"In Grubb's court. You know Grubb's court?—a kind of elbow going off from Rider's court. There's a room up there that you can get where even the police would hardly find you out."

"Thieves live there," said Pinky.

"No matter. They'll not trouble you or the baby."

"Is the room furnished?"

"Yes. There's a bed and a table and two chairs."

After farther consultation it was decided that Pinky should move at once from her present lodgings to the room in Grubb's court, and get, if possible, possession of the baby that very night. The moving was easily accomplished after the room was secured. Two small bundles of clothing constituted Pinky's entire effects; and taking these, the two girls went quietly out, leaving a week's rent unpaid.

The night that closed this early winter day was raw and cold, the easterly wind still prevailing, with occasional dashes of rain. In a cellar without fire, except a few bits of smouldering wood in an old clay furnace, that gave no warmth to the damp atmosphere, and with scarcely an article of furniture, a woman half stupid from drink sat on a heap of straw, her bed, with her hands clasped about her knees. She was rocking her body backward and forward, and crooning to herself in a maudlin way. A lighted tallow candle stood on the floor of the cellar, and near it a cup of water, in which was a spoon and some bread soaking.

"Mother Hewitt!" called a voice from the cellar door that opened on the street. "Here, take the baby!"

Mother Hewitt, as she was called, started up and made her way with an unsteady gait to the front part of the cellar, where a woman in not much better condition than herself stood holding out a bundle of rags in which a fretting baby was wrapped.

"Quick, quick!" called the woman. "And see here," she continued as Mother Hewitt reached her arms for the baby; "I don't believe you're doing the right thing. Did he have plenty of milk last night and this morning?"

"Just as much as he would take."

"I don't believe it. He's been frettin' and chawin' at the strings of his hood all the afternoon, when he ought to have been asleep, and he's looking punier every day. I believe you're giving him only bread and water."

But Mother Hewitt protested that she gave him the best of new milk, and as much as he would take.

"Well, here's a quarter," said the woman, handing Mother Hewitt some money; "and see that he is well fed to-night and to-morrow morning. He's getting 'most too deathly in his face. The people won't stand it if they think a baby's going to die—the women 'specially, and most of all the young things that have lost babies. One of these—I know 'em by the way they look out of their eyes—came twice to-day and stood over him sad and sorrowful like; she didn't give me anything. I've seen her before. Maybe she's his mother. As like as nor, for nobody knows where he came from. Wasn't Sally Long's baby; always thought she'd stole him from somebody. Now, mind, he's to have good milk every day, or I'll change his boarding-house. D'ye hear!"

And laughing at this sally, the woman turned away to spend in a night's debauch the money she had gained in half a day's begging.

Left to herself, Mother Hewitt went staggering back with the baby in her arms, and seated herself on the ground beside the cup of bread and water, which was mixed to the consistence of cream. As she did so the light of her poor candle fell on the baby's face. It was pinched and hungry and ashen pale, the thin lips wrought by want and suffering into such sad expressions of pain that none but the most stupid and hardened could look at them and keep back a gush of tears.

But Mother Hewitt saw nothing of this—felt nothing of this. Pity and tenderness had long since died out of her heart. As she laid the baby back on one arm she took a spoonful of the mixture prepared for its supper, and pushed it roughly into its mouth. The baby swallowed it with a kind of starving eagerness, but with no sign of satisfaction on its sorrowful little face. But Mother Hewitt was too impatient to get through with her work of feeding the child, and thrust in spoonful after spoonful until it choked, when she shook it angrily, calling it vile names.

The baby cried feebly at this. when she shook it again and slapped it with her heavy hand. Then it grew still. She put the spoon again to its lips, but it shut them tightly and turned its head away.

"Very well," said Mother Hewitt. "If you won't, you won't;" and she tossed the helpless thing as she would have tossed a senseless bundle over upon the heap of straw that served as a bed, adding, as she did so, "I never coaxed my own brats."

The baby did not cry. Mother Hewitt then blew out the candle, and groping her way to the door of the cellar that opened on the street, went out, shutting down the heavy door behind her, and leaving the child alone in that dark and noisome den—alone in its foul and wet garments, but, thanks to kindly drugs, only partially conscious of its misery.

Mother Hewitt's first visit was to the nearest dram-shop. Here she spent for liquor five cents of the money she had received. From the dram-shop she went to Sam McFaddon's policy-office. This was not hidden away, like most of the offices, in an upper room or a back building or in some remote cellar, concealed from public observation, but stood with open door on the very street, its customers going in and out as freely and unquestioned as the customers of its next-door neighbor, the dram-shop. Policemen passed Sam's door a hundred times in every twenty-four hours, saw his customers going in and out, knew their errand, talked with Sam about his business, some of them trying their luck occasionally after there had been an exciting "hit," but none reporting him or in any way interfering with his unlicensed plunder of the miserable and besotted wretches that crowded his neighborhood.

From the whisky-shop to the policy-shop went Mother Hewitt. Here she put down five cents more; she never bet higher than this on a "row." From the policy-shop she went back to the whisky-shop, and took another drink. By this time she was beginning to grow noisy. It so happened that the woman who had left the baby with her a little while before came in just then, and being herself much the worse for drink, picked a quarrel with Mother Hewitt, accusing her of getting drunk on the money she received for keeping the baby, and starving it to death. A fight was the consequence, in which they were permitted to tear and scratch and bruise each other in a shocking way, to the great enjoyment of the little crowd of debased and brutal men and women who filled the dram-shop. But fearing a visit from the police, the owner of the den, a strong, coarse Irishman, interfered, and dragging the women apart, pushed Mother Hewitt out, giving her so violent an impetus that she fell forward into the middle of the narrow street, where she lay unable to rise, not from any hurt, but from sheer intoxication.

"What's up now?" cried one and another as this little ripple of disturbance broke upon that vile and troubled sea of humanity.

"Only Mother Hewitt drunk again!" lightly spoke a young girl not out of her teens, but with a countenance that seemed marred by centuries of debasing evil. Her laugh would have made an angel shiver.

A policeman came along, and stood for a little while looking at the prostrate woman.

"It's Mother Hewitt," said one of the bystanders.

"Here, Dick," and the policeman spoke to a man near him. "Take hold of her feet."

The man did as told, and the policeman lifting the woman's head and shoulders, they carried her a short distance, to where a gate opened into a large yard used for putting in carts and wagons at night, and deposited her on the ground just inside.

"She can sleep it off there," said the policeman as he dropped his unseemly load. "She'll have a-plenty to keep her company before morning."

And so they left her without covering or shelter in the wet and chilly air of a late November night, drunk and asleep.

As the little crowd gathered by this ripple of excitement melted away, a single figure remained lurking in a corner of the yard and out of sight in its dark shadow. It was that of a man. The moment he was alone with the unconscious woman he glided toward her with the alert movements of an animal, and with a quickness that made his work seem instant, rifled her pockets. His gains were ten cents and the policy-slip she had just received at Sam McFaddon's. He next examined her shoes, but they were of no value, lifted her dirty dress and felt its texture for a moment, then dropped it with a motion of disgust and a growl of disappointment.

As he came out from the yard with his poor booty, the light from a street-lamp fell on as miserable a looking wretch as ever hid himself from the eyes of day—dirty, ragged, bloated, forlorn, with scarcely a trace of manhood in his swollen and disfigured face. His steps, quick from excitement a few moments before, were now shambling and made with difficulty. He had not far to walk for what he was seeking. The ministers to his appetite were all about him, a dozen in every block of that terrible district that seemed as if forsaken by God and man. Into the first that came in his way he went with nervous haste, for he had not tasted of the fiery stimulant he was craving with a fierce and unrelenting thirst for many hours. He did not leave the bar until he had drank as much of the burning poison its keeper dispensed as his booty would purchase. In less than half an hour he was thrown dead drunk into the street and then carried by policemen to the old wagon-yard, to take his night's unconscious rest on the ground in company with Mother Hewitt and a score besides of drunken wretches who were pitilessly turned out from the various dram-shops after their money was spent, and who were not considered by the police worth the trouble of taking to the station-house.

When Mother Hewitt crept back into her cellar at daylight, the baby was gone.

CHAPTER XI

FOR more than a week after Edith's call on Dr. Radcliffe she seemed to take but little interest in anything, and remained alone in her room for a greater part of the time, except when her father was in the house. Since her questions about her baby a slight reserve had risen up between them. During this time she went out at least once every day, and when questioned by her mother as to where she had been, evaded any direct answer. If questioned more closely, she would show a rising spirit and a decision of manner that had the effect to silence and at the same time to trouble Mrs. Dinneford, whose mind was continually on the rack.

One day the mother and daughter met in a part of the city where neither of them dreamed of seeing the other. It was not far from where Mrs. Bray lived. Mrs. Dinneford had been there on a purgational visit, and had come away lighter in purse and with a heavier burden of fear and anxiety on her heart.

"What are you doing here?" she demanded.

"I've been to St. John's mission sewing-school," replied Edith. "I have a class there."

"You have! Why didn't you tell me this before? I don't like

such doings. This is no place for you."

"My place is where I can do good," returned Edith, speaking slowly, but with great firmness.

"Good! You can do good if you want to without demeaning yourself to work like this. I don't want you mixed up with these low, vile people, and I won't have it!" Mrs. Dinneford spoke in a sharp, positive voice.

Edith made no answer, and they walked on together.

"I shall speak to your father about this," said Mrs. Dinneford. "It isn't reputable. I wouldn't have you seen here for the world."

"I shall walk unhurt; you need not fear," returned Edith.

There was silence between them for some time, Edith not caring to speak, and her mother in doubt as to what it were best to say.

"How long have you been going to St. John's mission school?" at length queried Mrs. Dinneford.

"I've been only a few times," replied Edith.

"And have a class of diseased and filthy little wretches, I suppose—gutter children?"

"They are God's children," said Edith, in a tone of rebuke.

"Oh, don't preach to me!" was angrily replied.

"I only said what was true," remarked Edith.

There was silence again.

"Are you going directly home?" asked Mrs. Dinneford, after they had walked the distance of several blocks. Edith replied that she was.

"Then you'd better take that car. I shall not be home for an hour yet."

They separated, Edith taking the car. As soon as she was alone Mrs. Dinneford quickened her steps, like a person who had been held back from some engagement. A walk of ten minutes brought her to one of the principal hotels of the city. Passing in, she went up to a reception-parlor, where she was met by a man who rose from a seat near the windows and advanced to the middle of the room. He was of low stature, with quick, rather nervous movements, had dark, restless eyes, and wore a heavy black moustache that was liberally sprinkled with gray. The lower part of his face was shaved clean. He showed some embarrassment as he came forward to meet Mrs. Dinneford.

"Mr. Feeling," she said, coldly.

The man bowed with a mixture of obsequiousness and familiarity, and tried to look steadily into Mrs. Dinneford's face, but was not able to do so. There was a steadiness and power in her eyes that his could not bear.

"What do you want with me, sir?" she demanded, a little sharply.

"Take a chair, and I will tell you," replied Freeling, and he turned, moving toward a corner of the room, she following. They sat down, taking chairs near each other.

T. S. Arthur

"There's trouble brewing," said the man, his face growing dark and anxious.

"What kind of trouble?"

"I had a letter from George Granger yesterday."

"What!" The color went out of the lady's face.

"A letter from George Granger. He wished to see me."

"Did you go?"

"Yes."

"What did he want?"

Freeling took a deep breath, and sighed. His manner was troubled.

"What did he want?" Mrs. Dinneford repeated the question.

"He's as sane as you or I," said Freeling.

"Is he? Oh, very well! Then let him go to the State's prison." Mrs. Dinneford said this with some bravado in her manner. But the color did not come back to her face.

"He has no idea of that," was replied.

"What then?" The lady leaned toward Freeling. Her hands moved nervously.

"He means to have the case in court again, but on a new issue."

"He does!"

"Yes; says that he's innocent, and that you and I know it—that he's the victim of a conspiracy, and that we are the conspirators!"

"Talk!—amounts to nothing," returned Mrs. Dinneford, with a faint little laugh.

"I don't know about that. It's ugly talk, and especially so, seeing that it's true."

"No one will give credence to the ravings of an insane criminal."

"People are quick to credit an evil report. They will pity and believe him, now that the worst is reached. A reaction in public feeling has already taken place. He has one or two friends left who do not hesitate to affirm that there has been foul play. One of these has been tampering with a clerk of mine, and I came upon them with their heads together on the street a few days ago, and had my suspicions aroused by their startled look when they saw me."

"'What did that man want with you?' I inquired, when the clerk came in."

"He hesitated a moment, and then replied, 'He was asking me something about Mr. Granger.'"

"'What about him?' I queried. 'He asked me if I knew anything in regard to the forgery,' he returned."

"I pressed him with questions, and found that suspicion was on the right track. This friend of Granger's asked particularly about your visits to the store, and whether he had ever

T. S. Arthur

noticed anything peculiar in our intercourse—anything that showed a familiarity beyond what would naturally arise between a customer and salesman."

"There's nothing in that," said Mrs. Dinneford. "If you and I keep our own counsel, we are safe. The testimony of a condemned criminal goes for nothing. People may surmise and talk as much as they please, but no one knows anything about those notes but you and I and George."

"A pardon from the governor may put a new aspect on the case."

"A pardon!" There was a tremor of alarm in Mrs. Dinneford's voice.

"Yes; that, no doubt, will be the first move."

"The first move! Why, Mr. Freeling, you don't think anything like this is in contemplation?"

"I'm afraid so. George, as I have said, is no more crazy than you or I. But he cannot come out of the asylum, as the case now stands, without going to the penitentiary. So the first move of his friends will be to get a pardon. Then he is our equal in the eyes of the law. It would be an ugly thing for you and me to be sued for a conspiracy to ruin this young man, and have the charge of forgery added to the count."

Mrs. Dinneford gave a low cry, and shivered.

"But it may come to that."

"Impossible!"

"The prudent man foreseeth the evil and hideth himself, but

the simple pass on and are punished," said Freeling. "It is for this that I have sent for you. It's an ugly business, and I was a weak fool ever to have engaged in it."

"You were a free agent."

"I was a weak fool."

"As you please," returned Mrs. Dinneford, coldly, and drawing herself away from him.

It was some moments before either of them spoke again. Then Freeling said,

"I was awake all night, thinking over this matter, and it looks uglier the more I think of it. It isn't likely that enough evidence could be found to convict either of us, but to be tried on such an accusation would be horrible."

"Horrible! horrible!" ejaculated Mrs. Dinneford. "What is to be done?" She gave signs of weakness and terror. Freeling observed her closely, then felt his way onward.

"We are in great peril," he said. "There is no knowing what turn affairs will take. I only wish I were a thousand miles from here. It would be safer for us both." Then, after a pause, he added, "If I were foot-free, I would be off to-morrow."

He watched Mrs. Dinneford closely, and saw a change creep over her face.

"If I were to disappear suddenly," he resumed, "suspicion, if it took a definite shape, would fall on me. You would not be thought of in the matter."

He paused again, observing his companion keenly but

T. S. Arthur

stealthily. He was not able to look her fully in the face.

"Speak out plainly," said Mrs. Dinneford, with visible impatience.

"Plainly, then, madam," returned Freeling, changing his whole bearing toward her, and speaking as one who felt that he was master of the situation, "it has come to this: I shall have to break up and leave the city, or there will be a new trial in which you and I will be the accused. Now, self-preservation is the first law of nature. I don't mean to go to the State's prison if I can help it. What I am now debating are the chances in my favor if Granger gets a pardon, and then makes an effort to drive us to the wall, which he most surely will. I have settled it so far—"

Mrs. Dinneford leaned toward him with an anxious expression on her countenance, waiting for the next sentence. But Freeling did not go on.

"How have you settled it?" she demanded, trembling as she spoke with the excitement of suspense.

"That I am not going to the wall if I can help it."

"How will you help it?"

"I have an accomplice;" and this time he was able to look at Mrs. Dinneford with such a fixed and threatening gaze that her eyes fell.

"You have?" she questioned, in a husky voice.

"Yes."

"Who?"

"Mrs. Helen Dinneford. And do you think for a moment that to save myself I would hesitate to sacrifice her?"

The lady's face grew white. She tried to speak, but could not.

"I am talking plainly, as you desired, madam," continued Freeling. "You led me into this thing. It was no scheme of mine; and if more evil consequences are to come, I shall do my best to save my own head. Let the hurt go to where it rightfully belongs."

"What do you mean?" Mrs. Dinneford tried to rally herself.

"Just this," was answered: "if I am dragged into court, I mean to go in as a witness, and not as a criminal. At the first movement toward an indictment, I shall see the district attorney, whom I know very well, and give him such information in the case as will lead to fixing the crime on you alone, while I will come in as the principal witness. This will make your conviction certain."

"Devil!" exclaimed Mrs. Dinneford, her white face convulsed and her eyes starting from their sockets with rage and fear. "Devil!" she repeated, not able to control her passion.

"Then you know me," was answered, with cool self-possession, "and what you have to expect."

Neither spoke for a considerable time. Up to this period they had been alone in the parlor. Guests of the house now came in and took seats near them. They arose and walked the floor for a little while, still in silence, then passed into an adjoining parlor that happened to be empty, and resumed the conference.

"This is a last resort," remarked Freeling, softening his voice

T. S. Arthur

as they sat down—"a card that I do not wish to play, and shall not if I can help it. But it is best that you should know that it is in my hand. If there is any better way of escape, I shall take it."

"You spoke of going away," said Mrs. Dinneford.

"Yes. But that involves a great deal."

"What?"

"The breaking up of my business, and loss of money and opportunities that I can hardly hope ever to regain."

"Why loss of money?"

"I shall have to wind up hurriedly, and it will be impossible to collect more than a small part of my outstanding claims. I shall have to go away under a cloud, and it will not be prudent to return. Most of these claims will therefore become losses. The amount of capital I shall be able to take will not be sufficient to do more than provide for a small beginning in some distant place and under an assumed name. On the other hand, if I remain and fight the thing through, as I have no doubt I can, I shall keep my business and my place in society here—hurt, it may be, in my good name, but still with the main chance all right. But it will be hard for you. If I pass the ordeal safely, you will not. And the question to consider is whether you can make it to my interest to go away, to drop out of sight, injured in fortune and good name, while you go unscathed. You now have it all in a nutshell. I will not press you to a decision to-day. Your mind is too much disturbed. To-morrow, at noon, I would like to see you again."

Freeling made a motion to rise, but Mrs. Dinneford did not stir.

"Perhaps," he said, "you decide at once to let things take their course. Understand me, I am ready for either alternative. The election is with yourself."

Mrs. Dinneford was too much stunned by all this to be able to come to any conclusion. She seemed in the maze of a terrible dream, full of appalling reality. To wait for twenty-four hours in this state of uncertainty was more than her thoughts could endure. And yet she must have time to think, and to get command of her mental resources.

"Will you be disengaged at five o'clock?" she asked.

"Yes."

"I will be here at five."

"Very well."

Mrs. Dinneford arose with a weary air.

"I shall want to hear from you very explicitly," she said. "If your demand is anywhere in the range of reason and possibility, I may meet it. If outside of that range, I shall of course reject it. It is possible that you may not hold all the winning cards—in fact, I know that you do not."

"I will be here at five," said Freeling.

"Very well. I shall be on time."

And they turned from each other, passing from the parlor by separate doors.

T. S. Arthur

CHAPTER XII

ONE morning, about two weeks later, Mr. Freeling did not make his appearance at his place of business as usual. At ten o'clock a clerk went to the hotel where he boarded to learn the cause of his absence. He had not been there since the night before. His trunks and clothing were all in their places, and nothing in the room indicated anything more than an ordinary absence.

Twelve o'clock, and still Mr. Freeling had not come to the store. Two or three notes were to be paid that day, and the managing-clerk began to feel uneasy. The bank and check books were in a private drawer in the fireproof of which Mr. Freeling had the key. So there was no means of ascertaining the balances in bank.

At one o'clock it was thought best to break open the private drawer and see how matters stood. Freeling kept three bank-accounts, and it was found that on the day before he had so nearly checked out all the balances that the aggregate on deposit was not over twenty dollars. In looking back over these bank-accounts, it was seen that within a week he had made deposits of over fifty thousand dollars, and that most of the checks drawn against these deposits were in sums of five thousand dollars each.

At three o'clock he was still absent. His notes went to protest, and on the next day his city creditors took possession of his effects. One fact soon became apparent—he had been paying the rogue's game on a pretty liberal scale, having borrowed on his checks, from business friends and brokers, not less than sixty or seventy thousand dollars. It was estimated, on a thorough examination of his business, that he had gone off with at least a hundred thousand dollars. To this amount Mrs. Dinneford had contributed from her private fortune the sum of twenty thousand dollars. Not until she had furnished him with that large amount would he consent to leave the city. He magnified her danger, and so overcame her with terrors that she yielded to his exorbitant demand.

On the day a public newspaper announcement of Freeling's rascality was made, Mrs. Dinneford went to bed sick of a nervous fever, and was for a short period out of her mind.

Neither Mr. Dinneford nor Edith had failed to notice a change in Mrs. Dinneford. She was not able to hide her troubled feelings. Edith was watching her far more closely than she imagined; and now that she was temporarily out of her mind, she did not let a word or look escape her. The first aspect of her temporary aberration was that of fear and deprecation. She was pursued by some one who filled her with terror, and she would lift her hands to keep him off, or hide her head in abject alarm. Then she would beg him to keep away. Once she said,

"It's no use; I can't do anything more. You're a vampire!"

"Who is a vampire?" asked Edith, hoping that her mother would repeat some name.

But the question seemed to put her on her guard. The expression of fear went out of her face, and she looked at her daughter curiously.

Edith did not repeat the question. In a little while the mother's wandering thoughts began to find words again, and she went on talking in broken sentences out of which little could be gleaned. At length she said, turning to Edith and speaking with the directness of one in her right mind,

"I told you her name was Gray, didn't I? Gray, not Bray."

It was only by a quick and strong effort that Edith could steady her voice as she replied:

"Yes; you said it was Gray."

"Gray, not Bray. You thought it was Bray."

"But it's Gray," said Edith, falling in with her mother's humor. Then she added, still trying to keep her voice even,

"She was my nurse when baby was born."

"Yes; she was the nurse, but she didn't—"

Checking herself, Mrs. Dinneford rose on one arm and looked at Edith in a frightened way, then said, hurriedly,

"Oh, it's dead, it's dead! You know that; and the woman's dead, too."

Edith sat motionless and silent as a statue, waiting for what more might come. But her mother shut her lips tightly, and turned her head away.

A long time elapsed before she was able to read in her mother's confused utterances anything to which she could attach a meaning. At last Mrs. Dinneford spoke out again, and with an abruptness that startled her:

"Not another dollar, sir! Remember, you don't hold *all* the winning cards!"

Edith held her breath, and sat motionless. Her mother muttered and mumbled incoherently for a while, and then said, sharply,

"I said I would ruin him, and I've done it!"

"Ruin who?" asked Edith, in a repressed voice.

This question, instead of eliciting an answer, as Edith had hoped, brought her mother back to semi-consciousness. She rose again in bed, and looked at her daughter in the same frightened way she had done a little while before, then laid herself over on the pillows again. Her lips were tightly shut.

Edith was almost wild with suspense. The clue to that sad and painful mystery which was absorbing her life seemed almost in her grasp. A word from those closely-shut lips, and she would have certainty for uncertainty. But she waited and waited until she grew faint, and still the lips kept silent.

But after a while Mrs. Dinneford grew uneasy, and began talking. She moved her head from side to side, threw her arms about restlessly and appeared greatly disturbed.

"Not dead, Mrs. Bray?" she cried out, at last, in a clear, strong voice.

Edith became fixed as a statue once more.

A few moments, and Mrs. Dinneford added,

T. S. Arthur

"No, no! I won't have her coming after me. More money! You're a vampire!"

Then she muttered, and writhed and distorted her face like one in some desperate struggle. Edith shuddered as she stood over her.

After this wild paroxysm Mrs. Dinneford grew more quiet, and seemed to sleep. Edith remained sitting by the bedside, her thoughts intent on the strange sentences that had fallen from her Mother's lips. What mystery lay behind them? Of what secret were they an obscure revelation? "Not dead!" Who not dead? And again, "It's dead! You know that; and the woman's dead, too." Then it was plain that she had heard aright the name of the person who had called on her mother, and about whom her mother had made a mystery. It was Bray; if not, why the anxiety to make her believe it Gray? And this woman had been her nurse. It was plain, also, that money was being paid for keeping secret. What secret? Then a life had been ruined. "I said I would ruin him, and I've done it!" Who? who could her mother mean but the unhappy man she had once called husband, now a criminal in the eyes of the law, and only saved by insanity from a criminal's cell?

Putting all together, Edith's mind quickly wrought out a theory, and this soon settled into a conviction—a conviction so close to fact that all the chief elements were true.

During her mother's temporary aberration, Edith never left her room except for a few minutes at a time. Not a word or sentence escaped her notice. But she waited and listened in vain for anything more. The talking paroxysm was over. A stupor of mind and body followed. Out of this a slow recovery came, but it did not progress to a full convales- cence. Mrs. Dinneford went forth from her sick-chamber weak and nervous, starting at sudden noises, and betraying a perpetual uneasiness and suspense. Edith was continually on the alert, watching every look and word and act with untiring scrutiny. Mrs. Dinneford soon became aware of this. Guilt made her wary, and danger inspired prudence. Edith's whole manner had changed. Why? was her natural query. Had she been wandering in her mind? Had she given any clue to the dark secrets she was hiding? Keen observation became mutual. Mother and daughter watched each other with a suspicion that never slept.

It was over a month from the time Freeling disappeared before Mrs. Dinneford was strong enough to go out, except in her carriage. In every case where she had ridden out, Edith had gone with her.

"If you don't care about riding, it's no matter," the mother would say, when she saw Edith getting ready. "I can go alone. I feel quite well and strong."

But Edith always had some reason for going against which her mother could urge no objections. So she kept her as closely under observation as possible. One day, on returning from a ride, as the carriage passed into the block where they lived, she saw a woman standing on the step in front of their residence. She had pulled the bell, and was waiting for a servant to answer it.

"There is some one at our door," said Edith.

Mrs. Dinneford leaned across her daughter, and then drew back quickly, saying,

"It's Mrs. Barker. Tell Henry to drive past. I don't want to see visitors, and particularly not Mrs. Barker."

She spoke hurriedly, and with ill-concealed agitation. Edith kept her eyes on the woman, and saw her go in, but did not tell the driver to keep on past the house. It was not Mrs. Barker. She knew that very well. In the next moment their carriage drew up at the door.

"Go on, Henry!" cried Mrs. Dinneford, leaning past her daughter, and speaking through the window that was open on that side. "Drive down to Loring's."

"Not till I get out, Henry," said Edith, pushing open the door and stepping to the pavement. Then with a quick movement she shut the door and ran across the pavement, calling back to the driver as she did so,

"Take mother to Loring's."

"Stop, Henry!" cried Mrs. Dinneford, and with an alertness that was surprising sprung from the carriage, and was on the steps of their house before Edith's violent ring had brought a servant to the door. They passed in, Edith holding her place just in advance.

"I will see Mrs. Barker," said Mrs. Dinneford, trying to keep out of her voice the fear and agitation from which she was suffering. "You can go up to your room."

"It isn't Mrs. Barker. You are mistaken." There was as much of betrayal in the voice of Edith as in that of her mother. Each was trying to hide herself from the other, but the veil in both cases was far too thin for deception.

Mother and daughter entered the parlor together. As they did so a woman of small stature, and wearing a rusty black dress, arose from a seat near the window. The moment she saw Edith she drew a heavy dark veil over her face with a quickness of movement that had in it as much of discomfiture as surprise.

Mrs. Dinneford was equal to the occasion. The imminent peril in which she stood calmed the wild tumult within, as the strong wind calms this turbulent ocean, and gave her thoughts clearness and her mind decision. Edith saw before the veil fell a startled face, and recognized the sallow countenance and black, evil eyes, the woman who had once before called to see her mother.

"Didn't I tell you not to come here, Mrs. Gray?" cried out Mrs. Dinneford, with an anger that was more real than feigned, advancing quickly upon the woman as she spoke. "Go!" and she pointed to the door, "and don't you dare to come here again. I told you when you were here last time that I wouldn't be bothered with you any longer. I've done all I ever intend doing. So take yourself away."

And she pointed again to the door. Mrs. Bray—for it was that personage—comprehended the situation fully. She was as good an actor as Mrs. Dinneford, and quite as equal to the occasion. Lifting her hand in a weak, deprecating way, and then shrinking like one borne down by the shock of a great disappointment, she moved back from the excited woman and made her way to the hall, Mrs. Dinneford following and assailing her in passionate language.

Edith was thrown completely off her guard by this unexpected scene. She did not stir from the spot where she stood on entering the parlor until the visitor was at the street door, whither her mother had followed the retreating figure. She did not hear the woman say in the tone of one who spoke more in command than entreaty,

"To-morrow at one o'clock, or take the consequences."

"It will be impossible to-morrow," Mrs. Dinneford whispered back, hurriedly; "I have been very ill, and have only just begun to ride out. It may be a week, but I'll surely come. I'm watched. Go now! go! go!"

And she pushed Mrs. Bray out into the vestibule and shut the door after her. Mrs. Dinneford did not return to the parlor, but went hastily up to her own room, locking herself in.

She did not come out until dinner-time, when she made an effort to seem composed, but Edith saw her hand tremble every time it was lifted. She drank three glasses of wine during the meal. After dinner she went to her own apartment immediately, and did not come down again that day.

On the next morning Mrs. Dinneford tried to appear cheerful and indifferent. But her almost colorless face, pinched about the lips and nostrils, and the troubled expression that would not go out of her eyes, betrayed to Edith the intense anxiety and dread that lay beneath the surface.

Days went by, but Edith had no more signs. Now that her mother was steadily getting back both bodily strength and mental self-poise, the veil behind which she was hiding herself, and which had been broken into rifts here and there during her sickness, grew thicker and thicker. Mrs. Dinneford had too much at stake not to play her cards with exceeding care. She knew that Edith was watching her with an intentness that let nothing escape. Her first care, as soon as she grew strong enough to have the mastery over herself, was so to control voice, manner and expression of countenance as not to appear aware of this surveillance. Her next was to re-establish the old distance between herself and daughter, which her illness had temporarily bridged over, and her next was to provide against any more visits from Mrs. Bray.

CHAPTER XIII

AS for Edith, all doubts and questionings as to her baby's fate were merged into a settled conviction that it was alive, and that her mother knew where it was to be found. From her mother's pity and humanity she had nothing to hope for the child. It had been cruelly cast adrift, pushed out to die; by what means was cared not, so that it died and left no trace.

The face of Mrs. Bray had, in the single glance Edith obtained of it, become photographed in her mind. If she had been an artist, she could have drawn it from memory so accurately that no one who knew the woman could have failed to recognize her likeness. Always when in the street her eyes searched for this face; she never passed a woman of small stature and poor dark clothing without turning to look at her. Every day she went out, walking the streets sometimes for hours looking for this face, but not finding it. Every day she passed certain corners and localities where she had seen women begging, and whenever she found one with a baby in her arms would stop to look at the poor starved thing, and question her about it.

Gradually all her thoughts became absorbed in the condition of poor, neglected and suffering children. Her attendance at the St. John's mission sewing-school, which was located in the neighborhood of one of the worst places in the city,

T. S. Arthur

brought her in contact with little children in such a wretched state of ignorance, destitution and vice that her heart was moved to deepest pity, intensified by the thought that ever and anon flashed across her mind: "And my baby may become like one of these!"

Sometimes this thought would drive her almost to madness. Often she would become so wild in her suspense as to be on the verge of openly accusing her mother with having knowledge of her baby's existence and demanding of her its restoration. But she was held back by the fear that such an accusation would only shut the door of hope for ever. She had come to believe her mother capable of almost any wickedness. Pressed to the wall she would never be if there was any way of escape, and to prevent such at thing there was nothing so desperate that she would not do it; and so Edith hesitated and feared to take the doubtful issue.

Week after week and month after month now went on without a single, occurrence that gave to Edith any new light. Mrs. Dinneford wrought with her accomplice so effectually that she kept her wholly out of the way. Often, in going and returning from the mission-school, Edith would linger about the neighborhood where she had once met her mother, hoping to see her come out of some one of the houses there, for she had got it into her mind that the woman called Mrs. Gray lived somewhere in this locality.

One day, in questioning a child who had come to the sewing-school as to her home and how she lived, the little girl said something about a baby that her mother said she knew must have been stolen.

"How old is the baby?" asked Edith, hardly able to keep the tremor out of her voice.

"It's a little thing," answered the child. "I don't know how old it is; maybe it's six months old, or maybe it's a year. It can sit upon the floor."

"Why does your mother think it has been stolen?"

"Because two bad girls have got it, and they pay a woman to take care of it. It doesn't belong to them, she knows. Mother says it would be a good thing if it died."

"Why does she say that?"

"Oh she always talks that way about babies—says she's glad when they die."

"Is it a boy or a girl?"

"It's a boy baby," answered the child.

"Does the woman take good care of it?"

"Oh dear, no! She lets it sit on the floor 'most all the time, and it cries so that I often go up and nurse it. The woman lives in the room over ours."

"Where do you live?"

"In Grubb's court."

"Will you show me the way there after school is over?"

The child looked up into Edith's face with an expression of surprise and doubt. Edith repeated her question.

"I guess you'd better not go," was answered, in a voice that meant all the words expressed.

"Why not?"

"It isn't a good place."

"But you live there?"

"Yes, but nobody's going to trouble me."

"Nor me," said Edith.

"Oh, but you don't know what kind of a place it is, nor what dreadful people live there."

"I could get a policeman to go with me, couldn't I?"

"Yes, maybe you could, or Mr. Paulding, the missionary. He goes about everywhere."

"Where can I find Mr. Paulding?"

"At the mission in Briar street."

"You'll show me the way there after school?"

"Oh yes; it isn't a nice place for you to go, but I guess nobody'll trouble you."

After the school closed, Edith, guided by the child, made her way to the Briar st. mission-house. As she entered the narrow street in which it was situated, the aspect of things was so strange and shocking to her eyes that she felt a chill creep to her heart. She had never imagined anything so forlorn and squalid, so wretched and comfortless. Miserable little hovels, many of them no better than pig-styes, and hardly cleaner within, were crowded together in all stages of dilapidation. Windows with scarcely a pane of glass, the chilly air kept out by old hats, bits of carpet or wads of newspaper, could be seen on all sides, with here and there, showing some remains of an orderly habit, a broken pane closed with a smooth piece of paper pasted to the sash. Instinctively she paused, oppressed by a sense of fear.

"It's only halfway down," said the child. "We'll 'go quick. I guess nobody'll speak to you. They're afraid of Mr. Paulding about here. He's down on 'em if they meddle with anybody that's coming to the mission."

Edith, thus urged, moved on. She had gone but a few steps when two men came in sight, advancing toward her. They were of the class to be seen at all times in that region— debased to the lowest degree, drunken, ragged, bloated, evil- eyed, capable of any wicked thing. They were singing when they came in sight, but checked their drunken mirth as soon as they saw Edith, whose heart sunk again. She stopped, trembling.

"They're only drunk," said the child. "I don't believe they'll hurt you."

Edith rallied herself and walked on, the men coming closer and closer. She saw them look at each other with leering eyes, and then at her in a way that made her shiver. When only a few paces distant, they paused, and with the evident intention of barring her farther progress.

"Good-afternoon, miss," said one of them, with a low bow. "Can we do anything for you?"

The pale, frightened face of Edith was noticed by the other, and it touched some remnant of manhood not yet wholly extinguished.

"Let her alone, you miserable cuss!" he cried, and giving his drunken companion a shove, sent him staggering across the street. This made the way clear, and Edith sprang forward, but she had gone only a few feet when she came face to face with another obstruction even more frightful, if possible, than the first. A woman with a red, swollen visage, black eye, soiled, tattered, drunk, with arms wildly extended, came rushing up to her. The child gave a scream. The wretched creature caught at a shawl worn by Edith, and was dragging it from her shoulders, when the door of one of the houses flew open, and a woman came out hastily. Grasping the assailant, she hurled her across the street with the strength of a giant.

"We're going to the mission," said the child.

"It's just down there. Go 'long. I'll stand here and see that no one meddles with you again."

Edith faltered her thanks, and went on.

"That's the queen," said her companion.

"The queen!" Edith's hasty tones betrayed her surprise.

"Yes; it's Norah. They're all afraid of her. I'm glad she saw us. She's as strong as a man."

In a few minutes they reached the mission, but in those few minutes Edith saw more to sadden the heart, more to make it ache for humanity, than could be described in pages.

The missionary was at home. Edith told him the purpose of her call and the locality she desired to visit.

"I wanted to go alone," she remarked, "but this little girl, who is in my class at the sewing-school, said it wouldn't be safe, and that you would go with me."

"I should be sorry to have you go alone into Grubb's court," said the missionary, kindly, and with concern in his voice, "for a worse place can hardly be found in the city—I was going to say in the world. You will be safe with me, however. But why do you wish to visit Grubb's court? Perhaps I can do all that is needed."

"This little girl who lives in there, has been telling me about a poor neglected baby that her mother says has no doubt been stolen, and—and—" Edith voice faltered, but she quickly gained steadiness under a strong effort of will: "I thought perhaps I might be able to do something for it—to get it into one of the homes, maybe. It is dreadful, sir, to think of little babies being neglected."

Mr. Paulding questioned the child who had brought Edith to the mission-house, and learned from her that the baby was merely boarded by the woman who had it in charge, and that she sometimes took it out and sat on the street, begging. The child repeated what she had said to Edith—that the baby was the property, so to speak, of two abandoned women, who paid its board.

"I think," said the missionary, after some reflection, "that if getting the child out of their hands is your purpose, you had better not go there at present. Your visit would arouse suspicion; and if the two women have anything to gain by keeping the child in their possession, it will be at once taken to a new place. I am moving about in these localities all the while, and can look in upon the baby without anything being thought of it."

This seemed so reasonable that Edith, who could not get over the nervous tremors occasioned by what she had already seen and encountered, readily consented to leave the matter for the present in Mr. Paulding's hands.

"If you will come here to-morrow," said the missionary, "I will tell you all I can about the baby."

Out of a region where disease, want and crime shrunk from common observation, and sin and death held high carnival, Edith hurried with trembling feet, and heart beating so heavily that she could hear it throb, the considerate missionary going with her until she had crossed the boundary of this morally infected district.

Mr. Dinneford met Edith at the door on her arrival home.

"My child," he exclaimed as he looked into her face, back to which the color had not returned since her fright in Briar street, "are you sick?"

"I don't feel very well;" and she tried to pass him hastily in the hall as they entered the house together. But he laid his hand on her arm and held her back gently, then drew her into the parlor. She sat down, trembling, weak and faint. Mr. Dinneford waited for some moments, looking at her with a tender concern, before speaking.

"Where have you been, my dear?" he asked, at length.

After a little hesitation, Edith told her father about her visit to Briar street and the shock she had received.

"You were wrong," he answered, gravely. "It is most fortunate for you that you took the child's advice and called at the mission. If you had gone to Grubb's court alone, you might not have come out alive."

"Oh no, father! It can't be so bad as that."

"It is just as bad as that," he replied, with a troubled face and manner. "Grubb's court is one of the traps into which unwary victims are drawn that they may be plundered. It is as much out of common observation almost as the lair of a wild beast in some deep wilderness. I have heard it described by those who have been there under protection of the police, and shudder to think of the narrow escape you have made. I don't want you to go into that vile district again. It is no place for such as you."

"There's a poor little baby there," said Edith, her voice trembling and tears filling her eyes. Then, after a brief struggle with her feelings, she threw herself upon her father, sobbing out, "And oh, father, it may be my baby!"

"My poor child," said Mr. Dinneford, not able to keep his voice firm—"my poor, poor child! It is all a wild dream, the suggestion of evil spirits who delight in torment."

"What became of my baby, father? Can you tell me?"

"It died, Edith dear. We know that," returned her father, trying to speak very confidently. But the doubt in his own mind betrayed itself.

"Do you know it?" she asked, rising and confronting her father.

"I didn't actually see it die. But—but—"

"You know no more about it than I do," said Edith; "if you did, you might set my heart at rest with a word. But you cannot. And so I am left to my wild fears, that grow stronger every day. Oh, father, help me, if you can. I must have certainty, or I shall lose my reason."

"If you don't give up this wild fancy, you surely will," answered Mr. Dinneford, in a distressed voice.

"If I were to shut myself up and do nothing," said Edith, with greater calmness, "I would be in a madhouse before a week went by. My safety lies in getting down to the truth of this wild fancy, as you call it. It has taken such possession of me that nothing but certainty can give me rest. Will you help me?"

"How can I help you? I have no clue to this sad mystery."

"Mystery! Then you are as much in the dark as I am—know no more of what became of my baby than I do! Oh, father, how could you let such a thing be done, and ask no questions —such a cruel and terrible thing—and I lying helpless and dumb? Oh, father, my innocent baby cast out like a dog to perish—nay, worse, like a lamb among wolves to be torn by their cruel teeth—and no one to put forth a hand to save! If I only knew that he was dead! If I could find his little grave and comfort my heart over it!"

Weak, naturally good men, like Mr. Dinneford, often permit great wrongs to be done in shrinking from conflict and evading the sterner duties of life. They are often the faithless guardians of immortal trusts.

There was a tone of accusation and rebuke in Edith's voice that smote painfully on her father's heart. He answered feebly:

"What could I do? How should I know that anything wrong was being done? You were very ill, and the baby was sent away to be nursed, and then I was told that it was dead."

"Oh, father! Sent away without your seeing it! My baby! Your little grandson! Oh, father!"

"But you know, dear, in what a temper of mind your mother was—how impossible it is for me to do anything with her when she once sets herself to do a thing."

"Even if it be murder!" said Edith, in a hoarse whisper.

"Hush, hush, my child! You must not speak so," returned the agitated father.

A silence fell between them. A wall of separation began to grow up. Edith arose, and was moving from the room.

"My daughter!" There was a sob in the father's voice.

Edith stopped.

"My daughter, we must not part yet. Come back; sit down with me, and let us talk more calmly. What is past cannot be changed. It is with the now of this unhappy business that we have to do."

Edith came back and sat down again, her father taking a seat beside her.

"That is just it," she answered, with a steadiness of tone and manner that showed how great was the self-control she was able to exert. "It is with the now of this unhappy affair that we have to do. If I spoke strongly of the past, it was that a higher and intenser life might be given to present duty."

"Let there be no distance between us. Let no wall of separation grow up," said Mr. Dinneford, tenderly. "I cannot bear to think of this. Confide in me, consult with me. I will help you in all possible ways to solve this mystery. But do not again venture alone into that dreadful place. I will go with you if you think any good will come of it."

"I must see Mr. Paulding in the morning," said Edith, with calm decision.

"Then I will go with you," returned Mr. Dinneford.

"Thank you, father;" and she kissed him. "Until then nothing more can be done." She kissed him again, and then went to her own room. After locking the door she sank on her knees, leaning forward, with her face buried in the cushion of a chair, and did not rise for a long time.

CHAPTER XIV

ON the next morning, after some persuasion, Edith consented to postpone her visit to Grubb's court until after her father had seen Mr. Paulding, the missionary.

"Let me go first and gain what information I can," he urged. "It may save you a fruitless errand."

It was not without a feeling of almost unconquerable repugnance that Mr. Dinneford took his way to the mission-house, in Briar street. His tastes, his habits and his naturally kind and sensitive feelings all made him shrink from personal contact with suffering and degradation. He gave much time and care to the good work of helping the poor and the wretched, but did his work in boards and on committees, rather than in the presence of the needy and suffering. He was not one of those who would pass over to the other side and leave a wounded traveler to perish, but he would avoid the road to Jericho, if he thought it likely any such painful incident would meet him in the way and shock his fine sensibilities. He was willing to work for the downcast, the wronged, the suffering and the vile, but preferred doing so at a distance, and not in immediate contact. Thus it happened that, although one of the managers of the Briar street mission and familiar with its work in a general way, he had never been at the mission-house—had never, in fact, set his foot

T. S. Arthur

within the morally plague-stricken district in which it stood. He had often been urged to go, but could not overcome his reluctance to meet humanity face to face in its sadder and more degraded aspects.

Now a necessity was upon him, and he had to go. It was about ten o'clock in the morning when, at almost a single step, he passed from what seemed paradise to purgatory, the sudden contrast was so great. There were but few persons in the little street; where the mission was situated at that early hour, and most of these were children—poor, half-clothed, dirty, wan-faced, keen-eyed and alert bits of humanity, older by far than their natural years, few of them possessing any higher sense of right and wrong than young savages. The night's late orgies or crimes had left most of their elders in a heavy morning sleep, from which they did not usually awaken before midday. Here and there one and another came creeping out, impelled by a thirst no water could quench. Now it was a bloated, wild-eyed man, dirty and forlorn beyond description, shambling into sight, but disappearing in a moment or two in one of the dram-shops, whose name was legion, and now it was a woman with the angel all gone out of her face, barefooted, blotched, coarse, red-eyed, bruised and awfully disfigured by her vicious, drunken life. Her steps too made haste to the dram-shop.

Such houses for men and women to live in as now stretched before his eyes in long dreary rows Mr. Dinneford had never seen, except in isolated cases of vice and squalor. To say that he was shocked would but faintly express his feelings. Hurrying along, he soon came in sight of the mission. At this moment a jar broke the quiet of the scene. Just beyond the mission-house two women suddenly made their appearance, one of them pushing the other out upon the street. Their angry cries rent the air, filling it with profane and obscene oaths. They struggled together for a little while, and then one of them, a woman with gray hair and not less than sixty years of age, fell across the curb with her head on the cobblestones.

As if a sorcerer had stamped his foot, a hundred wretched creatures, mostly women and children, seemed to spring up from the ground. It was like a phantasy. They gathered about the prostrate woman, laughing and jeering. A policeman who was standing at the corner a little way off came up leisurely, and pushing the motley crew aside, looked down at the prostrate woman.

"Oh, it's you again!" he said, in a tone of annoyance, taking hold of one arm and raising her so that she sat on the curbstone. Mr. Dinneford now saw her face distinctly; it was that of an old woman, but red, swollen and terribly marred. Her thin gray hair had fallen over her shoulders, and gave her a wild and crazy look.

"Come," said the policeman, drawing on the woman's arm and trying to raise her from the ground. But she would not move.

"Come," he said, more imperatively.

"Nature you going to do with me?" she demanded.

"I'm going to lock you up. So come along. Have had enough of you about here. Always drunk and in a row with somebody."

Her resistance was making the policeman angry.

"It'll take two like you to do that," returned the woman, in a spiteful voice, swearing foully at the same time.

T. S. Arthur

At this a cheer arose from the crowd. A negro with a push-cart came along at the moment.

"Here! I want you," called the policeman.

The negro pretended not to hear, and the policeman had to threaten him before he would stop.

Seeing the cart, the drunken woman threw herself back upon the pavement and set every muscle to a rigid strain. And now came one of those shocking scenes—too familiar, alas! in portions of our large Christian cities—at which everything pure and merciful and holy in our nature revolts: a gray-haired old woman, so debased by drink and an evil life that all sense of shame and degradation had been extinguished, fighting with a policeman, and for a time showing superior strength, swearing vilely, her face distorted with passion, and a crowd made up chiefly of women as vile and degraded as herself, and of all ages, and colors, laughing, shouting and enjoying the scene intensely.

At last, by aid of the negro, the woman was lifted into the cart and thrown down upon the floor, her head striking one of the sides with a sickening *thud*. She still swore and struggled, and had to be held down by the policeman, who stood over her, while the cart was pushed off to the nearest station-house, the excited crowd following with shouts and merry huzzas.

Mr. Dinneford was standing in a maze, shocked and distressed by this little episode, when a man at his side said in a grave, quiet voice,

"I doubt if you could see a sight just like that anywhere else in all Christendom." Then added, as he extended his hand,

"I am glad to see you here, Mr. Dinneford."

"Oh, Mr. Paulding!" and Mr. Dinneford put out his hand and grasped that of the missionary with a nervous grip. "This is awful! I am sixty years old, but anything so shocking my eyes have not before looked upon."

"We see things worse than this every day," said the missionary. "It is only one of the angry boils on the surface, and tells of the corrupt and vicious blood within. But I am right glad to find you here, Mr. Dinneford. Unless you see these things with your own eyes, it is impossible for you to comprehend the condition of affairs in this by-way to hell."

"Hell, itself, better say," returned Mr. Dinneford. "It is hell pushing itself into visible manifestation—hell establishing itself on the earth, and organizing its forces for the destruction of human souls, while the churches are too busy enlarging their phylacteries and making broader and more attractive the hems of their garments to take note of this fatal vantage-ground acquired by the enemy."

Mr. Dinneford stood and looked around him in a dazed sort of way.

"Is Grubb's court near this?" he asked, recollecting the errand upon which he had come.

"Yes."

"A young lady called to see you yesterday afternoon to ask about a child in that court?"

"Oh yes! You know the lady?"

"She is my daughter. One of the poor children in her sewing-class told her of a neglected baby in Grubb's court, and so drew upon her sympathies that she started to go there, but was warned by the child that it would be dangerous for a young lady like her to be seen in that den of thieves and harlots, and so she came to you. And now I am here in her stead to get your report about the baby. I would not consent to her visiting this place again."

Mr. Paulding took his visitor into the mission-house, near which they were standing. After they were seated, he said,

"I have seen the baby about which your daughter wished me to make inquiry. The woman who has the care of it is a vile creature, well known in this region—drunken and vicious. She said at first that it was her own baby, but afterward admitted that she didn't know who its mother was, and that she was paid for taking care of it. I found out, after a good deal of talking round, and an interview with the mother of the child who is in your daughter's sewing-class, that a girl of notoriously bad character, named Pinky Swett, pays the baby's board. There's a mystery about the child, and I am of the opinion that it has been stolen, or is known to be the offcast of some respectable family. The woman who has the care of it was suspicious, and seemed annoyed at my questions."

"Is it a boy?" asked Mr. Dinneford.

"Yes, and has a finely-formed head and a pair of large, clear, hazel eyes. Evidently it is of good parentage. The vicious, the sensual and the depraved mark their offspring with the unmistakable signs of their moral depravity. You cannot mistake them. But this baby has in its poor, wasted, suffering little face, in its well-balanced head and deep, almost spiritual eyes, the signs of a better origin."

"It ought at once to be taken away from the woman," said Mr. Dinneford, in a very decided manner.

"Who is to take it?" asked the missionary.

Mr. Dinneford was silent.

"Neither you nor I have any authority to do so. If I were to see it cast out upon the street, I might have it sent to the almshouse; but until I find it abandoned or shamefully abused, I have no right to interfere."

"I would like to see the baby," said Mr. Dinneford, on whose mind painful suggestions akin to those that were so disturbing his daughter were beginning to intrude themselves.

"It would hardly be prudent to go there to-day," said Mr. Paulding.

"Why not?"

"It would arouse suspicion; and if there is anything wrong, the baby would drop out of sight. You would not find it if you went again. These people are like birds with their wings half lifted, and fly away at the first warning of danger. As it is, I fear my visit and inquiries will be quite sufficient to the cause the child's removal to another place."

Mr. Dinneford mused for a while:

"There ought to be some way to reach a case like this, and there is, I am sure. From what you say, it is more than probable that this poor little waif may have drifted out of some pleasant home, where love would bless it with the tenderest care, into this hell of neglect and cruelty. It should be rescued on the instant. It is my duty—it is yours—to see

T. S. Arthur

that it is done, and that without delay. I will go at once to the mayor and state the case. He will send an officer with me, I know, and we will take the child by force. If its real mother then comes forward and shows herself at all worthy to have the care of it, well; if not, I will see that it is taken care of. I know where to place it."

To this proposition Mr. Paulding had no objection to offer.

"If you take that course, and act promptly, you can no doubt get possession of the poor thing. Indeed, sir"—and the missionary spoke with much earnestness—"if men of influence like yourself would come here and look the evil of suffering and neglected children in the face, and then do what they could to destroy that evil, there would soon be joy in heaven over the good work accomplished by their hands. I could give you a list of ten or twenty influential citizens whose will would be next to law in a matter like this who could in a month, if they put heart and hand to it, do such a work for humanity here as would make the angels glad. But they are too busy with their great enterprises to give thought and effort to a work like this."

A shadow fell across the missionary's face. There was a tone of discouragement in his voice.

"The great question is *what* to do," said Mr. Dinneford. "There are no problems so hard to solve as these problems of social evil. If men and women choose to debase themselves, who is to hinder? The vicious heart seeks a vicious life. While the heart is depraved the life will be evil. So long as the fountain is corrupt the water will be foul."

"There is a side to all this that most people do not consider," answered Mr. Paulding. "Self-hurt is one thing, hurt of the neighbor quite another. It may be questioned whether society has a right to touch the individual freedom of a member in anything that affects himself alone. But the moment he begins to hurt his neighbor, whether from ill-will or for gain, then it is the duty of society to restrain him. The common weal demands this, to say nothing of Christian obligation. If a man were to set up an exhibition in our city dangerous to life and limb, but so fascinating as to attract large numbers to witness and participate therein, and if hundreds were maimed or killed every year, do you think any one would question the right of our authorities to repress it? And yet to-day there are in our city more than twenty thousand persons who live by doing things a thousand times more hurtful to the people than any such exhibition could possibly be. And what is marvelous to think of, the larger part of these persons are actually licensed by the State to get gain by hurting, depraving and destroying the people. Think of it, Mr. Dinneford! The whole question lies in a nutshell. There is no difficulty about the problem. Restrain men from doing harm to each other, and the work is more than half done."

"Is not the law all the while doing this?"

"The law," was answered. "is weakly dealing with effect— how weakly let prison and police statistics show. Forty thousand arrests in our city for a single year, and the cause of these arrests clearly traced to the liquor licenses granted to five or six thousand persons to make money by debasing and degrading the people. If all of these were engaged in useful employments, serving, as every true citizen is bound to do, the common good, do you think we should have so sad and sickening a record? No, sir! We must go back to the causes of things. Nothing but radical work will do."

"You think, then," said Mr. Dinneford, "that the true remedy for all these dreadful social evils lies in restrictive legislation?"

"Restrictive only on the principles of eternal right," answered the missionary. "Man's freedom over himself must not be touched. Only his freedom to hurt his neighbor must be abridged. Here society has a right to put bonds on its members—to say to each individual, You are free to do anything by which your neighbor is served, but nothing to harm him. Here is where the discrimination must be made; and when the mass of the people come to see this, we shall have the beginning of a new day. There will then be hope for such poor wretches as crowd this region; or if most of them are so far lost as to be without hope, their places, when they die, will not be filled with new recruits for the army of perdition."

"If the laws we now have were only executed," said Mr. Dinneford, "there might be hope in our legislative restrictions. But the people are defrauded of justice through defects in its machinery. There are combinations to defeat good laws. There are men holding high office notoriously in league with scoundrels who prey upon the people. Through these, justice perpetually fails."

"The people are alone to blame," replied the missionary. "Each is busy with his farm and his merchandise with his own affairs, regardless of his neighbor. The common good is nothing, so that his own good is served. Each weakly folds his hands and is sorry when these troublesome questions are brought to his notice, but doesn't see that he can do anything. Nor can the people, unless some strong and influential leaders rally them, and, like great generals, lead them to the battle. As I said a little while ago, there are ten or twenty men in this city who, if they could be made to feel their high responsibility—who, if they could be induced to look away for a brief period from their great enterprises and concentrate thought and effort upon these questions of social evil, abuse of justice and violations of law—would in a single month inaugurate reforms and set agencies to work that would soon produce marvelous changes. They need not touch the rottenness of this half-dead carcass with knife or poultice. Only let them cut off the sources of pollution and disease, and the purified air will do the work of restoration where moral vitality remains, or hasten the end in those who are debased beyond hope."

"What could these men do? Where would their work begin?" asked Mr. Dinneford.

"Their own intelligence would soon discover the way to do this work if their hearts were in it. Men who can organize and successfully conduct great financial and industrial enterprises, who know how to control the wealth and power of the country and lead the people almost at will, would hardly be at fault in the adjustment of a matter like this. What would be the money influence of 'whisky rings' and gambling associations, set against the social and money influence of these men? Nothing, sir, nothing! Do you think we should long have over six thousand bars and nearly four hundred lottery-policy shops in our city if the men to whom I refer were to take the matter in hand?"

"Are there so many policy-shops?" asked Mr. Dinneford, in surprise.

"There may be more. You will find them by scores in every locality where poor and ignorant people are crowded together, sucking out their substance, and in the neighborhood of all the market-houses and manufactories, gathering in spoil. The harm they are doing is beyond computation. The men who control this unlawful business are rich and closely organized. They gather in their dishonest gains at the rate of hundreds of thousands of dollars every year, and know how and where to use this money for the protection of their agents in the work of defrauding the people, and the people are helpless because our men of wealth and influence have no time to give to public justice or the suppression of great social wrongs. With them, as things now are, rests the chief responsibility. They have the intelligence, the wealth and the public confidence, and are fully equal to the task if they will put their hands to the work. Let them but lift the standard and sound the trumpet of reform, and the people will rally instantly at the call. It must not be a mere spasmodic effort—a public meeting with wordy resolutions and strong speeches only—but organized work based on true principles of social order and the just rights of the people."

"You are very much in earnest about this matter," said Mr. Dinneford, seeing how excited the missionary had grown.

"And so would you and every other good citizen become if, standing face to face, as I do daily, with this awful debasement and crime and suffering, you were able to comprehend something of its real character. If I could get the influential citizens to whom I have referred to come here and see for themselves, to look upon this pandemonium in their midst and take in an adequate idea of its character, significance and aggressive force, there would be some hope of making them see their duty, of arousing them to action. But they stand aloof, busy with personal and material interest, while thousands of men, women and children are yearly destroyed, soul and body, through their indifference to duty and ignorance of their fellows' suffering."

"It is easy to say such things," answered Mr. Dinneford, who felt the remarks of Mr. Paulding as almost personal.

"Yes, it is easy to say them," returned the missionary, his voice dropping to a lower key, "and it may be of little use to say them. I am sometimes almost in despair, standing so nearly alone as I do with my feet on the very brink of this devastating flood of evil, and getting back only faint echoes to my calls for help. But when year after year I see some sheaves coming in as the reward of my efforts and of the few noble hearts that work with me, I thank God and take courage, and I lift my voice and call more loudly for help, trusting that I may be heard by some who, if they would only come up to the help of the Lord against the mighty, would scatter his foes like chaff on the threshing-floor. But I am holding you back from your purpose to visit the mayor; I think you had better act promptly if you would get possession of the child. I shall be interested in the result, and will take it as a favor if you will call at the mission again."

CHAPTER XV

WHEN Mr. Dinneford and the policeman sent by the mayor at his solicitation visited Grubb's court, the baby was not to be found. The room in which it had been seen by Mr. Paulding was vacant. Such a room as it was!—low and narrow, with bare, blackened walls, the single window having scarcely two whole panes of glass, the air loaded with the foulness that exhaled from the filth-covered floor, the only furniture a rough box and a dirty old straw bed lying in a corner.

As Mr. Dinneford stood at the door of this room and inhaled its fetid air, he grew sick, almost faint. Stepping back, with a shocked and disgusted look on his face, he said to the policeman,

"There must be a mistake. This cannot be the room."

Two or three children and a coarse, half-clothed woman, seeing a gentleman going into the house accompanied by a policeman, had followed them closely up stairs.

"Who lives in this room?" asked the policeman, addressing the woman.

"Don't know as anybody lives there now," she replied, with

evident evasion.

"Who did live here?" demanded the policeman.

"Oh, lots!" returned the woman, curtly.

"I want to know who lived here last," said the policeman, a little sternly.

"Can't say—never keep the run of 'em," answered the woman, with more indifference than she felt. "Goin' and comin' all the while. Maybe it was Poll Davis."

"Had she a baby?"

The woman gave a vulgar laugh as she replied: "I rather think not."

"It was Moll Fling," said one of the children, "and she had a baby."

"When was she here last?" inquired the policeman.

The woman, unseen by the latter, raised her fist and threatened the child, who did not seem to be in the least afraid of her, for she answered promptly:

"She went away about an hour ago."

"And took the baby?"

"Yes. You see Mr. Paulding was here asking about the baby, and she got scared."

"Why should that scare her?"

"I don't know, only it isn't her baby."

"How do you know that?"

"'Cause it isn't—I know it isn't. She's paid to take care of it."

"Who by?"

"Pinky Swett."

"Who's Pinky Swett?"

"Don't you know Pinky Swett?" and the child seemed half surprised.

"Where does Pinky Swett live?" asked the policeman.

"She did live next door for a while, but I don't know where she's gone."

Nothing beyond this could be ascertained. But having learned the names of the women who had possession of the child, the policeman said there would be no difficulty about discovering thcm. It might take a little time, but they could not escape the vigilance of the police.

With this assurance, Mr. Dinneford hastened from the polluted air of Grubb's court, and made his way to the mission in Briar street, in order to have some further conference with Mr. Paulding.

"As I feared," said the missionary, on learning that the baby could not be found. "These creatures are as keen of scent as Indians, and know the smallest sign of danger. It is very plain that there is something wrong—that these women have no natural right to the child, and that they are not using it to beg with."

"Do you know a woman called Pinky Swett?" asked the policeman.

"I've heard of her, but do not know her by sight. She bears a hard reputation even here, and adds to her many evil accomplishments the special one of adroit robbery. A victim lured to her den rarely escapes without loss of watch or pocket-book. And not one in a hundred dares to give information, for this would expose him to the public, and so her crimes are covered. Pinky Swett is not the one to bother herself about a baby unless its parentage be known, and not then unless the knowledge can be turned to advantage."

"The first thing to be done, then, is to find this woman," said the policeman.

"That will not be very hard work. But finding the baby, if she thinks you are after it, would not be so easy," returned Mr. Paulding. "She's as cunning as a fox."

"We shall see. If the chief of police undertakes to find the baby, it won't be out of sight long. You'd better confer with the mayor again," added the policeman, addressing Mr. Dinneford.

"I will do so without delay," returned that gentleman.

"I hope to see you here again soon," said the missionary as Mr. Dinneford was about going. "If I can help you in any way, I shall do so gladly."

"I have no doubt but that you can render good service." Then, in half apology, and to conceal the real concern at his heart, Mr. Dinneford added, "Somehow, and strangely enough when I come to think of it, I have allowed myself to get drawn into this thing, and once in, the natural persistence of my character leads me to go on to the end. I am one of those who cannot bear to give up or acknowledge a defeat; and so, having set my hand to this work, I am going to see it through."

When the little girl who had taken Edith to the mission-house in Briar street got home and told her story, there was a ripple of excitement in that part of Grubb's court where she lived, and a new interest was felt in the poor neglected baby. Mr. Paulding's visit and inquiries added to this interest. It had been several days since Pinky Swett's last visit to the child to see that it was safe. On the morning after Edith's call at the mission she came in about ten o'clock, and heard the news. In less than twenty minutes the child and the woman who had charge of it both disappeared from Grubb's court. Pinky sent them to her own room, not many squares distant, and then drew from the little girl who was in Edith's sewing-class all she knew about that young lady. It was not much that the child could tell. She was very sweet and good and handsome, and wore such beautiful clothes, was so kind and patient with the girls, but she did not remember her name, thought it was Edith.

"Now, see here," said Pinky, and she put some money into the child's hand; "I want you to find out for me what her name is and where she lives. Mind, you must be very careful to remember."

"What do you want to know for?" asked the little girl.

"That's none of your business. Do what I tell you," returned Pinky, with impatience; "and if you do it right, I'll give you a quarter more. When do you go again?"

"Next week, on Thursday."

"Not till next Thursday!" exclaimed Pinky, in a tone of disappointment.

"The school's only once a week."

Pinky chafed a good deal, but it was of no use; she must wait.

"You'll be sure and go next Thursday?" she said.

"If Mother lets me," replied the child.

"Oh, I'll see to that; I'll make her let you. What time does the school go in?"

"At three o'clock."

"Very well. You wait for me. I'll come round here at half-past two, and go with you. I want to see the young lady. They'll let me come into the school and learn to sew, won't they?"

"I don't know; you're too big, and you don't want to learn."

"How do you know I don't?"

"Because I do."

Pinky laughed, and then said,

"You'll wait for me?"

"Yes, if mother says so."

T. S. Arthur

"All right;" and Pinky hurried away to take measures for hiding the baby from a search that she felt almost sure was about being made. The first thing she did was to soundly abuse the woman in whose care she had placed the hapless child for her neglect and ill treatment, both of which were too manifest, and then to send her away under the new aspect of affairs she did not mean to trust this woman, nor indeed to trust anybody who knew anything of the inquiries which had been made about the child. A new nurse must be found, and she must live as far away from the old locality as possible. Pinky was not one inclined to put things off. Thought and act were always close together. Scarcely had the woman been gone ten minutes, before, bundling the baby in a shawl, she started off to find a safer hiding-place. This time she was more careful about the character and habits of the person selected for a nurse, and the baby's condition was greatly improved. The woman in whose charge she placed it was poor, but neither drunken nor depraved. Pinky arranged with her to take the care of it for two dollars a week, and supplied it with clean and comfortable clothing. Even she, wicked and vile as she was, could not help being touched by the change that appeared in the baby's shrunken face, and in its sad but beautiful eyes, after its wasted little body had been cleansed and clothed in clean, warm garments and it had taken its fill of nourishing food.

"It's a shame, the way it has been abused," said Pinky, speaking from an impulse of kindness, such as rarely swelled in her evil heart.

"A crying shame," answered the woman as she drew the baby close against her bosom and gazed down upon its pitiful face, and into the large brown eyes that were lifted to hers in mute appeal.

The real motherly tenderness that was in this woman's heart

was quickly perceived by the child, who did not move its eyes from hers, but lay perfectly still, gazing up at her in a kind of easeful rest such as it had never before known. She spoke to it in loving tones, touched its thin cheeks with her finger in playful caresses, kissed it on its lips and forehead, hugged it to her bosom; and still the eyes were fixed on hers in a strange baby-wonder, though not the faintest glinting of a smile played on its lips or over its serious face. Had it never learned to smile?

At last the poor thin lips curved a little, crushing out the lines of suffering, and into the eyes there came a loving glance in place of the fixed, wondering look that was almost a stare. A slight lifting of the hands, a motion of the head, a thrill through the whole body came next, and then a tender cooing sound.

"Did you ever see such beautiful eyes?" said the woman. "It will be a splendid baby when it has picked up a little."

"Let it pick up as fast as it can," returned Pinky; "but mind what I say: you are to be mum. Here's your pay for the first week, and you shall have it fair and square always. Call it your own baby, if you will, or your grandson. Yes, that's better. He's the child of your dead daughter, just sent to you from somewhere out of town. So take good care of him, and keep your mouth shut. I'll be round again in a little while."

And with this injunction Pinky went away. On the next Thursday she visited the St. John's mission sewing-school in company with the little girl from Grubb's court, but greatly to her disappointment, Edith did not make her appearance. There were four or five ladies in attendance on the school, which, under the superintendence of one of them, a woman past middle life, with a pale, serious face and a voice clear and sweet, was conducted with an order and decorum not often maintained among a class of children such as were there gathered together.

It was a long time since Pinky had found herself so repressed and ill at ease. There was a spiritual atmosphere in the place that did not vitalize her blood. She felt a sense of constriction and suffocation. She had taken her seat in the class taught usually by Edith, with the intention of studying that young lady and finding out all she could about her, not doubting her ability to act the part in hand with perfect self-possession. But she had not been in the room a minute before confidence began to die, and very soon she found herself ill at ease and conscious of being out of her place. The bold, bad woman felt weak and abashed. An unseen sphere of purity and Christian love surrounded and touched her soul with as palpable an impression as outward things give to the body. She had something of the inward distress and pain a devil would feel if lifted into the pure air of heaven, and the same desire to escape and plunge back into the dense and impure atmosphere in which evil finds its life and enjoyment. If she had come with any good purpose, it would have been different, but evil, and only evil, was in her heart; and when this felt the sphere of love and purity, her breast was constricted and life seemed going out of her.

It was little less than torture to Pinky for the short time she remained. As soon as she was satisfied that Edith would not be there, she threw down the garment on which she had been pretending to sew, and almost ran from the room.

"Who is that girl?" asked the lady who was teaching the class, looking in some surprise after the hurrying figure.

"It's Pinky Swett," answered the child from Grubb's court. "She wanted to see our teacher."

"Who is your regular teacher?" was inquired.

"Don't remember her name."

"It's Edith," spoke up one of the girls. "Mrs. Martin called her that."

"What did this Pinky Swett want to see her about?"

"Don't know," answered the child as she remembered the money Pinky had given her and the promise of more.

The teacher questioned no further, but went on with her work in the class.

CHAPTER XVI

IT was past midday when Mr. Dinneford returned home after his fruitless search. Edith, who had been waiting for hours in restless suspense, heard his step in the hall, and ran down to meet him.

"Did you see the baby?' she asked, trying to keep her agitation down.

Mr. Dinneford only shook his head,

"Why, not, father?" Her voice choked.

"It could not be found."

"You saw Mr. Paulding?"

"Yes."

"Didn't he find the baby?"

"Oh yes. But when I went to Grubb's court this morning, it was not there, and no one could or would give any information about it. As the missionary feared, those having possession of the baby had taken alarm and removed it to another place. But I have seen the mayor and some of the police, and got them interested. It will not be possible to hide the child for any length of time."

"You said that Mr. Paulding saw it?"

"Yes."

"What did he say?" Edith's voice trembled as she asked the question.

"He thinks there is something wrong."

"Did he tell you how the baby looked?"

"He said that it had large, beautiful brown eyes."

Edith clasped her hands, and drew them tightly against her bosom.

"Oh, father! if it should be my baby!"

"My dear, dear child," said Mr. Dinneford, putting his arms about Edith and holding her tightly, "you torture yourself with a wild dream. The thing is impossible."

"It is somebody's baby," sobbed Edith, her face on her father's breast, "and it may be mine. Who knows?"

"We will do our best to find it," returned Mr. Dinneford, "and then do what Christian charity demands. I am in earnest so far, and will leave nothing undone, you may rest assured. The police have the mayor's instructions to find the baby and give it into my care, and I do not think we shall have long to wait."

An ear they thought not of, heard all this. Mrs. Dinneford's suspicions had been aroused by many things in Edith's manner and conduct of late, and she had watched her every look and word and movement with a keenness of observation that let nothing escape. Careful as her husband and daughter were in their interviews, it was impossible to conceal anything from eyes that never failed in watchfulness. An unguarded word here, a look of mutual intelligence there, a sudden silence when she appeared, an unusual soberness of demeanor and evident absorbed interest in something they were careful to conceal, had the effect to quicken all Mrs. Dinneford's alarms and suspicions.

She had seen from the top of the stairs a brief but excited interview pass between Edith and her father as the latter stood in the vestibule that morning, and she had noticed the almost wild look on her daughter's face as she hastened back along the hall and ran up to her room. Here she stayed alone for over an hour, and then came down to the parlor, where she remained restless, moving about or standing by the window for a greater part of the morning.

There was something more than usual on hand. Guilt in its guesses came near the truth. What could all this mean, if it had not something to do with the cast-off baby? Certainty at last came. She was in the dining-room when Edith ran down to meet her father in the hall, and slipped noiselessly and unobserved into one of the parlors, where, concealed by a curtain, she heard everything that passed between her husband and daughter.

Still as death she stood, holding down the strong pulses of her heart. From the hall Edith and her father turned into one of the parlors—the same in which Mrs. Dinneford was concealed behind the curtain—and sat down.

"It had large brown eyes?" said Edith, a yearning tenderness in her voice.

"Yes, and a finely-formed bead, showing good parentage," returned the father.

"Didn't you find out who the women were—the two bad women the little girl told me about? If we had their names, the police could find them. The little girl's mother must know who they are."

"We have the name of one of them," said Mr. Dinneford. "She is called Pinky Swett, and it can't be long before the police are on her track. She is said to be a desperate character. Nothing more can be done now; we must wait until the police work up the affair. I will call at the mayor's office in the morning and find out what has been done."

Mrs. Dinneford heard no more. The bell rang, and her husband and daughter left the parlor and went up stairs. The moment they were beyond observation she glided noiselessly through the hall, and reached her chamber without being noticed. Soon afterward she came down dressed for visiting, and went out hastily, her veil closely drawn. Her manner was hurried. Descending the steps, she stood for a single moment, as if hesitating which way to go, and then moved off rapidly. Soon she had passed out of the fashionable neighborhood in which she lived. After this she walked more slowly, and with the air of one whose mind was in doubt or hesitation. Once she stopped, and turning about, slowly retraced her steps for the distance of a square. Then she wheeled around, as if from some new and strong resolve, and went on again. At last she paused before a respectable-looking house of moderate size in a neighborhood remote from the busier and more thronged parts of the city. The shutters were all bowed down to the parlor, and the house had a quiet, unobtrusive look. Mrs. Dinneford gave a quick, anxious glance up and down the street, and then hurriedly ascended the steps and rang the bell.

"Is Mrs. Hoyt in?" she asked of a stupid-looking girl who came to the door.

"Yes, ma'am," was answered.

"Tell her a lady wants to see her;" and she passed into the plainly-furnished parlor. There were no pictures on the walls nor ornaments on the mantel-piece, nor any evidence of taste—nothing home-like—in the shadowed room, the atmosphere of which was close and heavy. She waited here for a few moments, when there was a rustle of garments and the sound of light, quick feet on the stairs. A small, dark-eyed, sallow-faced woman entered the parlor.

"Mrs. Bray—no, Mrs. Hoyt."

"Mrs. Dinneford;" and the two women stood face to face for a few moments, each regarding the other keenly.

"Mrs. Hoyt—don't forget," said the former, with a warning emphasis in her voice. "Mrs. Bray is dead."

In her heart Mrs. Dinneford wished that it were indeed so.

"Anything wrong?" asked the black-eyed little woman.

"Do you know a Pinky Swett?" asked Mrs. Dinneford, abruptly.

Mrs. Hoyt—so we must now call her—betrayed surprise at this question, and was about answering "No," but checked herself and gave a half-hesitating "Yes," adding the question, "What about her?"

Before Mrs. Dinneford could reply, however, Mrs. Hoyt took hold of her arm and said, "Come up to my room. Walls have ears sometimes, and I will not answer for these."

Mrs. Dinneford went with her up stairs to a chamber in the rear part of the building.

"We shall be out of earshot here," said Mrs. Hoyt as she closed the door, locking it at the same time. "And now tell me what's up, and what about Pinky Swett."

"You know her?"

"Yes, slightly."

"More than slightly, I guess."

Mrs. Hoyt's eyes flashed impatiently. Mrs. Dinneford saw it, and took warning.

"She's got that cursed baby."

"How do you know?"

"No matter how I know. It's enough that I know. Who is she?"

"That question may be hard to answer. About all I know of her is that she came from the country a few years ago, and has been drifting about here ever since."

"What is she doing with that baby? and how did she get hold of it?"

"Questions more easily asked than answered."

T. S. Arthur

"Pshaw! I don't want any beating about the bush, Mrs. Bray."

"Mrs. Hoyt," said the person addressed.

"Oh, well, Mrs. Hoyt, then. We ought to understand each other by this time."

"I guess we do;" and the little woman arched her brows.

"I don't want any beating about the bush," resumed Mrs. Dinneford. "I am here on business."

"Very well; let's to business, then;" and Mrs. Hoyt leaned back in her chair.

"Edith knows that this woman has the baby," said Mrs. Dinneford.

"What!" and Mrs. Hoyt started to her feet.

"The mayor has been seen, and the police are after her."

"How do you know?"

"Enough that I know. And now, Mrs. Hoyt, this thing must come to an end, and there is not an instant to be lost. Has Pinky Swett, as she is called, been told where the baby came from?"

"Not by me."

"By anybody?"

"That is more than I can say."

"What has become of the woman I gave it to?"

"She's about somewhere."

"When did you see her?"

Mrs. Hoyt pretended to think for some moments, and then replied:

"Not for a month or two."

"Had she the baby then?"

"No; she was rid of it long before that."

"Did she know this Pinky Swett?"

"Yes."

"Curse the brat! If I'd thought all this trouble was to come, I'd have smothered it before it was half an hour old."

"Risky business," remarked Mrs. Hoyt.

"Safer than to have let it live," said Mrs. Dinneford, a hard, evil expression settling around her mouth. "And now I want the thing done. You understand. Find this Pinky Swett. The police are after her, and may be ahead of you. I am desperate, you see. Anything but the discovery and possession of this child by Edith. It must be got out of the way. If it will not starve, it must drown."

Mrs. Dinneford's face was distorted by the strength of her evil passions. Her eyes were full of fire, flashing now, and now glaring like those of a wild animal.

"It might fall out of a window," said Mrs. Hoyt, in a low, even voice, and with a faint smile on her lips. "Children fall out of windows sometimes."

"But don't always get killed," answered Mrs. Dinneford, coldly.

"Or, it might drop from somebody's arms into the river—off the deck of a ferryboat, I mean," added Mrs. Hoyt.

"That's better. But I don't care how it's done, so it's done."

"Accidents are safer," said Mrs. Hoyt.

"I guess you're right about that. Let it be an accident, then."

It was half an hour from the time Mrs. Dinneford entered this house before she came away. As she passed from the door, closely veiled, a gentleman whom she knew very well was going by on the opposite side of the street. From something in his manner she felt sure that he had recognized her, and that the recognition had caused him no little surprise. Looking back two or three times as she hurried homeward, she saw, to her consternation, that he was following her, evidently with the purpose of making sure of her identity.

To throw this man off of her track was Mrs. Dinneford's next concern. This she did by taking a street-car that was going in a direction opposite to the part of the town in which she lived, and riding for a distance of over a mile. An hour afterward she came back to her own neighborhood, but not without a feeling of uneasiness. Just as she was passing up to the door of her residence a gentleman came hurriedly around the nearest corner. She recognized him at a glance. It seemed as if the servant would never answer her ring. On he came, until the sound of his steps was in her ears. He was scarcely ten paces distant when the door opened and she passed in. When she gained her room, she sat down faint and trembling. Here was a new element in the danger and disgrace that were digging her steps so closely.

As we have seen, Edith did not make her appearance at the mission sewing-school on the following Thursday, nor did she go there for many weeks afterward. The wild hope that had taken her to Briar street, the nervous strain and agitation attendant on that visit, and the reaction occasioned by her father's failure to get possession of the baby, were too much for her strength, and an utter prostration of mind and body was the consequence. There was no fever nor sign of any active disease—only weakness, Nature's enforced quietude, that life and reason might be saved.

T. S. Arthur

CHAPTER XVII

THE police were at fault. They found Pinky Swett, but were not able to find the baby. Careful as they were in their surveillance, she managed to keep them on the wrong track and to baffle every effort to discover what had been done with the child.

In this uncertainty months went by. Edith came up slowly from her prostrate condition, paler, sadder and quieter, living in a kind of waking dream. Her father tried to hold her back from her mission work among the poor, but she said, "I must go, father; I will die if I do not."

And so her life lost itself in charities. Now and then her mother made an effort to draw her into society. She had not yet given up her ambition, nor her hope of one day seeing her daughter take social rank among the highest, or what she esteemed the highest. But her power over Edith was entirely gone. She might as well have set herself to turn the wind from its course as to influence her in anything. It was all in vain. Edith had dropped out of society, and did not mean to go back. She had no heart for anything outside of her home, except the Christian work to which she had laid her hands.

The restless, watchful, suspicious manner exhibited for a long time by Mrs. Dinneford, and particularly noticed by

Edith, gradually wore off. She grew externally more like her old self, but with something new in the expression of her face when in repose, that gave a chill to the heart of Edith whenever she saw its mysterious record, that seemed in her eyes only an imperfect effort to conceal some guilty secret.

Thus the mother and daughter, though in daily personal contact, stood far apart—were internally as distant from each other as the antipodes.

As for Mr. Dinneford, what he had seen and heard on his first visit to Briar street had aroused him to a new and deeper sense of his duty as a citizen. Against all the reluctance and protests of his natural feelings, he had compelled himself to stand face to face with the appalling degradation and crime that festered and rioted in that almost Heaven-deserted region. He had heard and read much about its evil condition; but when, under the protection of a policeman, he went from house to house, from den to den, through cellar and garret and hovel, comfortless and filthy as dog-kennels and pig-styes, and saw the sick and suffering, the utterly vile and debauched, starving babes and children with faces marred by crime, and the legion of harpies who were among them as birds of prey, he went back to his home sick at heart, and with a feeling of helplessness and hopelessness out of which he found it almost impossible to rise.

We cannot stain our pages with a description of what he saw. It is so vile and terrible, alas, so horrible, that few would credit it. The few imperfect glimpses of life in that region which we have already given are sad enough and painful enough, but they only hint at the real truth.

"What can be done?" asked Mr. Dinneford of the missionary, at their next meeting, in a voice that revealed his utter despair of a remedy. "To me it seems as if nothing but fire could purify this region."

"The causes that have produced this would soon create another as bad," was answered.

"What are the causes?"

"The primary cause," said Mr. Paulding, "is the effort of hell to establish itself on the earth for the destruction of human souls; the secondary cause lies in the indifference and supineness of the people. 'While the husband-men slept the enemy sowed tares.' Thus it was of old, and thus it is to-day. The people are sleeping or indifferent, the churches are sleeping or indifferent, while the enemy goes on sowing tares for the harvest of death."

"Well may you say the harvest of death," returned Mr. Dinneford, gloomily.

"And hell," added the missionary, with a stern emphasis. "Yes, sir, it is the harvest of death and hell that is gathered here, and such a full harvest! There is little joy in heaven over the sheaves that are garnered in this accursed region. What hope is there in fire, or any other purifying process, if the enemy be permitted to go on sowing his evil seed at will?"

"How will you prevent it?" asked Mr. Dinneford.

"Not by standing afar off and leaving the enemy in undisputed possession—not by sleeping while he sows and reaps and binds into bundles for the fires, his harvests of human souls! We must be as alert and wise and ready of hand as he; and God being our helper, we can drive him from the field!"

"You have thought over this sad problem a great deal," said Mr. Dinneford. "You have stood face to face with the enemy for years, and know his strength and his resources. Have you any well-grounded hope of ever dislodging him from this stronghold?"

"I have just said it, Mr. Dinneford. But until the churches and the people come up to the help of the Lord against the mighty, he cannot be dislodged. I am standing here, sustained in my work by a small band of earnest Christian men and women, like an almost barren rock in the midst of a down-rushing river on whose turbulent surface thousands are being swept to destruction. The few we are able to rescue are as a drop in the bucket to the number who are lost. In weakness and sorrow, almost in despair sometimes, we stand on our rock, with the cry of lost souls mingling with the cry of fiends in our ears, and wonder at the churches and the people, that they stand aloof—nay, worse, turn from us coldly often—when we press the claims of this worse than heathen people who are perishing at their very doors.

"Sir," continued the missionary, warming on his theme, "I was in a church last Sunday that cost its congregation over two hundred thousand dollars. It was an anniversary occasion, and the collections for the day were to be given to some foreign mission. How eloquently the preacher pleaded for the heathen! What vivid pictures of their moral and spiritual destitution he drew! How full of pathos he was, even to tears! And the congregation responded in a contribution of over three thousand dollars, to be sent somewhere, and to be disbursed by somebody of whom not one in a hundred of the contributors knew anything or took the trouble to inform themselves. I felt sick and oppressed at such a waste of money and Christian sympathy, when heathen more destitute and degraded than could be found in any foreign land were dying at home in thousands every

T. S. Arthur

year, unthought of and uncared for. I gave no amens to his prayers—I could not. They would have stuck in my throat. I said to myself, in bitterness and anger, 'How dare a watchman on the walls of Zion point to an enemy afar off, of whose movements and power and organization he knows but little, while the very gates of the city are being stormed and its walls broken down?' But you must excuse me, Mr. Dinneford. I lose my calmness sometimes when these things crowd my thoughts too strongly. I am human like the rest, and weak, and cannot stand in the midst of this terrible wickedness and suffering year after year without being stirred by it to the very inmost of my being. In my intense absorption I can see nothing else sometimes."

He paused for a little while, and then said, in a quiet, business way,

"In seeking a remedy for the condition of society found here, we must let common sense and a knowledge of human nature go hand in hand with Christian charity. To ignore any of these is to make failure certain. If the whisky-and policy-shops were all closed, the task would be easy. In a single month the transformation would be marvelous. But we cannot hope for this, at least not for a long time to come—not until politics and whisky are divorced, and not until associations of bad men cease to be strong enough in our courts to set law and justice at defiance. Our work, then, must be in the face of these baleful influences."

"Is the evil of lottery-policies so great that you class it with the curse of rum?" asked Mr. Dinneford.

"It is more concealed, but as all-pervading and almost as disastrous in its effects. The policy-shops draw from the people, especially the poor and ignorant, hundreds of thousands of dollars every year. There is no more chance of thrift for one who indulges in this sort of gambling than there is for one who indulges in drink. The vice in either case drags its subject down to want, and in most cases to crime. I could point you to women virtuous a year ago, but who now live abandoned lives; and they would tell you, if you would question them, that their way downward was through the policy-shops. To get the means of securing a hoped-for prize—of getting a hundred or two hundred dollars for every single one risked, and so rising above want or meeting some desperate exigency—virtue was sacrificed in an evil moment."

"The whisky-shops brutalize, benumb and debase or madden with cruel and murderous passions; the policy-shops, more seductive and fascinating in their allurements, lead on to as deep a gulf of moral ruin and hopeless depravity. I have seen the poor garments of a dying child sold at a pawn-shop for a mere trifle by its infatuated mother, and the money thrown away in this kind of gambling. Women sell or pawn their clothing, often sending their little children to dispose of these articles, while they remain half clad at home to await the daily drawings and receive the prize they fondly hope to obtain, but which rarely, if ever, comes.

"Children learn early to indulge this vice, and lie and steal in order to obtain money to gratify it. You would be amazed to see the scores of little boys and girls, white and black, who daily visit the policy-shops in this neighborhood to put down the pennies they have begged or received for stolen articles on some favorite numbers—quick-witted, sharp, eager little wretches, who talk the lottery slang as glibly as older customers. What hope is there in the future for these children? Will their education in the shop of a policy-dealer fit them to become honest, industrious citizens?"

All this was so new and dreadful to Mr. Dinneford that be

was stunned and disheartened; and when, after an interview with the missionary that lasted over an hour, he went away, it was with a feeling of utter discouragement. He saw little hope of making head against the flood of evil that was devastating this accursed region.

CHAPTER XVIII

MRS. HOYT, alias Bray, found Pinky Swett, but she did not find the poor cast-off baby. Pinky had resolved to make it her own capital in trade. She parleyed and trifled with Mrs. Hoyt week after week, and each did her best to get down to the other's secret, but in vain. Mutually baffled, they parted at last in bitter anger.

One day, about two months after the interview between Mrs. Dinneford and Mrs. Hoyt described in another chapter, the former received in an envelope a paragraph cut from a newspaper. It read as follows:

"A CHILD DROWNED.—A sad accident occurred yesterday on board the steamer Fawn as she was going down the river. A woman was standing with a child in her arms near the railing on the lower deck forward. Suddenly the child gave a spring, and was out of her arms in a moment. She caught after it frantically, but in vain. Every effort was made to recover the child, but all proved fruitless. It did not rise to the surface of the water."

Mrs. Dinneford read the paragraph twice, and then tore it into little bits. Her mouth set itself sternly. A long sigh of relief came up from her chest. After awhile the hard lines began slowly to disappear, giving place to a look of

T. S. Arthur

satisfaction and comfort.

"Out of my way at last," she staid, rising and beginning to move about the room. But the expression of relief and confidence which had come into her face soon died out. The evil counselors that lead the soul into sin become its tormentors after the sin is committed, and torture it with fears. So tortured they this guilty and wretched woman at every opportunity. They led her on step by step to do evil, and then crowded her mind with suggestions of perils and consequences the bare thought of which filled her with terror.

It was only a few weeks after this that Mrs. Dinneford, while looking over a morning paper, saw in the court record the name of Pinky Swett. This girl had been tried for robbing a man of his pocket-book, containing five hundred dollars, found guilty, and sentenced to prison for a term of two years.

"Good again!" exclaimed Mrs. Dinneford, with satisfaction. "The wheel turns."

After that she gradually rose above the doubts and dread of exposure that haunted her continually, and set herself to work to draw her daughter back again into society. But she found her influence over Edith entirely gone. Indeed, Edith stood so far away from her that she seemed more like a stranger than a child.

Two or three times had Pinky Swett gone to the mission sewing-school in order to get a sight of Edith. Her purpose was to follow her home, and so find out her name and were she lived. With this knowledge in her possession, she meant to visit Mrs. Bray, and by a sudden or casual mention by name of Edith as the child's mother throw her off her guard, and lead her to betray the fact if it were really so. But Edith was sick at home, and did not go to the school. After a few weeks the little girl who was to identify Edith as the person who had shown so much interest in the baby was taken away from Grubb's court by her mother, and nobody could tell where to find her. So, Pinky had to abandon her efforts in this direction, and Edith, when she was strong enough to go back to the sewing-school, missed the child, from whom she was hoping to hear something that might give a clue to where the poor waif had been taken.

Up to the time of her arrest and imprisonment, Pinky had faithfully paid the child's board, and looked in now and then upon the woman who had it in charge, to see that it was properly cared for. How marvelously the baby had improved in these two or three months! The shrunken limb's were rounded into beautiful symmetry, and the pinched face looked full and rosy. The large brown eyes, in which you once saw only fear or a mystery of suffering, were full of a happy light, and the voice rang out often in merry child-laughter. The baby had learned to walk, and was daily growing more and more lovable.

But after Pinky's imprisonment there was a change. The woman—Mrs. Burke by name—in whose care the child had been placed could not afford to keep him for nothing. The two dollars week received for his board added just enough to her income to enable her to remain at home. But failing to receive this, she must go out for day's work in families at least twice in every week.

What, then, was to be done with little Andy, as the baby was called? At first Mrs. Burke thought of getting him into one of the homes for friendless children, but the pleasant child had crept into her affections, and she could not bear the thought of giving him up. His presence stirred in her heart old and tender things long buried out of sight, and set the past, with

T. S. Arthur

its better and purer memories, side by side with the present. She had been many times a mother, but her children were all dead but one, and she—Alas! the thought of her, whenever it came, made her heart heavy and sad.

"I will keep him a while and see, how it comes out," she said, on getting the promise of a neighbor to let Andy play with her children and keep an eye on him whenever she was out. He had grown strong, and could toddle about and take care of himself wonderfully well for a child of his age.

And now began a new life for the baby—a life in which he must look out for himself and hold his own in a hand-to-hand struggle. He had no rights that the herd of children among whom he was thrown felt bound to respect; and if he were not able to maintain his rights, he must go down helplessly, and he did go down daily, often hourly. But he had will and vital force, and these brought him always to his feet again, and with strength increased rather than lost. On the days that Mrs. Burke went out he lived for most of the time in the little street, playing with the children that swarmed its pavements, often dragged from before wheels or horses' hoofs by a friendly hand, or lifted from some gutter in which he had fallen, dripping with mud.

When Mrs. Burke came home on the evening of her first day out, the baby was a sight to see. His clothes were stiff with dirt, his shoes and stockings wet, and his face more like that of a chimney-sweep than anything else. But this was not all; there was a great lump as large as a pigeon's egg on the back of his head, a black-and-blue spot on his forehead and a bad cut on his upper lip. His joy at seeing her and the tearful cry he gave as he threw his arm's about her neck quite overcame Mrs. Burke, and caused her eyes to grow dim. She was angry at the plight in which she found him, and said some hard things to the woman who had promised to look after the child, at which the latter grew angry in turn, and told her to stay at home and take care of the brat herself, or put him in one of the homes.

The fresh care and anxiety felt by Mrs. Burke drew little Andy nearer and made her reject more decidedly the thought of giving him up. She remained at home on the day following, but did not find it so easy as before to keep the baby quiet. He had got a taste of the free, wild life of the street, of its companionship and excitement, and fretted to go out. Toward evening she put by her work and went on the pavement with Andy. It was swarming with children. At the sight of them he began to scream with pleasure. Pulling his hand free from that of Mrs. Burke, he ran in among them, and in a moment after was tumbled over on the pavement. His head got a hard knock, but he didn't seem to mind it, for he scrambled to his feet and commenced tossing his hands about, laughing and crying out as wildly as the rest. In a little while, over he was knocked again, and as he fell one of the children stepped on his hand and hurt him so that he screamed with pain. Mrs. Burke caught him in her arms; but when he found that she was going to take him in the house he stopped crying and struggled to get down. He was willing to take the knocks and falls. The pleasure of this free life among children was more to him than any of the suffering it brought.

On the next day Mrs. Burke had to go out again. Another neighbor promised to look after Andy. When she returned at night, she found things worse, if anything, than before. The child was dirtier, if that were possible, and there were two great lumps on his head, instead of one. He had been knocked down by a horse in the street, escaping death by one of the narrowest of chances, and had been discovered and removed from a ladder up which he had climbed a distance of twenty feet.

T. S. Arthur

What help was there? None that Mrs. Burke knew, except to give up the child, and she was not unselfish enough for this. The thought of sending him away was always attended with pain. It would take the light out of her poor lonely life, into which he had brought a few stray sunbeams.

She could not, she would not, give him up. He must take his chances. Ah, but they were hard chances! Children mature fast under the stimulus of street-training. Andy had a large brain and an active, nervous organization. Life in the open air gave vigor and hardness to his body. As the months went by he learned self-reliance, caution, self-protection, and took a good many lessons in the art of aggression. A rapidly-growing child needs a large amount of nutritious food to supply waste and furnish material for the daily-increasing bodily structure. Andy did not get this. At two years of age he had lost all the roundness of babyhood. His limbs were slender, his body thin and his face colorless and hungry-looking.

About this time—that is, when Andy was two years old—Mrs. Burke took sick and died. She had been failing for several months, and unable to earn sufficient even to pay her rent. But for the help of neighbors and an occasional supply of food or fuel from some public charity, she would have starved. At her death Andy had no home and no one to care for him. One pitying neighbor after another would take him in at night, or let him share a meal with her children, but beyond this he was utterly cast out and friendless. It was summer-time when Mrs. Burke died, and the poor waif was spared for a time the suffering of cold.

Now and then a mother's heart would be touched, and after a half-reluctantly given supper and a place where he might sleep for the night would mend and wash his soiled clothes and dry them by the fire, ready for morning. The pleased look that she saw in his large, sad eyes—for they had grown wistful and sad since the only one he had known as a mother died—was always her reward, and something not to be put out of her memory. Many of the children took kindly to Andy, and often supplied him with food.

"Andy is so hungry, mamma; can't I take him something to eat?" rarely failed to bring the needed bread for the poor little cast-adrift. And if he was discovered now and then sound asleep in bed with some pitying child who had taken him in stealthily after dark, few were hard-hearted enough to push him into the street, or make him go down and sleep on the kitchen floor. Yet this was not unfrequently done. Poverty is sometimes very cruel, yet often tender and compassionate.

One day, a few months after Mrs. Burke's death, Andy, who was beginning to drift farther and farther away from the little street, yet always managing to get back into it as darkness came on, that he might lay his tired body in some friendly place, got lost in strange localities. He had wandered about for many hours, sitting now on some step or cellar-door or horse-block, watching the children at play and sometimes joining in their sports, when they would let him, with the spontaneous abandon of a puppy or a kitten, and now enjoying some street-show or attractive shop-window. There was nothing of the air of a lost child about him. For all that his manner betrayed, his home might have been in the nearest court or alley. So, he wandered along from street to street without attracting the special notice of any—a bare-headed, bare-footed, dirty, half-clad atom of humanity not three years old.

Hungry, tired and cold, for the summer was gone and mid-autumn had brought its chilly nights, Andy found himself, as darkness fell, in a vile, narrow court, among some children as forlorn and dirty as himself. It was Grubb's court—his old home—though in his memory there was of course no record of the place.

Too tired and hungry for play, Andy was sitting on the step of a wretched hovel, when the door opened and a woman called sharply the names of her two children. They answered a little way off. "Come in this minute, and get your suppers," she called again, and turning back without noticing Andy, left the door open for her children. The poor cast-adrift looked in and saw light and food and comfort—a home that made him heartsick with longing, mean and disordered and miserable as it would have appeared to your eyes and mine, reader. The two children, coming at their mother's call, found him standing just on the threshold gazing in wistfully; and as they entered, he, drawn by their attraction, went in also. Then, turning toward her children, the mother saw Andy.

"Out of this!" she cried, in quick anger, raising her hand and moving hastily toward the child. "Off home with you!"

Andy might well be frightened at the terrible face and threatening words of this woman, and he was frightened. But he did not turn and fly, as she meant that he should. He had learned, young as he was, that if he were driven off by every rebuff, he would starve. It was only through importunity and perseverance that he lived. So he held his ground, his large, clear eyes fixed steadily on the woman's face as she advanced upon him. Something in those eyes and in the firmly-set mouth checked the woman's purpose if she had meant violence, but she thrust him out into the damp street, nevertheless, though not roughly, and shut the door against him.

Andy did not cry; poor little baby that he was, he had long since learned that for him crying did no good. It brought him nothing. Just across the street a door stood open. As a stray kitten creeps in through an open door, so crept he through this one, hoping for shelter and a place of rest.

"Who're you?" growled the rough but not unkindly voice of a man, coming from the darkness. At the same moment a light gleamed out from a match, and then the steadier flame of a candle lit up the small room, not more than eight or nine feet square, and containing little that could be called furniture. The floor was bare. In one corner were some old bits of carpet and a blanket. A small table, a couple of chairs with the backs broken off and a few pans and dishes made up the inventory of household goods.

As the light made all things clear in this poor room, Andy saw the bloodshot eyes, and grizzly face of a man, not far past middle life.

"Who are you, little one?" he growled again as the light gave him a view of Andy's face. This growl had in it a tone of kindness and welcome to the ears of Andy who came forward, saying,

"I'm Andy."

"Indeed! You're Andy, are you?" and he reached out one of his hands.

"Yes; I'm Andy," returned the child, fixing his eyes with a look so deep and searching on the man's face that they held him as by a kind of fascination.

"Well, Andy, where did you come from?" asked the man.

"Don't know," was answered.

"Don't know!"

T. S. Arthur

Andy shook his head.

"Where do you live?"

"Don't live nowhere," returned the child; "and I'm hungry."

"Hungry?" The man let the hand he was still holding drop, and getting up quickly, took some bread from a closet and set it on the old table.

Andy did not wait for an invitation, but seized upon the bread and commenced eating almost ravenously. As he did so the man fumbled in his pockets. There were a few pennies there. He felt them over, counting them with his fingers, and evidently in some debate with himself. At last, as he closed the debate, he said, with a kind of compelled utterance,

"I say, young one, wouldn't you like some milk with your bread?"

"Milk! oh my I oh goody! yes," answered the child, a gleam of pleasure coming into his face.

"Then you shall have some;" and catching up a broken mug, the man went out. In a minute or two he returned with a pint of milk, into which he broke a piece of bread, and then sat watching Andy as he filled himself with the most delicious food he had tasted for weeks, his marred face beaming with a higher satisfaction than he had known for a long time.

"Is it good?" asked the man.

"I bet you!" was the cheery answer.

"Well, you're a little brick," laughed the man as he stroked Andy's head. "And you don't live anywhere?"

"No."

"Is your mother dead?"

"Yes."

"And your father?"

"Hain't got no father."

"Would you like to live here?"

Andy looked toward the empty bowl from which he had made such a satisfying meal, and said,

"Yes."

"It will hold us both. You're not very big;" and as he said this the man drew his arm about the boy in a fond sort of way.

"I guess you're tired," he added, for Andy, now that an arm was drawn around him, leaned against it heavily.

"Yes, I'm tired," said the child.

"And sleepy too, poor little fellow! It isn't much of a bed I can give you, but it's better than a door-step or a rubbish corner."

Then he doubled the only blanket he had, and made as soft a bed as possible. On this he laid Andy, who was fast asleep almost as soon as down.

"Poor little chap!" said the man, in a tender, half-broken voice, as he stood over the sleeping child, candle in hand. "Poor little chap!"

T. S. Arthur

The sight troubled him. He turned with a quick, disturbed movement and put the candle down. The light streaming upward into his face showed the countenance of a man so degraded by intemperance that everything attractive had died out of it. His clothes were scanty, worn almost to tatters, and soiled with the slime and dirt of many an ash-heap or gutter where he had slept off his almost daily fits of drunkenness. There was an air of irresolution about him, and a strong play of feeling in his marred, repulsive face, as he stood by the table on which he had set the candle. One hand was in his pocket, fumbling over the few pennies yet remaining there.

As if drawn by an attraction he could not resist, his eyes kept turning to the spot where Andy lay sleeping. Once, as they came back, they rested on the mug from which the child had taken his supper of bread and milk.

"Poor little fellow!" came from his lips, in a tone of pity.

Then he sat down by the table and leaned his head on his hand. His face was toward the corner of the room where the child lay. He still fumbled the small coins in his pocket, but after a while his fingers ceased to play with them, then his hand was slowly withdrawn from the pocket, a deep sigh accompanying the act.

After the lapse of several minutes he took up the candle, and going over to the bed, crouched down and let the light fall on Andy's face. The large forehead, soiled as it was, looked white to the man's eyes, and the brown matted hair, as he drew it through his fingers, was soft and beautiful. Memory had taken him back for years, and he was looking at the fair forehead and touching the soft brown hair of another baby. His eyes grew dim. He set the candle upon the floor, and putting his hands over his face, sobbed two or three times.

When this paroxysm of feeling went off, he got up with a steadier air, and set the light back upon the table. The conflict going on in his mind was not quite over, but another look at Andy settled the question. Stooping with a hurried movement, he blew out the candle, then groped his way over to the bed, and lying down, took the child in his arms and drew him close to his breast. So the morning found them both asleep.

T. S. Arthur

CHAPTER XIX

MR. DINNEFORD had become deeply interested in the work that was going on in Briar street, and made frequent visits to the mission house. Sometimes he took heart in the work, but oftener he suffered great discouragement of feeling. In one of his many conversations with Mr. Paulding he said,

"Looking as I do from the standpoint gained since I came here, I am inclined to say there is no hope. The enemy is too strong for us."

"He is very strong," returned the missionary, "but God is stronger, and our cause is his cause. We have planted his standard here in the very midst of the enemy's territory, and have not only held our ground for years, but gained some victories. If we had the people, the churches and the law-officers on our side, we could drive him out in a year. But we have no hope of this—at least not for a long time to come; and so, as wisely as we can, as earnestly as we can, and with the limited means at our control, we are fighting the foe and helping the weak, and gaining a little every year."

"And you really think there is gain?"

"I know it," answered the missionary, with a ringing confidence in his voice. "It is by comparisons that we are able to get at true results. Come with me into our school-room, next door."

They passed from the office of the mission into the street.

"These buildings," said Mr. Paulding, "erected by that true Christian charity which hopeth all things, stand upon the very site of one of the worst dens once to be found in this region. In them we have a chapel for worship, two large and well ventilated school-rooms, where from two to three hundred children that would not be admitted into any public school are taught daily, a hospital and dispensary and bathrooms. Let me show you the school. Then I will give you a measure of comparison."

Mr. Dinneford went up to the school-rooms. He found them crowded with children, under the care of female teachers, who seemed to have but little trouble in keeping them in order. Such a congregation of boys and girls Mr. Dinneford had never seen before. It made his heart ache as he looked into some of their marred and pinched, faces, most of which bore signs of pain, suffering, want and evil. It moved him to tears when he heard them sing, led by one of the teachers, a tender hymn expressive of the Lord's love for poor neglected children.

"The Lord Jesus came to seek and to save that which was lost," said the missionary as they came down from the school-room, "and we are trying to do the same work. And that our labor is not all in vain will be evident when I show you what this work was in the beginning. You have seen a little of what it is now."

They went back to the office of the missionary.

"It is nearly twenty years," said Mr. Paulding, "since the

organization of our mission. The question of what to do for the children became at once the absorbing one. The only building in which to open a Sunday-school that could be obtained was an old dilapidated frame house used as a receptacle for bones, rags, etc.; but so forbidding was its aspect, and so noisome the stench arising from the putrefying bones and rotting rags, that it was feared for the health of those who might occupy it. However it was agreed to try the effect of scraping, scrubbing, white-washing and a liberal use of chloride of lime. This was attended with such good effects that, notwithstanding the place was still offensive to the olfactories, the managers concluded to open in it our first Sabbath-school.

"No difficulty was experienced in gathering in a sufficient number of children to compose a school; for, excited by such a novel spectacle as a Sabbath-school in that region, they came in crowds. But such a Sabbath-school as that first one was beyond all doubt the rarest thing of the kind that any of those interested in its formation had ever witnessed. The jostling, tumbling, scratching, pinching, pulling of hair, little ones crying and larger ones punching each other's heads and swearing most profanely, altogether formed a scene of confusion and riot that disheartened the teachers in the start, and made them begin to think they had undertaken a hopeless task.

"As to the appearance of these young Ishmaelites, it was plain that they had rarely made the acquaintance of soap and water. Hands, feet and face exhibited a uniform crust of mud and filth. As it was necessary to obtain order, the superintendent, remembering that 'music hath charms to soothe the savage breast,' decided to try its effects on the untamed group before him; and giving out a line of a hymn adapted to the tune of 'Lily Dale,' he commenced to sing. The effect was instantaneous. It was like oil on troubled waters. The delighted youngsters listened to the first line, and then joined in with such hearty good-will that the old shanty rang again.

"The attempt to engage and lead them in prayer was, however, a matter of great difficulty. They seemed to regard the attitude of kneeling as very amusing, and were reluctant to commit themselves so far to the ridicule of their companions as to be caught in such a posture. After reading to them a portion of the Holy Scriptures and telling them of Jesus, they were dismissed, greatly pleased with their first visit to a Sabbath-school.

"As for ourselves, we had also received a lesson. We found —what indeed we had expected—that the poor children were very ignorant, but we also found what we did not expect— namely, such an acute intelligence and aptitude to receive instruction as admonished us of the danger of leaving them to grow up under evil influences to become master-spirits in crime and pests to society. Many of the faces that we had just seen were very expressive—indeed, painfully so. Some of them seemed to exhibit an unnatural and premature develop- ment of those passions whose absence makes childhood so attractive.

"Hunger! ay, its traces were also plainly written there. It is painful to see the marks of hunger on the human face, but to see the cheeks of childhood blanched by famine, to behold the attenuated limbs and bright wolfish eyes, ah! that is a sight.

"The organization of a day-school came next. There were hundreds of children in the district close about the mission who were wholly without instruction. They were too dirty, vicious and disorderly to be admitted into any of the public schools; and unless some special means of education were provided, they must grow up in ignorance. It was therefore resolved to open a day-school, but to find a teacher with her heart in such a work was a difficulty hard to be met; moreover, it was thought by many unsafe for a lady to remain in this locality alone, even though a suitable one should offer. But one brave and self-devoted was found, and one Sunday it was announced to the children in the Sabbath-school that a day school would be opened in the same building at nine o'clock on Monday morning.

"About thirty neglected little ones from the lanes and alleys around the mission were found at the schoolroom door at the appointed hour. But when admitted, very few of them had any idea of the purpose for which they were collected. The efforts of the teacher to seat them proved a failure. The idea among them seemed to be that each should take some part in amusing the company. One would jump from the back of a bench upon which he had been seated, while others were creeping about the floor; another, who deemed himself a proficient in turning somersaults, would be trying his skill in this way, while his neighbor, equally ambitious, would show the teacher how he could stand on his head. Occasionally they would pause and listen to the singing of a hymn or the reading of a little story; then all would be confusion again; and thus the morning wore away. The first session having closed, the teacher retired to her home, feeling that a repetition of the scenes through which she had passed could scarcely be endured.

"Two o'clock found her again at the door, and the children soon gathered around her. Upon entering the schoolroom, most of them were induced to be seated, and a hymn was sung which they had learned in the Sabbath-school. When it was finished, the question was asked, 'Shall we pray?' With one accord they answered, 'Yes.' 'And will you be quiet?' They replied in the affirmative. All were then requested to be silent and cover their faces. In this posture they remained until the prayer was closed; and after resuming their seats, for some minutes order was preserved. This was the only encouraging circumstance of the day.

"For many weeks a stranger would scarcely have recognized a school in this disorderly gathering which day after day met in the old gloomy building. Very many difficulties which we may not name were met and conquered. Fights were of common occurrence. A description of one may give the reader an idea of what came frequently under our notice.

"A rough boy about fourteen years of age, over whom some influence had been gained, was chosen monitor one morning; and as he was a leader in all the mischief, it was hoped that putting him upon his honor would assist in keeping order. Talking aloud was forbidden. For a few minutes matters went on charmingly, until some one, tired of the restraint, broke silence. The monitor, feeling the importance of his position, and knowing of but one mode of redress, instantly struck him a violent blow upon the ear, causing him to scream with pain. In a moment the school was a scene of confusion, the friends of each boy taking sides, and before the cause of trouble could be ascertained most of the boys were piled upon each other in the middle of the room, creating sounds altogether indescribable. The teacher, realizing that she was alone, and not well understanding her influence, feared for a moment to interfere; but as matters were growing worse, something must be done. She made an effort to gain the ear of the monitor, and asked why he did so. He, confident of being in the right, answered,

"Teacher, he didn't mind you; he spoke, and I licked him; and I'll do it again if be don't mind you."

"His services were of course no longer required, although he had done his duty according to his understanding of the case.

"Thus it was at the beginning of this work nearly twenty years ago," said the missionary. "Now we have an orderly school of over two hundred children, who, but for the opportunity here given, would grow up without even the rudiments of all education. Is not this a gain upon the enemy? Think of a school like this doing its work daily among these neglected little ones for nearly a score of years, and you will no longer feel as if nothing had been done—as if no headway had been gained. Think, too, of the Sabbath-school work in that time, and of the thousands of children who have had their memories filled with precious texts from the Bible, who have been told of the loving Saviour who came into the world and suffered and died for them, and of his tender love and perpetual care over his children, no matter how poor and vile and afar off from him they may be. It is impossible that the good seed of the word scattered here for so long a time should not have taken root in many hearts. We know that they have, and can point to scores of blessed instances—can take you to men and women, now good and virtuous people, who, but for our day-and Sabbath-schools, would, in all human probability, be now among the outcast, the vicious and the criminal.

"So much for what has been done among the children. Our work with men and women has not been so fruitful as might well be supposed, and yet great good has been accomplished even among the hardened, the desperate and the miserably vile and besotted. Bad as things are to-day—awful to see and to contemplate, shocking and disgraceful to a Christian community—they were nearly as bad again at the time this mission set up the standard of God and made battle in his name. Our work began as a simple religious movement, with street preaching."

"And with what effect?" asked Mr. Dinneford.

"With good effect, in a limited number of cases, I trust. In a degraded community like this there will always be some who had a different childhood from that of the crowds of young heathen who swarm its courts and alleys; some who in early life had religious training, and in whose memories were stored up holy things from Scripture; some who have tender and sweet recollection of a mother and home and family prayer and service in God's temples. In the hearts of such God's Spirit in moving could touch and quicken and flush with reviving life these old memories, and through them bring conviction of sin, and an intense desire to rise out of the horrible pit into which they had fallen and the clay wherein their feet were mired. Angels could come near to these by what of good and true was to be found half hidden, but not erased from their book of life, and so help in the work of their recovery and salvation.

"But, sir, beyond this class there is small hope, I fear, in preaching and praying. The great mass of these wretched beings have had little or no early religious instruction. There, are but few, if any, remains of things pure and good and holy stored away since childhood in their memories to be touched and quickened by the Spirit of God. And so we must approach them in another and more external way. We must begin with their physical evils, and lessen these as fast as possible; we must remove temptation from their doors, or get them as far as possible out of the reach of temptation, but in this work not neglecting the religious element as an agency, of untold power.

"Christ fed the hungry, and healed the sick, and clothed the naked, and had no respect unto the persons of men. And we, if we would lift up fallen humanity, must learn by his example. It is not by preaching and prayer and revival

T. S. Arthur

meetings that the true Christian philanthropist can hope to accomplish any great good among the people here, but by doing all in his power to change their sad external condition and raise them out of their suffering and degradation. Without some degree of external order and obedience to the laws of natural life, it is, I hold, next to impossible, to plant in the mind any seeds of spiritual truth. There is no ground there. The parable of the sower that went forth to sow illustrates this law. Only the seed that fell on good ground brought forth fruit. Our true work, then, among this heathen people, of whom the churches take so little care, is first to get the ground in order for the planting, of heavenly seed. Failing in this, our hope is small."

"This mission has changed its attitude since the beginning," said Mr. Dinneford.

"Yes. Good and earnest men wrought for years with the evil elements around them, trusting in God's Spirit to change the hearts of the vile and abandoned sinners among whom they preached and prayed. But there was little preparation of the ground, and few seeds got lodgment except in stony places, by the wayside and among thorns. Our work now is to prepare the ground, and in this work, slowly as it is progressing, we have great encouragement. Every year we can mark the signs of advancement. Every year we make some head against the enemy. Every year our hearts take courage and are refreshed by the smell of grasses and the odor of flowers and the sight of fruit-bearing plants in once barren and desolate places. The ground is surely being made ready for the sower."

"I am glad to hear you speak so encouragingly," returned Mr. Dinneford. "To me the case looked desperate—wellnigh hopeless. Anything worse than I have witnessed here seemed impossible."

"It is only by comparisons, as I said before, that we can get at the true measure of change and progress," answered the missionary. "Since we have been at work in earnest to improve the external life of this region, we have had much to encourage us. True, what we have done has made only a small impression on the evil that exists here; but the value of this impression lies in the fact that it shows what can be done with larger agencies. Double our effective force, and we can double the result. Increase it tenfold, and ten times as much can be done."

"What is your idea of this work?" said Mr. Dinneford. "In other words, what do you think the best practical way to purify this region?"

"If you draw burning brands and embers close together, your fire grows stronger; if you scatter them apart, it will go out," answered the missionary. "Moral and physical laws correspond to each other. Crowd bad men and women together, and they corrupt and deprave each other. Separate them, and you limit their evil power and make more possible for good the influence of better conditions. Let me give you an instance: A man and his wife who had lived in a wretched way in one of the poorest hovels in Briar street for two years, and who had become idle and intemperate, disappeared from among us about six months ago. None of their neighbors knew or cared much what had become of them. They had two children. Last week, as I was passing the corner of a street in the south-western part of the city in which stood a row of small new houses, a neatly-dressed woman came out of a store with a basket in her hand. I did not know her, but by the brightening look in her face I saw that she knew me.

"'Mr. Paulding,' she said, in a pleased way, holding out her hand; 'you don't know me,' she added, seeing the doubt in my face. 'I am Mrs.—.'"

T. S. Arthur

"'Impossible!' I could not help exclaiming."

"'But it's true, Mr. Paulding,' she averred, a glow of pleasure on her countenance. 'We've turned over a new leaf.'"

"'So I should think from your appearance,' I replied. 'Where do you live?'"

"'In the third house from the corner,' pointing to the neat row of small brick houses I have mentioned. 'Come and look at our new home. I want to tell you about it!'"

"I was too much pleased to need a second invitation."

"'I've got as clean steps as my neighbors,' she said, with pride in her voice, 'and shades to my windows, and a bright doorknob. It wasn't so in Briar street. One had no heart there. Isn't this nice?'"

"And she glanced around the little parlor we had entered."

"It was nice, compared to the dirty and disorderly place they had called their home in Briar street. The floor was covered with a new ingrain carpet. There were a small table and six cane-seat chairs in the room, shades at the windows, two or three small pictures on the walls and some trifling ornaments on the mantel. Everything was clean and the air of the room sweet."

"'This is my little Emma,' she said as a cleanly-dressed child came into the room; 'You remember she was in the school.'"

"I did remember her as a ragged, dirty-faced child, forlorn and neglected, like most of the children about here. It was a wonderful transformation."

"'And now,' I said, 'tell me how all this has come about.'"

"'Well, you see, Mr. Paulding,' she answered, 'there was no use in John and me trying to be anything down there. It was temptation on every hand, and we were weak and easily tempted. There was nothing to make us look up or to feel any pride. We lived like our neighbors, and you know what kind of a way that was."

"One day John said to me, 'Emma,' says he, 'it's awful, the way we're living; we'd better be dead.' His voice was shaky-like, and it kind of made me feel bad. 'I know it, John,' said I, 'but what can we do?' 'Go 'way from here,' he said. 'But where?' I asked. 'Anywhere. I'm not all played out yet;' and he held up his hand and shut it tight. 'There's good stuff in me yet, and if you're willing to make a new start, I am.' I put my hand in his, and said, 'God helping me, I will try, John.' He went off that very day and got a room in a decent neighborhood, and we moved in it before night. We had only one cart-load, and a wretched load of stuff it was. But I can't tell you how much better it looked when we got it into our new room, the walls of which were nicely papered, and the paint clean and white. I fixed up everything and made it as neat as possible. John was so pleased. 'It feels something like old times,' he said. He had been knocking about a good while, picking up odd jobs and not half working, but he took heart now, quit drinking and went to work in good earnest, and was soon making ten dollars a week, every cent of which he brought home. He now gets sixteen dollars. We haven't made a back step since. But it wouldn't have been any use trying if we'd stayed in Briar street. Pride helped us a good deal in the beginning, sir. I was ashamed not to have my children looking as clean as my neighbors, and ashamed not to keep things neat and tidy-like. I didn't care anything about it in Briar street."

T. S. Arthur

"I give you this instance, true in nearly every particular," said the missionary, "in order to show you how incurable is the evil condition of the people here; unless we can get the burning brands apart, they help to consume each other."

"But how to get them apart? that is the difficult question," said Mr. Dinneford.

"There are two ways," was replied—"by forcing the human brands apart, and by interposing incombustible things between them. As we have no authority to apply force, and no means at hand for its exercise if we had the authority, our work has been in the other direction. We have been trying to get in among these burning brands elements that would stand the fire, and, so lessen the ardor of combustion."

"How are you doing this?"

"By getting better houses for the people to live in. Improve the house, make it more sightly and convenient, and in most cases you will improve the person who lives in it. He will not kindle so easily, though he yet remain close to the burning brands."

"And are you doing this?"

"A little has been done. Two or three years ago a building association was organized by a few gentlemen of means, with a view to the purchase of property in this district and the erection of small but good houses, to be rented at moderate cost to honest and industrious people. A number of such houses have already been built, and they are now occupied by tenants of a better class, whose influence on their neighbors is becoming more and more apparent every day. Brady street—once the worst place in all this district—has changed wonderfully. There is scarcely a house in the two blocks through which it runs that does not show some improvement since the association pulled down half a dozen of its worst frame tenements and put neat brick dwellings in their places. It is no uncommon thing now to see pavement sweeping and washing in front of some of the smallest and poorest of the houses in Brady street where two years ago the dirt would stick to your feet in passing. A clean muslin half curtain, a paper shade or a pot of growing plants will meet your eyes at a window here and there as you pass along. The thieves who once harbored in this street, and hid their plunder in cellars and garrets until it could be sold or pawned, have abandoned the locality. They could not live side by side with honest industry."

"And all this change may be traced to the work of our building association, limited as are its means and half-hearted as are its operations. The worst of our population—the common herd of thieves, beggars and vile women who expose themselves shamelessly on the street—are beginning to feel less at home and more in danger of arrest and exposure. The burning brands are no longer in such close contact, and so the fires of evil are raging less fiercely. Let in the light, and the darkness flees. Establish the good, and evil shrinks away, weak and abashed."

CHAPTER XX

SO the morning found them fast asleep. The man awoke first and felt the child against his bosom, soft and warm. It was some moments ere he understood what it meant. It seemed as if the wretched life he had been leading was all a horrible dream out of which he had awakened, and that the child sleeping in his bosom was his own tenderly-loved baby. But the sweet illusions faded away, and the hard, sorrowful truth stood out sternly before him.

Then Andy's eyes opened and looked into his face. There was nothing scared in the look-hardly an expression of surprise. But the man saw a mute appeal and a tender confidence that made his heart swell and yearn toward the homeless little one.

"Had a nice sleep?" he asked, in a tone of friendly encouragement.

Andy nodded his head, and then gazed curiously about the room.

"Want some breakfast?"

The hungry face lit up with a flash of pleasure.

"Of course you do, little one."

The man was on his feet by this time, with his hand in his pocket, from which he drew a number of pennies. These he counted over carefully twice. The number was just ten. If there had been only himself to provide for, it would not have taken long to settle the question of expenditure. Five cents at an eating-shop where the caterer supplied himself from the hodge-podge of beggars' baskets would have given him a breakfast fit for a dog or pig, while the remaining five cents would have gone for fiery liquor to quench a burning thirst.

But another mouth had too be fed. All at once this poor degraded man had risen to a sense of responsibility, and was practicing the virtue of self-denial. A little child was leading him.

He had no toilette to make, no ablutions to practice. There was neither pail nor wash-basin in his miserable kennel. So, without any delay of preparation, he caught up the broken mug and went out, as forlorn a looking wretch as was to be seen in all that region. Almost every house that he passed was a grog-shop, and his nerves were all unstrung and his mouth and throat dry from a night's abstinence. But he was able to go by without a pause. In a few minutes he returned with a loaf of bread, a pint of milk and a single dried sausage.

What a good breakfast the two made. Not for a long time had the man so enjoyed a meal. The sight of little Andy, as he ate with the fine relish of a hungry child, made his dry bread and sausage taste sweeter than anything that had passed his lips for weeks.

Something more than the food he had taken steadied the man's nerves and allayed his thirst. Love was beating back

T. S. Arthur

into his heart—love for this homeless wanderer, whose coming had supplied the lost links in the chain which bound him to the past and called up memories that had slept almost the sleep of death for years. Good resolutions began forming in his mind.

"It may be," he said to himself as new and better impressions than he had known for a long time began to crowd upon him, "that God has led this baby here."

The thought sent a strange thrill to his soul. He trembled with excess of feeling. He had once been a religious man; and with the old instinct of dependence on God, he clasped his hands together with a sudden, desperate energy, and looking up, cried, in a half-despairing, half-trustful voice,

"Lord, help me!"

No earnest cry like that ever goes up without an instant answer in the gift of divine strength. The man felt it in a stronger purpose and a quickening hope. He was conscious of a new power in himself.

"God being my helper," he said in the silence of his heart, "I will be a man again."

There was a long distance between him and a true manhood. The way back was over very rough and difficult places, and through dangers and temptations almost impossible to resist. Who would have faith in him? Who would help him in his great extremity? How was he to live? Not any longer by begging or petty theft. He must do honest work. There was no hope in anything else. If God were to be his helper, he must be honest, and work. To this conviction he had come.

But what was to be done with Andy while he was away

trying to earn something? The child might get hurt in the street or wander off in his absence and never find his way back. The care he felt for the little one was pleasure compared to the thought of losing him.

As for Andy, the comfort of a good breakfast and the feeling that he had a home, mean as it was, and somebody to care for him, made his heart light and set his lips to music.

When before had the dreary walls of that poor hovel echoed to the happy voice of a light-hearted child? But there was another echo to the voice, and from walls as long a stranger to such sounds as these—the walls in the chambers of that poor man's memory. A wellnigh lost and ruined soul was listening to the far-off voices of children. Sunny-haired little ones were thronging about him; he was looking into their tender eyes; their soft arms were clinging to his neck; he was holding them tightly clasped to his bosom.

"Baby," he said. It was the word that came most naturally to his lips.

Andy, who was sitting where a few sunbeams came in through a rent in the wall, with the warm light on his head, turned and looked into the bleared but friendly eyes gazing at him so earnestly.

"I'm going out, baby. Will you stay here till I come back?"

"Yes," answered the child, "I'll stay."

"I won't be gone very long, and I'll bring you an apple and something good for dinner."

Andy's face lit up and his eyes danced.

"Don't go out until I come back. Somebody might carry you off, and then I couldn't give you the nice red apple."

"I'll stay right here," said Andy, in a positive tone.

"And won't go into the street till I come back?"

"No, I won't." Andy knit his brows and closed his lips firmly.

"All right, little one," answered the man, in a cheery sort of voice that was so strange to his own ears that it seemed like the voice of somebody else.

Still, he could not feel satisfied. He was living in the midst of thieves to whom the most insignificant thing upon which they could lay their hands was booty. Children who had learned to be hard and cruel thronged the court, and he feared, if he left Andy alone in the hovel, that it would not only be robbed of its meagre furniture, but the child subjected to ill-treatment. He had always fastened the door on going out, but hesitated now about locking Andy in.

All things considered, it was safest, he felt, to lock the door. There was nothing in the room that could bring harm to the child—no fire or matches, no stairs to climb or windows out of which he could fall.

"I guess I'd better lock the door, hadn't I, so that nobody can carry off my little boy?" he asked of Andy.

Andy made no objections. He was ready for anything his kind friend might propose.

"And you mustn't cry or make a noise. The police might break in if you did."

"All right," said Andy, with the self-assertion of a boy of ten. The man stroked the child's head and ran his fingers through his hair in a fond way; then, as one who tore himself from an object of attraction, went hastily out and locked the door.

And now was to begin a new life. Friendless, debased, repulsive in appearance, everything about him denoting the abandoned drunkard, this man started forth to get honest bread. Where should he go? What could he do? Who would give employment to an object like him? The odds were fearfully against him—no, not that, either. In outward respects, fearful enough were the odds, but on the other side agencies invisible to mortal sight were organizing for his safety. In to his purpose to lead a new life and help a poor homeless child God's strength was flowing. Angels were drawing near to a miserable wreck of humanity with hands outstretched to save. All heaven was coming to the rescue.

He was shuffling along in the direction of a market-house, hoping to earn a little by carrying home baskets, when he came face to face with an old friend of his better days, a man with whom he had once held close business relations.

"Mr. Hall!" exclaimed this man in a tone of sorrowful surprise, stopping and looking at him with an expression of deepest pity on his countenance. "This is dreadful!"

"You may well say that, Mr. Graham. It dreadful enough. No one knows that better than I do," was answered, with a bitterness that his old friend felt to be genuine.

"Why, then, lead this terrible life a day longer?" asked the friend.

"I shall not lead it a day longer if God will help me," was replied, with a genuineness of purpose that was felt by

T. S. Arthur

Mr. Graham.

"Give me your hand on that, Andrew Hall," he exclaimed. Two hands closed in a tight grip.

"Where are you going now?" inquired the friend.

"I'm in search of something to do—something that will give me honest bread. Look at my hand."

He held it up.

"It shakes, you see. I have not tasted liquor this morning. I could have bought it, but I did not."

"Why?"

"I said, 'God being my helper, I will be a man again,' and I am trying."

"Andrew Hall," said his old friend, solemnly, as he laid his hand on his shoulder, "if you are really in earnest—if you do mean, in the help of God, to try—all will be well. But in his help alone is there any hope. Have you seen Mr. Paulding?"

"No."

"Why not?"

"He has no faith in me. I have deceived him too often."

"What ground of faith is there now?" asked Mr. Graham.

"This," was the firm but hastily spoken answer. "Last night as I sat in the gloom of my dreary hovel, feeling so wretched that I wished I could die, a little child came in—a poor, motherless, homeless wanderer, almost a baby—and crept down to my heart, and he is lying there still, Mr. Graham, soft, and warm and precious, a sweet burden to bear. I bought him a supper and a breakfast of bread and milk with the money, I had saved for drink, and now, both for his sake and mine, I am out seeking for work. I have locked him in, so that no one can harm or carry him away while I earn enough to buy him his dinner, and maybe something better to wear, poor little homeless thing!"

There was a genuine earnestness and pathos about the man that could not be mistaken.

"I think," said Mr. Graham, his voice not quite steady, "that God brought us together this morning. I know Mr. Paulding. Let us go first to the mission, and have some talk with him. You must have a bath and better, and cleaner clothes before you are in a condition to get employment."

The bath and a suit of partly-worn but good clean clothes were supplied at the mission house.

"Now come with me, and I will find you something to do," said the old friend.

But Andrew Hall stood hesitating.

"The little child—I told him I'd come back soon. He's locked up all alone, poor baby!"

He spoke with a quiver in his voice.

"Oh, true, true!" answered Mr. Graham; "the baby must be looked after;" and he explained to the missionary.

"I will go round with you and get the child," said Mr.

Paulding. "My wife will take care of him while you are away with Mr. Graham."

They found little Andy sitting patiently on the floor. He did not know the friend who had given him a home and food and loving words, and looked at him half scared and doubting. But his voice made the child spring to his feet with a bound, and flushed his thin-face with the joy of a glad recognition.

Mrs. Paulding received him with a true motherly kindness, and soon a bath and clean clothing wrought as great a change in the child as they had done in the man.

"I want your help in saving him," said Mr. Graham, aside, to the missionary. "He was once among our most respectable citizens, a good church-member, a good husband and father, a man of ability and large influence. Society lost much when it lost him. He is well worth saving, and we must do it if possible. God sent him this little child to touch his heart and flood it with old memories, and then he led me to come down here that I might meet and help him just when his good purposes made help needful and salvation possible. It is all of his loving care and wise providence of his tender mercy, which is over the poorest and weakest and most degraded of his children. Will you give him your special care?"

"It is the work I am here to do," answered the missionary. "The Master came to seek and to save that which was lost, and I am his humble follower."

"The child will have to be provided for," said Mr. Graham. "It cannot, of course, be left with him. It needs a woman's care."

"It will not do to separate them," returned the missionary. "As you remarked just now, God sent him this little child to touch his heart and lead him back from the wilderness in which he has strayed. His safety depends on the touch of that hand. So long as he feels its clasp and its pull, he will walk in the new way wherein God is setting his feet. No, no; the child must be left with him—at least for the present. We will take care of it while he is at work during the day, and at night it can sleep in his arms, a protecting angel."

"What kind of a place does he live in?" asked Mr. Graham.

"A dog might dwell there in comfort, but not a man," replied the missionary.

Mr. Graham gave him money: "Provide a decent room. If more is required, let me know."

He then went away, taking Mr. Hall with him.

"You will find the little one here when you come back," said Mr. Paulding as he saw the anxious, questioning look that was cast toward Andy.

Clothed and in his right mind, but in no condition for work, was Andrew Hall. Mr. Graham soon noticed, as he walked by his side, that he was in a very nervous condition.

"What had you for breakfast this morning" he asked, the right thought coming into his mind.

"Not much. Some bread and a dried sausage."

"Oh dear! that will never do! You must have something more nutritious—a good beefsteak and a cup of coffee to steady your nerves. Come."

And in a few minutes they were in an eating-house. When

T. S. Arthur

they came out, Hall was a different man. Mr. Graham then took him to his store and set him to work to arrange and file a number of letters and papers, which occupied him for several hours. He saw that he had a good dinner and at five o'clock gave him a couple of dollars for his day's work, aid after many kind words of advice and assurance told him to come back in the morning, and he would find something else for him to do.

Swiftly as his feet would carry him, Andrew Hall made his way to the Briar street mission. He did not at first know the clean, handsome child that lifted his large brown eyes to his face as he came in, nor did the child know him until he spoke. Then a cry of pleasure broke from the baby's lips, and he ran to the arms reached out to clasp him.

"We'll go home now," he said, as if anxious to regain possession of the child.

"Not back to Grubb's court," was answered by Mr. Paulding. "If you are going to be a new man, you must have a new and better home, and I've found one for you just a little way from here. It's a nice clean room, and I'll take you there. The rent is six dollars a month, but you can easily pay that when you get fairly to work."

The room was in the second story of a small house, better kept than most of its neighbors, and contained a comfortable bed, with other needed furniture, scanty, but clean and good. It was to Mr. Hall like the chamber of a prince compared with what he had known for a long time; and as he looked around him and comprehended something of the blessed change that was coming over his life, tears filled his eyes.

"Bring Andy around in the morning," said the missionary as he turned to go. "Mrs. Paulding will take good care of him."

That night, after undressing the child and putting on him the clean night-gown which good Mrs. Paulding had not forgotten, he said,

"And now Andy will say his prayers."

Andy looked at him with wide-open, questioning eyes. Mr. Hall saw that he was not understood.

"You know, 'Now I lay me'?" he said.

"No, don't know it," replied Andy.

"'Our Father,' then?"

The child knit his brow. It was plain that he did not understand what his good friend meant.

"You've said your prayers?"

Andy shook his head in a bewildered way.

"Never said your prayers!" exclaimed Mr. Hall, in a voice so full of surprise and pain that Andy grew half frightened.

"Poor baby!" was said, pityingly, a moment after. Then the question, "Wouldn't you like to say your prayers?" brought the quick answer, "Yes."

"Kneel down, then, right here." Andy knelt, looking up almost wonderingly into the face that bent over him.

"We have a good Father in heaven," said Mr. Hall, with tender reverence in his tone, pointing upward as he spoke, "He loves us and takes care of us. He brought you to me, and told me to love you and take care of you for him, and I'm going to do it. Now, I want you to say a little prayer to this good and kind Father before you go to bed. Will you?"

"Yes, I will," came the ready answer.

"Say it over after me. 'Now I lay me down to sleep.'"

Andy repeated the words, his little hands clasped together, and followed through the verse which thousands of little children in thousands of Christian homes were saying at the very same hour.

There was a subdued expression on the child's face as he rose from his knees; and when Mr. Hall lifted him from the floor to lay him in bed, he drew his arms about his neck and hugged him tightly.

How beautiful the child looked as he lay with shut eyes, the long brown lashes fringing his flushed cheeks, that seemed already to have gained a healthy roundness! The soft breath came through his parted lips, about which still lingered the smile of peace that rested there after his first prayer was said; his little hands lay upon his breast.

As Mr. Hall sat gazing at this picture there came a rap on his door. Then the missionary entered. Neither of the men spoke for some moments. Mr. Paulding comprehended the scene, and felt its sweet and holy influence.

"Blessed childhood!" he said, breaking the silence. "Innocent childhood! The nearer we come to it, the nearer we get to heaven." Then, after a pause, he added, "And heaven is our only hope, Mr. Hall."

"I have no hope but in God's strength," was answered, in a tone of solemn earnestness.

"God is our refuge, our rock of defence, our hiding-place, our sure protector. If we trust in him, we shall dwell in safety," said the mission. "I am glad to hear you speak of hoping in God. He will give you strength if you lean upon him, and there is not power enough in all hell to drag you down if you put forth this God-given strength. But remember, my friend, that you must use it as if it were your own. You must resist. God's strength outside of our will and effort is of no use to any of us in temptation. But looking to our Lord and Saviour in humble yet earnest prayer for help in the hour of trial and need if we put forth our strength in resistance of evil, small though it be, then into our weak efforts will come an influx of divine power that shall surely give us the victory. Have you a Bible?"

Mr. Hall shook his head.

"I have brought you one;" and the missionary drew a small Bible from his pocket. "No man is safe without a Bible."

"Oh, I am glad! I was just wishing for a Bible," said Hall as he reached out his hand to receive the precious book.

"If you read it every night and morning—if you treasure its holy precepts in your memory, and call them up in times of trial, or when evil enticements are in your way—God can come near to your soul to succor and to save, for the words of the holy book are his words, and he is present in them. If we take them into our thoughts, reverently seeking to obey them, we make a dwelling-place for the Lord, so that he can abide with us; and in his presence there is safety."

"And nowhere else," responded Hall, speaking from a deep sense of personal helplessness.

"Nowhere else," echoed the missionary. "And herein lies the

T. S. Arthur

hope or the despair of men. It is pitiful, it is heart-aching, to see the vain but wild and earnest efforts made by the slaves of intemperance to get free from their cruel bondage. Thousands rend their fetters every year after some desperate struggle, and escape. But, alas! how many are captured and taken back into slavery! Appetite springs upon them in some unguarded moment, and in their weakness there is none to succor. They do not go to the Strong for strength, but trust in themselves, and are cast down. Few are ever redeemed from the slavery of intemperance but those who pray to God and humbly seek his aid. And so long as they depend on him, they are safe. He will be as a wall of fire about them."

As the missionary talked, the face of Mr. Hall underwent a remarkable change. It grew solemn and very thoughtful. His hands drew together and the fingers clasped. At the last words of Mr. Paulding a deep groan came from his heart; and lifting his gaze upward, he cried out,

"Lord, save me, or I perish!"

"Let us pray," said the missionary, and the two men knelt together, one with bowed head and crouching body, the other with face uplifted, tenderly talking to Him who had come down to the lowliest and the vilest that he might make them pure as the angels, about the poor prodigal now coming back to his Father's house.

After the prayer, Mr. paulding read a chapter from the Bible aloud, and then, after words of hope and comfort, went away.

CHAPTER XXI

"*I TAKE* reproof to myself," said Mr. Dinneford. "As one of your board of managers, I ought to have regarded my position as more than a nominal one. I understand better now what you said about the ten or twenty of our rich and influential men who, if they could be induced to look away for a brief period from their great enterprises, and concentrate thought and effort upon the social evils, abuse of justice, violations of law, poverty and suffering that exist here and in other parts of our city, would inaugurate reforms and set beneficent agencies at work that would soon produce marvelous changes for good."

"Ah, yes," sighed Mr. Paulding. "If we had for just a little while the help of our strong men—the men of brains and will and money, the men who are used to commanding success, whose business it is to organize forces and set impediments at defiance, the men whose word is a kind of law to the people—how quickly, and as if by magic, would all this change!

"But we cannot now hope to get this great diversion in our favor. Until we do we must stand in the breach, small in numbers and weak though we are—must go on doing our best and helping when we may. Help is help and good is good, be it ever so small. If I am able to rescue but a single

T. S. Arthur

life where many are drowning, I make just so much head against death and destruction. Shall I stand off and refuse to put forth my hand because I cannot save a score?

"Take heart, Mr. Dinneford. Our work is not in vain. Its fruits may be seen all around. Bad as you find everything, it is not so bad as it was. When our day-school was opened, the stench from the filthy children who were gathered in was so great that the teachers were nauseated. They were dirty in person as well as dirty in their clothing. This would not do. There was no hope of moral purity while such physical impurity existed. So the mission set up baths, and made every child go in and thoroughly wash his body. Then they got children's clothing—new and old—from all possible sources, and put clean garments on their little scholars. From the moment they were washed and cleanly clad, a new and better spirit came upon them. They were more orderly and obedient, and more teachable. There was, or seemed to be, a tenderer quality in their voices as they sang their hymns of praise."

Just then there came a sudden outcry and a confusion of voices from the street. Mr. Dinneford arose quickly and went to the window. A man, apparently drunk and in a rage, was holding a boy tightly gripped by the collar with one hand and cuffing him about the head and face with the other.

"It's that miserable Blind Jake!" said Mr. Paulding.

In great excitement, Mr. Dinneford threw up the window and called for the police. At this the man stopped beating the boy, but swore at him terribly, his sightless eyes rolling and his face distorted in a frightful way. A policeman who was not far off came now upon the scene.

"What's all this about?" he asked, sternly.

"Jake's drunk again, that's the row," answered a voice.

"Lock him up, lock him up!" cried two or three from the crowd.

An expression of savage defiance came into the face of the blind man, and he moved his arms and clenched his fist like one who was bent on desperate resistance. He was large and muscular, and, now that he was excited by drink and bad passions, had a look that was dangerous.

"Go home and behave yourself," said the policeman, not caring to have a single-handed tussle with the human savage, whose strength and desperate character he well knew.

Blind Jake, as he was called, stood for a few moments half defiant, growling and distorting his face until it looked more like a wild animal's than a man's, then jerked out the words,

"Where's that Pete?" with a sound like the crack of a whip.

The boy he had been beating in his drunken fury, and who did not seem to be much hurt, came forward from the crowd, and taking him by the hand, led him away.

"Who is this blind man? I have seen him before," said Mr. Dinneford.

"You may see him any day standing at the street corners, begging, a miserable-looking object, exciting the pity of the humane, and gathering in money to spend in drunken debauchery at night. He has been known to bring in some days as high as ten and some fifteen dollars, all of which is wasted in riot before the next morning. He lives just over the way, and night after night I can hear his howls and curses and laughter mingled with those of the vile women with whom he herds."

"Surely this cannot be?" said Mr. Dinneford.

"Surely it is," was replied. "I know of what I speak. There is hardly a viler wretch in all our city than this man, who draws hundreds—I might say, without exaggeration, thousands—of dollars from weak and tender-hearted people every year to be spent as I have said; and he is not the only one. Out of this district go hundreds of thieves and beggars every day, spreading themselves over the city and gathering in their harvests from our people. I see them at the street corners, coming out of yards and alley-gates, skulking near unguarded premises and studying shop-windows. They are all impostors or thieves. Not one of them is deserving of charity. He who gives to them wastes his money and encourages thieving and vagrancy. One half of the successful burglaries committed on dwelling-houses are in consequence of information gained by beggars. Servant-girls are lured away by old women who come in the guise of alms-seekers, and by well-feigned poverty and a seeming spirit of humble thankfulness—often of pious trust in God—win upon their sympathy and confidence. Many a poor weak girl has thus been led to visit one of these poor women in the hope of doing her some good, and many a one has thus been drawn into evil ways. If the people only understood this matter as I understand it, they would shut hearts and hands against all beggars. I add beggary as a vice to drinking and policy-buying as the next most active agency in the work of making paupers and criminals."

"But there are deserving poor," said Dinneford. "We cannot shut our hearts against all who seek for help."

"The deserving poor," replied Mr. Paulding, "are never common beggars—never those who solicit in the street or importune from house to house. They try always to help themselves, and ask for aid only when in great extremity. They rarely force themselves on your attention; they suffer and die often in dumb despair. We find them in these dreary and desolate cellars and garrets, sick and starving and silent, often dying, and minister to them as best we can. If the money given daily to idle and vicious beggars could be gathered into a fund and dispensed with a wise Christian charity, it would do a vast amount of good; now it does only evil."

"You are doubtless right in this," returned Mr. Dinneford. "Some one has said that to help the evil is to hurt the good, and I guess his saying is near the truth."

"If you help the vicious and the idle," was answered, "you simply encourage vice and idleness, and these never exist without doing a hurt to society. Withhold aid, and they will be forced to work, and so not only do something for the common good, but be kept out of the evil ways into which idleness always leads.

"So you see, sir, how wrong it is to give alms to the vast crew of beggars that infest our cities, and especially to the children who are sent out daily to beg or steal as opportunity offers.

"But there is another view of the case, continued Mr. Paulding, "that few consider, and which would, I am sure, arouse the people to immediate action if they understood it as I do. We compare the nation to a great man. We call it a 'body politic.' We speak of its head, its brain, its hands, its feet, its arteries and vital forces. We know that no part of the nation can be hurt without all the other parts feeling in some degree the shock and sharing the loss or suffering. What is true of the great man of the nation is true of our smaller

T. S. Arthur

communities, our States and cities and towns. Each is an aggregate man, and the health and well-being of this man depend on the individual men and the groups and societies of men by which it is constituted. There cannot be an unhealthy organ in the human system without a communication of disease to the whole body. A diseased liver or heart or lung, a useless hand or foot, an ulcer or local obstruction, cannot exist without injury and impediment to the whole. In the case of a malignant ulcer, how soon the blood gets poisoned!

"Now, here is a malignant ulcer in the body politic of our city. Is it possible, do you think, for it to exist, and in the virulent condition we find it, and not poison the blood of our whole community? Moral and spiritual laws are as unvarying in their action, out of natural sight though they be, as physical laws. Evil and good are as positive entities as fire, and destroy or consume as surely. As certainly as an ulcer poisons with its malignant ichor this blood that visits every part of the body, so surely is this ulcer poisoning every part of our community. Any one who reflects for a moment will see that it cannot be otherwise. From this moral ulcer there flows out daily and nightly an ichor as destructive as that from a cancer. Here theft and robbery and murder have birth, nurture and growth until full formed and organized, and then go forth to plunder and destroy. The life and property of no citizen is safe so long as this community exists. It has its schools of instruction for thieves and housebreakers, where even little children are educated to the business of stealing and robbery. Out from it go daily hundreds of men and women, boys and girls, on their business of beggary, theft and the enticement of the weak and unwary into crime. In it congregate human vultures and harpies who absorb most of the plunder that is gained outside, and render more brutal and desperate the wretches they rob in comparative safety.

"Let me show you how this is done. A man or a woman

thirsting for liquor will steal anything to get money for whisky. The article stolen may be a coat, a pair of boots or a dress—something worth from five to twenty dollars. It is taken to one of these harpies, and sold for fifty cents or a dollar—anything to get enough for a drunken spree. I am speaking only of what I know. Then, again, a man or a woman gets stupidly drunk in one of the whisky-shops. Before he or she is thrown out upon the street, the thrifty liquor-seller 'goes through' the pockets of the insensible wretch, and confiscates all he finds. Again, a vile woman has robbed one of her visitors, and with the money in her pocket goes to a dram-shop. The sum may be ten dollars or it may be two hundred. A glass or so unlooses her tongue; she boasts of her exploit, and perhaps shows her booty. Not once in a dozen times will she take this booty away. If there are only a few women in the shop, the liquor-seller will most likely pounce on her at once and get the money by force. There is no redress. To inform the police is to give information against herself. He may give her back a little to keep her quiet or he may not, just as he feels about it. If he does not resort to direct force, he will manage in some other way to get the money. I could take you to the dram-shop of a man scarcely a stone's throw from this place who came out of the State's prison less than four years ago and set up his vile trap where it now stands. He is known to be worth fifty thousand dollars to-day. How did he make this large sum? By the profits of his bar? No one believes this. It has been by robbing his drunken and criminal customers whenever he could get them in his power."

"I am oppressed by all this," said Mr. Dinneford. "I never dreamed of such a state of things."

"Nor does one in a hundred of our good citizens, who live in quiet unconcern with this pest-house of crime and disease in their midst. And speaking of disease, let me give you another

T. S. Arthur

fact that should be widely known. Every obnoxious epidemic with which our city has been visited in the last twenty years has originated here—ship fever, relapsing fever and small-pox—and so, getting a lodgment in the body politic, have poured their malignant poisons into the blood and diseased the whole. Death has found his way into the homes of hundreds of our best citizens through the door opened for him here."

"Can this be so?" exclaimed Mr. Dinneford.

"It is just as I have said," was replied. "And how could it be otherwise? Whether men take heed or not, the evil they permit to lie at their doors will surely do them harm. Ignorance of a statute, a moral or a physical law gives no immunity from consequence if the law be transgressed—a fact that thousands learn every year to their sorrow. There are those who would call this spread of disease, originating here, all over our city, a judgment from God, to punish the people for that neglect and indifference which has left such a hell as this in their midst. I do not so read it. God has no pleasure in punishments and retributions. The evil comes not from him. It enters through the door we have left open, just as a thief enters our dwellings, invited through our neglect to make the fastenings sure. It comes under the operations of a law as unvarying as any law in physics. And so long as we have this epidemic-breeding district in the very heart of our city, we must expect to reap our periodical harvests of disease and death. What it is to be next year, or the next, none can tell."

"Does not your perpetual contact with all this give your mind an unhealthy tone—a disposition to magnify its disastrous consequences?" said Mr. Dinneford.

The missionary dropped his eyes. The flush and animation

went out of his face.

"I leave you to judge for yourself," he answered, after a brief silence, and in a voice that betrayed a feeling of disappointment. "You have the fact before you in the board of health, prison, almshouse, police, house of refuge, mission and other reports that are made every year to the people. If they hear not these, neither will they believe, though one rose from the dead."

"All is too dreadfully palpable for unbelief," returned Mr. Dinneford. "I only expressed a passing thought."

"My mind may take an unhealthy tone—does often, without doubt," said Mr. Paulding. "I wonder, sometimes, that I can keep my head clear and my purposes steady amid all this moral and physical disorder and suffering. But exaggeration of either this evil or its consequences is impossible. The half can never be told."

Mr. Dinneford rose to go. As he did so, two little Italian children, a boy and a girl, not over eight years of age, tired, hungry, pinched and starved-looking little creatures, the boy with a harp slung over his shoulder, and the girl carrying a violin, went past on the other side.

"Where in the world do all of these little wretches come from?" asked Mr. Dinneford. "They are swarming our streets of late. Yesterday I saw a child who could not be over two years of age tinkling her triangle, while an older boy and girl were playing on a harp and violin. She seemed so cold and tired that it made me sad to look at her. There is something wrong about this."

"Something very wrong," answered the missionary. "Doubt-less you think these children are brought here by their parents or near relatives. No such thing. Most of them are slaves. I speak advisedly. The slave-trade is not yet dead. Its abolition on the coast of Africa did not abolish the cupidity that gave it birth. And the 'coolie' trade, one of its new forms, is not confined to the East."

"I am at a loss for your meaning," said Mr. Dinneford.

"I am not surprised. The new slave-trade, which has been carried on with a secresy that is only now beginning to attract attention, has its source of supply in Southern Italy, from which large numbers of children are drawn every year and brought to this country.

"The headquarters of this trade—cruel enough in some of its features to bear comparison with the African slave-trade itself—are in New York. From this city agents are sent out to Southern Italy every year, where little intelligence and great poverty exist. These agents tell grand stories of the brilliant prospects offered to the young in America. Let me now read to you from the published testimony of one who has made a thorough investigation of this nefarious business, so that you may get a clear comprehension of its extent and iniquity.

"He says: 'One of these agents will approach the father of a family, and after commenting upon the beauty of his children, will tell him that his boys "should be sent at once to America, where they must in time become rich." "There are no poor in America." "The children should go when young, so that they may grow up with the people and the better acquire the language." "None are too young or too old to go to America." The father, of course, has not the means to go himself or to send his children to this delightful country. The agent then offers to take the children to America, and to pay forty or fifty dollars to the father upon his signing an indenture abandoning all claims upon them. He often, also, promises to pay a hundred or more at the end of a year, but, of course, never does it.

"After the agent has collected a sufficient number of children, they are all supplied with musical instruments, and the trip on foot through Switzerland and France begins. They are generally shipped to Genoa, and often to Marseilles, and accomplish the remainder of the journey to Havre or Calais by easy stages from village to village. Thus they become a paying investment from the beginning. This journey occupies the greater portion of the summer months; and after a long trip in the steerage of a sailing-vessel, the unfortunate children land at Castle Garden. As the parents never hear from them again, they do not know whether they are doing well or not."

"They are too young and ignorant to know how to get themselves delivered from oppression; they do not speak our language, and find little or no sympathy among the people whom they annoy. They are thus left to the mercy of their masters, who treat them brutally, and apparently without fear of the law or any of its officers. They are crowded into small, ill-ventilated, uncarpeted rooms, eighteen or twenty in each, and pass the night on the floor, with only a blanket to protect them from the severity of the weather. In the mornings they are fed by their temporary guardian with maccaroni, served in the filthiest manner in a large open dish in the centre of the room, after which they are turned out into the streets to beg or steal until late at night."

"More than all this, when the miserable little outcasts return to their cheerless quarters, they are required to deliver every cent which they have gathered during the day; and if the same be deemed insufficient, the children are carefully searched and soundly beaten."

T. S. Arthur

"The children are put through a kind of training in the arts of producing discords on their instruments, and of begging, in the whole of which the cruelty of the masters and the stolid submission of the pupils are the predominant features. The worst part of all is that the children become utterly unfitted for any occupation except vagrancy and theft."

"You have the answer to your question, 'Where do all these little wretches come from?'" said the missionary as he laid aside the paper from which he had been reading. "Poor little slaves!"

CHAPTER XXII

EDITH'S life, as we have seen, became lost, so to speak, in charities. Her work lay chiefly with children, She was active in mission-schools and in two or three homes for friendless little ones, and did much to extend their sphere of usefulness. Her garments were plain and sombre, her fair young face almost colorless, and her aspect so nun-like as often to occasion remark.

Her patience and tender ways with poor little children, especially with the youngest, were noticed by all who were associated with her. Sometimes she would show unusual interest in a child just brought to one of the homes, particularly if it were a boy, and only two or three years old. She would hover about it and ask it questions, and betray an eager concern that caused a moment's surprise to those who noticed her. Often, at such times, the pale face would grow warm with the flush of blood sent out by her quicker heartbeats, and her eyes would have a depth of expression and a brightness that made her beauty seem the reflection of some divine beatitude. Now and then it was observed that her manner with these little waifs and cast-adrifts that were gathered in from the street had in it an expression of pain, that her eyes looked at them sadly, sometimes tearfully. Often she came with light feet and a manner almost cheery, to go away with eyes cast down and lips set and curved and steps that were slow and heavy.

Time had not yet solved the mystery of her baby's life or death; and until it was solved, time had no power to abate the yearning at her heart, to dull the edge of anxious suspense or to reconcile her to a Providence that seemed only cruel. In her daily prayers this thought of cruelty in God often came in to hide his face from her, and she rose from her knees more frequently in a passion of despairing tears than comforted. How often she pleaded with God, weeping bitter tears, that he would give her certainty in place of terrible doubts! Again, she would implore his loving care over her poor baby, wherever it might be.

So the days wore on, until nearly three years had elapsed since Edith's child was born.

It was Christmas eve, but there were no busy hands at work, made light by loving hearts, in the home of Mr. Dinneford. All its chambers were silent. And yet the coming anniversary was not to go uncelebrated. Edith's heart was full of interest for the children of the poor, the lowly, the neglected and the suffering, whom Christ came to save and to bless. Her anniversary was to be spent with them, and she was looking forward to its advent with real pleasure.

"We have made provision for four hundred children, said her father. "The dinner is to be at twelve o'clock, and we must be there by nine or ten. We shall be busy enough getting everything ready. There are forty turkeys to cut up and four hundred plates to fill."

"And many willing hands to do it," remarked Edith, with a quiet smile; "ours among the rest."

"You'd better keep away from there," spoke up Mrs.

Dinneford, with a jar in her voice. "I don't see what possesses you. You can find poor little wretches anywhere, if you're so fond of them, without going to Briar street. You'll bring home the small-pox or something worse."

Neither Edith nor her father made any reply, and there fell a silence on the group that was burdensome to all. Mrs. Dinneford felt it most heavily, and after the lapse of a few minutes withdrew from the room.

"A good dinner to four hundred hungry children, some of them half starved," said Edith as her mother shut the door. "I shall enjoy the sight as much as they will enjoy the feast."

A little after ten o'clock on the next morning, Mr. Dinneford and Edith took their way to the mission-school in Briar street. They found from fifteen to twenty ladies and gentlemen already there, and at work helping to arrange the tables, which were set in the two long upper rooms. There were places for nearly four hundred children, and in front of each was an apple, a cake and a biscuit, and between every four a large mince pie. The forty turkeys were at the baker's, to be ready at a little before twelve o'clock, the dinner-hour, and in time for the carvers, who were to fill the four hundred plates for the expected guests.

At eleven o'clock Edith and her father went down to the chapel on the first floor, where the children had assembled for the morning exercises, that were to continue for an hour.

Edith had a place near the reading-desk where she could see the countenances of all those children who were sitting side by side in row after row and filling every seat in the room, a restless, eager, expectant crowd, half disciplined and only held quiet by the order and authority they had learned to respect. Such faces as she looked into! In scarcely a single

T. S. Arthur

one could she find anything of true childhood, and they were so marred by suffering and evil! In vain she turned from one to another, searching for a sweet, happy look or a face unmarked by pain or vice or passion. It made her heart ache. Some were so hard and brutal in their expression, and so mature in their aspect, that they seemed like the faces of debased men on which a score of years, passed in sensuality and crime, had cut their deep deforming lines, while others were pale and wasted, with half-scared yet defiant eyes, and thin, sharp, enduring lips, making one tearful to look at them. Some were restless as caged animals, not still for a single instant, hands moving nervously and bodies swaying to and fro, while others sat stolid and almost as immovable as stone, staring at the little group of men and women in front who were to lead them in the exercises of the morning.

At length one face of the many before her fixed the eyes of Edith. It was the face of a little boy scarcely more than three years old. He was only a few benches from her, and had been hidden from view by a larger boy just in front of him. When Edith first noticed this child, he was looking at her intently from a pair of large, clear brown eyes that had in them a wistful, hungry expression. His hair, thick and wavy, had been smoothly brushed by some careful hand, and fell back from a large forehead, the whiteness and smoothness of which was noticeable in contrast with those around him. His clothes were clean and good.

As Edith turned again and again to the face of this child, the youngest perhaps in the room, her heart began to move toward him. Always she found him with his great earnest eyes upon her. There seemed at last to be a mutual fascination. His eyes seemed never to move from her face; and when she tried to look away and get interested in other faces, almost unconsciously to herself her eyes would wander back, and she would find herself gazing at the child.

At eleven o'clock Mr. Paulding announced that the exercises for the morning would begin, when silence fell on the restless company of undisciplined children. A hymn was read, and then, as the leader struck the tune, out leaped the voices of these four hundred children, each singing with a strange wild abandon, many of them swaying their heads and bodies in time to the measure. As the first lines of the hymn,

"Jesus, gentle Shepherd, lead us, Much we need thy tender care,"

swelled up from the lips of those poor neglected children, the eyes of Edith grew blind with tears.

After a prayer was offered up, familiar addresses, full of kindness and encouragement, were made to the children, interspersed with singing and other appropriate exercises. These were continued for an hour. At their close the children were taken up stairs to the two long school-rooms, in which their dinner was to be served. Here were Christmas trees loaded with presents, wreaths of evergreen on the walls and ceilings, and illuminated texts hung here and there, and everything was provided to make the day's influence as beautiful and pleasant as possible to the poor little ones gathered in from cheerless and miserable homes.

Meantime, the carvers had been very busy at work on the forty turkeys—large, tender fellows, full of dressing and cooked as nicely as if they had been intended for a dinner of aldermen—cutting them up and filling the plates. There was no stinting of the supply. Each plate was loaded with turkey, dressing, potatoes that had been baked with the fowls, and a heaping spoonful of cranberry sauce, and as fast as filled conveyed to the tables by the lady attendants, who had come, many of them, from elegant homes, to assist the good missionary's wife and the devoted teachers of the mission-school in this labor of love. And so, when the four hundred hungry children came streaming into the rooms, they found tables spread with such bounty as the eyes of many of them had never looked upon, and kind gentlemen and beautiful ladies already there to place them at these tables and serve them while eating.

It was curious and touching, and ludicrous sometimes, to see the many ways in which the children accepted this bountiful supply of food. A few pounced upon it like hungry dogs, devouring whole platefuls in a few minutes, but most of them kept a decent restraint upon themselves in the presence of the ladies and gentlemen, for whom they could not but feel an instinctive respect. Very few of them could use at fork except in the most awkward manner. Some tried to cut their meat, but failing in the task, would seize it with their hands and eagerly convey it to their hungry mouths. Here and there would be seen a mite of a boy sitting in a kind of maze before a heaped-up dinner-plate, his hands, strangers, no doubt, to knife or fork, lying in his lap, and his face wearing a kind of helpless look. But he did not have to wait long. Eyes that were on the alert soon saw him; ready hands cut his food, and a cheery voice encouraged him to eat. If these children had been the sons and daughters of princes, they could not have been ministered to with a more gracious devotion to their wants and comfort than was shown by their volunteer attendants.

Edith, entering into the spirit of the scene, gave herself to the work in hand with an interest that made her heart glow with pleasure. She had lost sight of the little boy in whom she had felt so sudden and strong an interest, and had been searching about for him ever since the children came up from the chapel. At last she saw him, shut in and hidden between two larger boys, who were eating with a hungry eagerness and forgetfulness of everything around them almost painful to see. He was sitting in front of his heaped-up plate, looking at the tempting food, with his knife and fork lying untouched on the table. There was a dreamy, half-sad, half-bewildered look about him.

"Poor little fellow!" exclaimed Edith as soon as she saw him, and in a moment she was behind his chair.

"Shall I cut it up for you?" she asked as she lifted his knife and fork from the table.

The child turned almost with a start, and looked up at her with a quick flash of feeling on his face. She saw that he remembered her.

"Let me fix it all nicely," she said as she stooped over him and commenced cutting up his piece of turkey. The child did not look at his plate while she cut the food, but with his head turned kept his large eyes on her countenance.

"Now it's all right," said Edith, encouragingly, as she laid the knife and fork on his plate, taking a deep breath at the same time, for her heart beat so rapidly that her lungs was oppressed with the inflowing of blood. She felt, at the same time, an almost irresistible desire to catch him up into her arms and draw him lovingly to her bosom. The child made no attempt to eat, and still kept looking at her.

"Now, my little man," she said, taking his fork and lifting a piece of the turkey to his mouth. It touched his palate, and appetite asserted its power over him; his eyes went down to his plate with a hungry eagerness. Then Edith put the fork into his hand, but he did not know how to use it, and made but awkward attempts to take up the food.

Mrs. Paulding, the missionary's wife, came by at the moment,

T. S. Arthur

and seeing the child, put her hand on him, and said, kindly.

"Oh, it's little Andy," and passed on.

"So your name's Andy?"

"Yes, ma'am." It was the first time Edith had heard his voice. It fell sweet and tender on her ears, and stirred her heart strangely.

"Where do you live?"

He gave the name of a street she had never heard of before.

"But you're not eating your dinner. Come, take your fork just so. There! that's the way;" and Edith took his hand, in which he was still holding the fork, and lifted two or three mouthfuls, which he ate with increasing relish. After that he needed no help, and seemed to forget in the relish of a good dinner the presence of Edith, who soon found others who needed her service.

The plentiful meal was at last over, and the children, made happy for one day at least, were slowly dispersing to their dreary homes, drifting away from the better influences good men and women had been trying to gather about them even for a little while. The children were beginning to leave the tables when Edith, who had been busy among them, remembered the little boy who had so interested her, and made her way to the place where he had been sitting. But he was not there. She looked into the crowd of boys and girls who were pressing toward the door, but could not see the child. A shadow of disappointment came over her feelings, and a strange heaviness weighed over her heart.

"Oh, I'm so sorry," she said to herself. "I wanted to see

him again."

She pressed through the crowd of children, and made her way down among them to the landing below and out upon the street, looking this way and that, but could not see the child. Then she returned to the upper rooms, but her search was in vain. Remembering that Mrs. Paulding had called him by name, she sought for the missionary's wife and made inquiry about him.

"Do you mean the little fellow I called Andy?" said Mrs. Paulding.

"Yes, that's the one," returned Edith.

"A beautiful boy, isn't he?"

"Indeed he is. I never saw such eyes in a child. Who is he, Mrs. Paulding, and what is he doing here? He cannot be the child of depraved or vicious parents."

"I do not think he is. But from whence he came no one knows. He drifted in from some unknown land of sorrow to find shelter on our inhospitable coast. I am sure that God, in his wise providence, sent him here, for his coming was the means of saving a poor debased man who is well worth the saving."

Then she told in a few words the story of Andy's appearance at Mr. Hall's wretched hovel and the wonderful changes that followed—how a degraded drunkard, seemingly beyond the reach of hope and help, had been led back to sobriety and a life of honest industry by the hand of a little child cast somehow adrift in the world, yet guarded and guided by Him who does not lose sight in his good providence of even a single sparrow.

T. S. Arthur

"Who is this man, and where does he live?" asked Mr. Dinneford, who had been listening to Mrs. Paulding's brief recital.

"His name is Andrew Hall," was replied.

"Andrew Hall!" exclaimed Mr. Dinneford, with a start and a look of surprise.

"Yes, sir. That is his name, and he is now living alone with the child of whom we have been speaking, not very far from here, but in a much better neighborhood. He brought Andy around this morning to let him enjoy the day, and has come for him, no doubt, and taken him home."

"Give me the street and number, if you please, Mr. Paulding," said Mr. Dinneford, with much repressed excitement. "We will go there at once," he added, turning to his daughter.

Edith's face had become pale, and her father felt her hand tremble as she laid it on his arm.

At this moment a man came up hurriedly to Mrs. Paulding, and said, with manifest concern,

"Have you seen Andy, ma'am? I've been looking all over, but can't find him."

"He was here a little while ago," answered the missionary's wife. "We were just speaking of him. I thought you'd taken him home."

"Mr. Hall!" said Edith's father, in a tone of glad recognition, extending his hand at the same time.

"Mr. Dinneford!" The two men stood looking at each other, with shut lips and faces marked by intense feeling, each grasping tightly the other's hand.

"It is going to be well with you once more, my dear old friend!" said Mr. Dinneford.

"God being my helper, yes!" was the firm reply. "He has taken my feet out of the miry clay and set them on firm ground, and I have promised him that they shall not go down into the pit again. But Andy! I must look for him."

And he was turning away.

"I saw Andy a little while ago," now spoke up a woman who had come in from the street and heard the last remark.

"Where?" asked Mr. Hall.

"A girl had him, and she was going up Briar street on the run, fairly dragging Andy after her. She looked like Pinky Swett, and I do believe it was her. She's been in prison, you know but I guess her time's up."

Mr. Hall stopped to hear no more, but ran down stairs and up the street, going in the direction said to have been taken by the woman. Edith sat down, white and faint.

"Pinky Swett!" exclaimed Mrs. Paulding. "Why, that's the girl who had the child you were looking after a long time ago, Mr. Dinneford."

"Yes; I remember the name, and no doubt this is the very child she had in her possession at that time. Are you sure she has been in prison for the last two years?" and Mr. Dinneford turned to the woman who had mentioned her name.

T. S. Arthur

"Oh yes, Sir; I remember all about it," answered the woman. "She stole a man's pocket-book, and got two years for it."

"You know her?"

"Oh yes, indeed! And she's a bad one, I can tell you. She had somebody's baby round in Grubb's court, and it was 'most starved to death. I heard it said it belonged to some of the big people up town, and that she was getting hush-money for it, but I don't know as it was true. People will talk."

"Do you know what became of that baby?" asked Edith, with ill-repressed excitement. Her face was still very pale, and her forehead contracted as by pain.

"No, ma'am. The police came round asking questions, and the baby wasn't seen in Grubb's court after that."

"You think it was Pinky Swett whom you saw just now?"

"I'm dead sure of it, sir," turning to Mr. Dinneford, who had asked the question.

"And you are certain it was the little boy named Andy that she had with her?"

"I'm as sure as death, sir."

"Did he look frightened?"

"Oh dear, yes, sir—scared as could be. He pulled back all his might, but she whisked him along as if he'd been only a chicken. I saw them go round the corner of Clayton street like the wind."

Mr. Paulding now joined them, and became advised of what

had happened. He looked very grave.

"We shall find the little boy," he said. "He cannot be concealed by this wretched woman as the baby was; he is too old for that. The police will ferret him out. But I am greatly concerned for Mr. Hall. That child is the bond which holds him at safe anchorage. Break this bond, and he may drift to sea again. I must go after him."

And the missionary hurried away.

For over an hour Edith and her father remained at the mission waiting for some news of little Andy. At the end of this time Mr. Paulding came back with word that nothing could be learned beyond the fact that a woman with a child answering to the description of Andy had been seen getting into an up-town car on Clayton street about one o'clock. She came, it was said by two or three who professed to have seen her, from the direction of Briar street. The chief of police had been seen, and he had already telegraphed to all the stations. Mr. Hall was at the central station awaiting the result.

After getting a promise from Mr. Paulding to send a messenger the moment news of Andy was received, Mr. Dinneford and Edith returned home.

T. S. Arthur

CHAPTER XXIII

AS Edith glanced up, on arriving before their residence, she saw for a moment her mother's face at the window. It vanished like the face of a ghost, but not quick enough to prevent Edith from seeing that it was almost colorless and had a scared look. They did not find Mrs. Dinneford in the parlor when they came in, nor did she make her appearance until an hour afterward, when dinner was announced. Then it was plain to both her husband and daughter that something had occurred since morning to trouble her profoundly. The paleness noticed by Edith at the window and the scared look remained. Whenever she turned her eyes suddenly upon her mother, she found her looking at her with a strange, searching intentness. It was plain that Mrs. Dinneford saw in Edith's face as great a change and mystery as Edith saw in hers, and the riddle of her husband's countenance, so altered since morning, was harder even than Edith's to solve.

A drearier Christmas dinner, and one in which less food was taken by those who ate it, could hardly have been found in the city. The Briar-street feast was one of joy and gladness in comparison. The courses came and went with unwonted quickness, plates bearing off the almost untasted viands which they had received. Scarcely a word was spoken during the meal. Mrs. Dinneford asked no question about the dinner in Briar street, and no remark was made about it by either

Edith or her father. In half the usual time this meal was ended. Mrs. Dinneford left the table first, and retired to her own room. As she did so, in taking her handkerchief from her pocket, she drew out a letter, which fell unnoticed by her upon the floor. Mr. Dinneford was about calling her attention to it when Edith, who saw his purpose and was near enough to touch his hand, gave a quick signal to forbear. The instant her mother was out of the room she sprang from her seat, and had just secured the letter when the dining-room door was pushed open, and Mrs. Dinneford came in, white and frightened. She saw the letter in Edith's hand, and with a cry like some animal in pain leaped upon her and tried to wrest it from her grasp. But Edith held it in her closed hand with a desperate grip, defying all her mother's efforts to get possession of it. In her wild fear and anger Mrs. Dinneford exclaimed,

"I'll kill you if you don't give me that letter!" and actually, in her blind rage, reached toward the table as if to get a knife. Mr. Dinneford, who had been for a moment stupefied, now started forward, and throwing his arms about his wife, held her tightly until Edith could escape with the letter, not releasing her until the sound of his daughter's retiring feet were no longer heard. By this time she had ceased to struggle; and when he released her, she stood still in a passive, dull sort of way, her arms falling heavily to her sides. He looked into her face, and saw that the eyes were staring wildly and the muscles in a convulsive quiver. Then starting and reaching out helplessly, she fell forward. Catching her in his arms, Mr. Dinneford drew her toward a sofa, but she was dead before he could raise her from the floor.

When Edith reached her room, she shut and locked the door. Then all her excitement died away. She sat down, and opening the letter with hands that gave no sign of inward

T. S. Arthur

agitation or suspense, read it through. It was dated at Havana, and was as follows:

"MRS. HELEN DINNEFORD: MADAM—My physician tells me that I cannot live a week—may die at any moment; and I am afraid to die with one unconfessed and unatoned sin upon my conscience—a sin into which I was led by you, the sharer of my guilt. I need not go into particulars. You know to what I refer—the ruin of an innocent, confiding young man, your daughter's husband. I do not wonder that he lost his reason! But I have information that his insanity has taken on the mildest form, and that his friends are only keeping him at the hospital until they can get a pardon from the governor. It is in your power and mine to establish his innocence at once. I leave you a single mouth in which to do this, and at the same time screen yourself, if that be possible. If, at the end of a month, it is not done, then a copy of this letter, with a circumstantial statement of the whole iniquitous affair, will be placed in the hands of your husband, and another in the hands of your daughter. I have so provided for this that no failure can take place. So be warned and make the innocence of George Granger as clear as noonday.

"LLOYD FREELING."

Twice Edith read this letter through before a sign of emotion was visible. She looked about the room, down at herself, and again at the letter.

"Am I really awake?" she said, beginning to tremble. Then the glad but terrible truth grappled with her convictions, and through the wild struggle and antagonism, of feeling that shook her soul there shone into her face a joy so great that the pale features grew almost radiant.

"Innocent! innocent!" fell from her lips, over which crept a smile of ineffable love. But it faded out quickly, and left in its place a shadow of ineffable pain.

"Innocent! innocent!" she repeated, now clasping her hands and lifting her eyes heavenward. "Dear Lord and Saviour! My heart is full of thankfulness! Innocent! Oh, let it be made as clear as noonday! And my baby, Lord—oh, my baby, my baby! Give him back to me!"

She fell forward upon her bed, kneeling, her face hidden among the pillows, trembling and sobbing.

"Edith! Edith!" came the agitated voice of her father from without. She rose quickly, and opening the door, saw his pale, convulsed countenance.

"Quick! quick! Your mother!" and Mr. Dinneford turned and ran down stairs, she following. On reaching the dining-room, Edith found her mother lying on a sofa, with the servants about her in great excitement. Better than any one did she comprehend what she saw.

"Dead," fell almost coldly from her lips.

"I have sent for Dr. Radcliffe. It may only be a fainting fit," answered Mr. Dinneford.

Edith stood a little way off from her mother, as if held from personal contact by an invisible barrier, and looked upon her ashen face without any sign of emotion.

"Dead, and better so," she said, in an undertone heard only by her father.

"My child! don't, don't!" exclaimed Mr. Dinneford in a deprecating whisper.

"Dead, and better so," she repeated, firmly.

While the servants chafed the hands and feet of Mrs. Dinneford, and did what they could in their confused way to bring her back to life, Edith stood a little way off, apparently undisturbed by what she saw, and not once touching her mother's body or offering a suggestion to the bewildered attendants.

When Dr. Radcliffe came and looked at Mrs. Dinneford, all saw by his countenance that he believed her dead. A careful examination proved the truth of his first impression. She was done with life in this world.

As to the cause of her death, the doctor, gathering what he could from her husband, pronounced it heart disease. The story told outside was this—so the doctor gave it, and so it was understood: Mrs. Dinneford was sitting at the table when her head was seen to sink forward, and before any one could get to her she was dead. It was not so stated to him by either Mr. Dinneford or Edith, but he was a prudent man, and careful of the good fame of his patients. Family affairs he held as sacred trusts. We'll he knew that there had been a tragedy in this home—a tragedy for which he was in part, he feared, responsible; and he did not care to look into it too closely. But of all that was involved in this tragedy he really knew little. Social gossip had its guesses at the truth, often not very remote, and he was familiar with these, believing little or much as it suited him.

It is not surprising that Edith's father, on seeing the letter of Lloyd Freeling, echoed his daughter's words, "Better so!"

Not a tear was shed on the grave of Mrs. Dinneford. Husband and daughter saw her body carried forth and buried out of sight with a feeling of rejection and a sense of relief.

Death had no power to soften their hearts toward her. Charity had no mantle broad enough to cover her wickedness; filial love was dead, and the good heart of her husband turned away at remembrance with a shudder of horror.

Yes, it was "better so!" They had no grief, but thankfulness, that she was dead.

On the morning after the funeral there came a letter from Havana addressed to Mr. Dinneford. It was from the man Freeling. In it he related circumstantially all the reader knows about the conspiracy to destroy Granger. The letter enclosed an affidavit made by Freeling, and duly attested by the American consul, in which he stated explicitly that all the forgeries were made by himself, and that George Granger was entirely ignorant of the character of the paper he had endorsed with the name of the firm.

Since the revelation made to Edith by Freeling's letter to her mother, all the repressed love of years, never dead nor diminished, but only chained, held down, covered over, shook itself free from bonds and the wrecks and debris of crushed hopes. It filled her heart with an agony of fullness. Her first passionate impulse was to go to him and throw herself into his arms. But a chilling thought came with the impulse, and sent all the outgoing heart-beats back. She was no longer the wife of George Granger. In a weak hour she had yielded to the importunities of her father, and consented to an application for divorce. No, she was no longer the wife of George Granger. She had no right to go to him. If it were true that reason had been in part or wholly restored, would he not reject her with scorn? The very thought made her heart stand still. It would be more than she could bear.

　　　　　　　T. S. Arthur

CHAPTER XXIV

NO other result than the one that followed could have been hoped for. The strain upon Edith was too great. After the funeral of her mother mind and body gave way, and she passed several weeks in a half-unconscious state.

Two women, leading actors in this tragedy of life, met for the first time in over two years—Mrs. Hoyt, *alias* Bray, and Pinky Swett. It had not gone very well with either of them during that period. Pinky, as the reader knows, had spent the time in prison, and Mrs. Bray, who had also gone a step too far in her evil ways, was now hiding from the police under a different name from any heretofore assumed. They met, by what seemed an accident, on the street.

"Pinky!"

"Fan!"

Dropped from their lips in mutual surprise and pleasure. A little while they held each other's hands, and looked into each other's faces with keenly-searching, sinister eyes, one thought coming uppermost in the minds of both—the thought of that long-time-lost capital in trade, the cast-adrift baby.

From the street they went to Mrs. Bray's hiding-place a small ill-furnished room in one of the suburbs of the city—and there took counsel together.

"What became of that baby?" was one of Mrs. Bray's first questions.

"It's all right," answered Pinky.

"Do you know where it is?"

"Yes."

"And can you put your hand on it?"

"At any moment."

"Not worth the trouble of looking after now," said Mrs. Bray, assuming an indifferent manner.

"Why?" Pinky turned on her quickly.

"Oh, because the old lady is dead."

"What old lady?"

"The grandmother."

"When did she die?"

"Three or four weeks ago."

"What was her name?" asked Pinky.

Mrs. Bray closed her lips tightly and shook her head.

"Can't betray that secret," she replied.

"Oh, just as you like;" and Pinky gave her head an impatient toss. "High sense of honor! Respect for the memory of a departed friend! But it won't go down with me, Fan. We know each other too well. As for the baby—a pretty big one now, by the way, and as handsome a boy as you'll find in all this city—he's worth something to somebody, and I'm on that somebody's track. There's mother as well as a grandmother in the case, Fan."

Mrs. Bray's eyes flashed, and her face grew red with an excitement she could not hold back. Pinky watched her keenly.

"There's somebody in this town to-day who would give thousands to get him," she added, still keeping her eyes on her companion. "And as I was saying, I'm on that some-body's track. You thought no one but you and Sal Long knew anything, and that when she died you had the secret all to yourself. But Sal didn't keep mum about it."

"Did she tell you anything?" demanded Mrs. Bray, thrown off her guard by Pinky's last assertion.

"Enough for me to put this and that together and make it nearly all out," answered Pinky, with great coolness. "I was close after the game when I got caught myself. But I'm on the track once more, and don't mean to be thrown off. A link or two in the chain of evidence touching the parentage of this child, and I am all right. You have these missing links, and can furnish them if you will. If not, I am bound to find them. You know me, Fan. If I once set my heart on doing a thing, heaven and earth can't stop me."

"You're devil enough for anything, I know, and can lie as

fast as you can talk," returned Mrs. Bray, in considerable irritation. "If I could believe a word you said! But I can't."

"No necessity for it," retorted Pinky, with a careless toss of her head. "If you don't wish to hunt in company, all right. I'll take the game myself."

"You forget," said Mrs. Bray, "I can spoil your game."

"Indeed! how?"

"By blowing the whole thing to Mr.—"

"Mr. who?" asked Pinky, leaning forward eagerly as her companion paused without uttering the name that was on her lips.

"Wouldn't you like to know?" Mrs. Bray gave a low tantalizing laugh.

"I'm not sure that I would, from you. I'm bound to know somehow, and it will be cheapest to find out for myself," replied Pinky, hiding her real desire, which was to get the clue she sought from Mrs. Bray, and which she alone could give. "As for blowing on me, I wouldn't like anything better. I wish you'd call on Mr. Somebody at once, and tell him I've got the heir of his house and fortune, or on Mrs. Somebody, and tell her I've got her lost baby. Do it, Fan; that's a deary."

"Suppose I were to do so?" asked Mrs. Bray, repressing the anger that was in her heart, and speaking with some degree of calmness.

"What then?"

"The police would be down on you in less than an hour."

"And what then?"

"Your game would be up."

Pinky laughed derisively:

"The police are down on me now, and have been coming down on me for nearly a month past. But I'm too much for them. I know how to cover my tracks."

"Down on you! For what?"

"They're after the boy."

"What do they know about him? Who set them after him?"

"I grabbed him up last Christmas down in Briar street after being on his track for a week, and them that had him are after him sharp."

"Who had him?"

"I'm a little puzzled at the rumpus it has kicked up," said Pinky, in reply. "It's stirred things amazingly."

"How?"

"Oh, as I said, the police are after me sharp. They've had me before the mayor twice, and got two or three to swear they saw me pick up the child in Briar street and run off with him. But I denied it all."

"And I can swear that you confessed it all to me," said Mrs. Bray, with ill-concealed triumph.

"It won't do, Fan," laughed Pinky. "They'll not be able to find him any more then than now. But I wish you would. I'd like to know this Mr. Somebody of whom you spoke. I'll sell out to him. He'll bid high, I'm thinking."

Baffled by her sharper accomplice, and afraid to trust her with the secret of the child's parentage lest she should rob her of the last gain possible to receive out of this great iniquity, Mrs. Bray became wrought up to a state of ungovernable passion, and in a blind rage pushed Pinky from her room. The assault was sudden and unexpected—so sudden that Pinky, who was the stronger, had no time to recover herself and take the offensive before she was on the outside and the door shut and locked against her. A few impotent threats and curses were interchanged between the two infuriated women, and then Pinky went away.

On the day following, as Mr. Dinneford was preparing to go out, he was informed that a lady had called and was waiting down stairs to see him. She did not send her card nor give her name. On going into the room where the visitor had been shown, he saw a little woman with a dark, sallow complexion. She arose and came forward a step or two in evident embarrassment.

"Mr. Dinneford?" she said.

"That is my name, madam," was replied.

"You do not know me?"

Mr. Dinneford looked at her closely, and then answered,

"I have not that pleasure, madam."

The woman stood for a moment or two, hesitating.

"Be seated, madam," said Mr. Dinneford.

She sat down, seeming very ill at ease. He took a chair in front of her.

"You wish to see me?"

"Yes, sir, and on a matter that deeply concerns you. I was your daughter's nurse when her baby was born."

She paused at this. Mr. Dinneford had caught his breath. She saw the almost wild interest that flushed his face.

After waiting a moment for some response, she added, in a low, steady voice,

"That baby is still alive, and I am the only person who can clearly identify him."

Mr. Dinneford did not reply immediately. He saw by the woman's face that she was not to be trusted, and that in coming to him she had only sinister ends in view. Her story might be true or false. He thought hurriedly, and tried to regain exterior calmness. As soon as he felt that he could speak without betraying too much eagerness, he said, with an appearance of having recognized her,

"You are Mrs.—?"

He paused, but she did not supply the name.

"Mrs.—? Mrs.—? what is it?"

"No matter, Mr. Dinneford," answered Mrs. Bray, with the coolness and self-possession she had now regained. "What I have just told you is true. If you wish to follow up the matter—wish to get possession of your daughter's child—you have the opportunity; if not, our interview ends, of course;" and she made a feint, as if going to rise.

"Is it the child a woman named Pinky Swett stole away from Briar street on Christmas day?" asked Mr. Dinneford, speaking from a thought that flashed into his mind, and so without premeditation. He fixed his eyes intently on Mrs. Bray's face, and saw by its quick changes and blank surprise that he had put the right question. Before she could recover herself and reply, he added,

"And you are, doubtless, this same Pinky Swett."

The half smile, half sneer, that curved the woman's lips, told Mr. Dinneford that he was mistaken.

"No, sir," was returned, with regained coolness. "I am not 'this same Pinky Swett.' You are out there."

"But you know her?"

"I don't know anything just now, sir," answered the woman, with a chill in her tones. She closed her lips tightly, and shrunk back in her chair.

"What, then, are your here for?" asked Mr. Dinneford, showing considerable sternness of manner.

"I thought you understood," returned the woman. "I was explicit in my statement."

"Oh, I begin to see. There is a price on your information," said Mr. Dinneford.

"Yes, sir. You might have known that from the first. I will be frank with you."

"But why have you kept this secret for three years? Why did you not come before?" asked Mr. Dinneford.

"Because I was paid to keep the secret. Do you understand?"

Too well did Mr. Dinneford understand, and it was with difficulty he could suppress a groan as his head drooped forward and his eyes fell to the floor.

"It does not pay to keep it any longer," added the woman.

Mr. Dinneford made no response.

"Gain lies on the other side. The secret is yours, if you will have it."

"At what price?" asked Mr. Dinneford, without lifting his eyes.

"One thousand dollars, cash in hand."

"On production of the child and proof of its identity?"

Mrs. Bray took time to answer. "I do not mean to have any slip in this matter," she said. "It was a bad business at the start, as I told Mrs. Dinneford, and has given me more trouble than I've been paid for, ten times over. I shall not be sorry to wash my hands clean of it; but whenever I do so, there must be compensation and security. I haven't the child, and you may hunt me to cover with all the police hounds in the city, and yet not find him."

"If I agree to pay your demand," replied Mr. Dinneford, "it

can only be on production and identification of the child."

"After which your humble servant will be quickly handed over to the police," a low, derisive laugh gurgling in the woman's throat.

"The guilty are ever in dread, and the false always in fear of betrayal," said Mr. Dinneford. "I can make no terms with you for any antecedent reward. The child must be in my possession and his parentage clearly proved before I give you a dollar. As to what may follow to yourself, your safety will lie in your own silence. You hold, and will still hold, a family secret that we shall not care to have betrayed. If you should ever betray it, or seek, because of its possession, to annoy or prey upon us, I shall consider all honorable contract we may have at an end, and act accordingly."

"Will you put in writing, an obligation to pay me one thousand dollars in case I bring the child and prove its identity?"

"No; but I will give you my word of honor that this sum shall be placed in your hands whenever you produce the child."

Mrs. Bray remained silent for a considerable time, then, as if satisfied, arose, saying,

"You will hear from me by to-morrow or the day after, at farthest. Good-morning."

As she was moving toward the door Mr. Dinneford said,

"Let me have your name and residence, madam."

The woman quickened her steps, partly turning her head as

she did so, and said, with a sinister curl of the lip,

"No, I thank you, sir."

In the next moment she was gone.

CHAPTER XXV

NOTHING of all this was communicated to Edith. After a few weeks of prostration strength came slowly back to mind and body, and with returning strength her interest in her old work revived. Her feet went down again into lowly ways, and her hands took hold of suffering.

Immediately on receipt of Freeling's letter and affidavit, Mr. Dinneford had taken steps to procure a pardon for George Granger. It came within a few days after the application was made, and the young man was taken from the asylum where he had been for three years.

Mr. Dinneford went to him with Freeling's affidavit and the pardon, and placing them in his hands, watched him closely to see the effect they would produce. He found him greatly changed in appearance, looking older by many years. His manner was quiet, as that of one who had learned submission after long suffering. But his eyes were clear and steady, and without sign of mental aberration. He read Freeling's affidavit first, folded it in an absent kind of way, as if he were dreaming, reopened and read it through again. Then Mr. Dinneford saw a strong shiver pass over him; he became pale and slightly convulsed. His face sunk in his hands, and he sat for a while struggling with emotions that he found it almost impossible to hold back.

T. S. Arthur

When he looked up, the wild struggle was over.

"It is too late," he said.

"No, George, it is never too late," replied Mr. Dinneford. "You have suffered a cruel wrong, but in the future there are for you, I doubt not, many compensations."

He shook his head in a dreary way, murmuring,

"I have lost too much."

"Nothing that may not be restored. And in all you have not lost a good conscience."

"No, thank God!" answered the young man, with a sudden flush in his face. "But for that anchor to my soul, I should have long ago drifted out to sea a helpless wreck. No thank God! I have not lost a good conscience."

"You have not yet read the other paper," said Mr. Dinneford. "It is your pardon."

"Pardon!" An indignant flash came into Granger's eyes. "Oh, sir, that hurts too deeply. Pardon! I am not a criminal."

"Falsely so regarded in the eyes of the law, but now proved to be innocent, and so expressed by the governor. It is not a pardon in any sense of remission, but a declaration of innocence and sorrow for the undeserved wrongs you have suffered."

"It is well," he answered, gloomily—"the best that can be done; and I should be thankful."

"You cannot be more deeply thankful than I am, George."

Mr. Dinneford spoke with much feeling. "Let us bury this dreadful past out of our sight, and trust in God for a better future. You are free again, and your innocence shall, so far as I have power to do it, be made as clear as noonday. You are at liberty to depart from here at once. Will you go with me now?"

Granger lifted a half-surprised look to Mr. Dinneford's face.

"Thank you," he replied, after a few moments' thought. "I shall never forget your kindness, but I prefer remaining here for a few days, until I can confer with my friends and make some decision as to the future."

Granger's manner grew reserved, almost embarrassed. Mr. Dinneford was not wrong in his impression of the cause. How could he help thinking of Edith, who, turning against him with the rest, had accepted the theory of guilt and pronounced her sentence upon him, hardest of all to bear? So it appeared to him, for he had nothing but the hard fact before him that she had applied for and obtained a divorce.

Yes, it was the thought of Edith that drew Granger back and covered him with reserve. What more could Mr. Dinneford say? He had not considered all the hearings of this unhappy case; but now that he remembered the divorce, he began to see, how full of embarrassment it was, and how delicate the relation he bore to this unhappy victim of his wife's dreadful crime.

What could he say for Edith? Nothing! He knew that her heart had never turned itself away from this man, though she had, under a pressure she was not strong enough to resist, turned her back upon him and cast aside his dishonored name, thus testifying to the world that she believed him base and criminal. If he should speak of her, would not the young

T. S. Arthur

man answer with indignant scorn?

"Give me the address of your friends, and I will call upon them immediately," said Mr. Dinneford, replying, after a long silence, to Granger's last remark. "I am here to repair, to any extent that in me lies the frightful wrongs you have suffered. I shall make your cause my own, and never rest until every false tarnish shall be wiped from your name. In honor and conscience I am bound to this."

Looking at the young man intently, he saw a grateful response in the warmer color that broke into his face and in the moisture that filled his eyes.

"I would be base if I were not thankful, Mr. Dinneford," Granger replied. "But you cannot put yourself in my place, cannot know what I have suffered, cannot comprehend the sense of wrong and cruel rejection that has filled my soul with the very gall of bitterness. To be cast out utterly, suddenly and without warning from heaven into hell, and for no evil thought or act! Ah, sir! you do not understand."

"It was a frightful ordeal, George," answered Mr. Dinneford, laying his hand on Granger with the tenderness of a father. "But, thank God! it is over. You have stood the terrible heat, and now, coming out of the furnace, I shall see to it that not even the smell of fire remain upon your garments."

Still the young man could not be moved from his purpose to remain at the asylum until he had seen and conferred with his friends, in whose hands Mr. Dinneford placed the governor's pardon and the affidavit of Lloyd Freeling setting forth his innocence.

Mrs. Bray did not call on Mr. Dinneford, as she had promised. She had quarreled with Pinky Swett, as the reader will remember, and in a fit of blind anger thrust her from the room. But in the next moment she remembered that she did not know where the girl lived, and if she lost sight of her now, might not again come across her for weeks or months. So putting on her hat and cloak hurriedly, she waited until she heard Pinky going down stairs, and then came out noiselessly, and followed her into the street. She had to be quick in her movements, for Pinky, hot with anger, was dashing off at a rapid speed. For three or four blocks Mrs. Bray kept her in view; but there being only a few persons in the street, she had to remain at a considerable distance behind, so as not to attract her attention. Suddenly, she lost sight of Pinky. She had looked back on hearing a noise in the street; turning again, she could see nothing of the girl. Hurrying forward to the corner which Pinky had in all probability turned, Mrs. Bray looked eagerly up and down, but to her disappointment Pinky was not in sight.

"Somewhere here. I thought it was farther off," said Mrs. Bray to herself. "It's too bad that I should have lost sight of her."

She stood irresolute for a little while, then walked down one of the blocks and back on the other side. Halfway down, a small street or alley divided the block.

"It's in there, no doubt," said Mrs. Bray, speaking to herself again. On the corner was a small shop in which notions and trimmings were sold. Going into this, she asked for some trifling articles, and while looking over them drew the woman who kept the shop into conversation.

"What kind of people live in this little street?" she inquired, in a half-careless tone.

The woman smiled as she answered, with a slight toss of

T. S. Arthur

the head,

"Oh, all kinds."

"Good, bad and indifferent?"

"Yes, white sheep and black."

"So I thought. The black sheep will get in. You can't keep 'em out."

"No, and 'tisn't much use trying," answered the shop-keeper, with a levity of manner not unmarked by Mrs. Bray, who said,

"The black sheep have to live as well as the white ones."

"Just so. You hit the nail there."

"And I suppose you find their money as good as that of the whitest?"

"Oh yes."

"And quite as freely spent?"

"As to that," answered the woman, who was inclined to be talkative and gossipy, "we make more out of the black sheep than out of the white ones. They don't higgle so about prices. Not that we have two prices, but you see they don't try to beat us down, and never stop to worry about the cost of a thing if they happen to fancy it. They look and buy, and there's the end of it."

"I understand," remarked Mrs. Bray, with a familiar nod. "It may be wicked to say so; but if I kept a store like this, I'd rather have the sinners for customers than the saints."

She had taken a seat at the counter; and now, leaning forward upon her arms and looking at the shop-woman in a pleasant, half-confidential way, said,

"You know everybody about here?"

"Pretty much."

"The black sheep as well as the white?"

"As customers."

"Of course; that's all I mean," was returned. "I'd be sorry if you knew them in any other way—some of them, at least." Then, after a pause, "Do you know a girl they call Pinky?"

"I may know her, but not by that name. What kind of a looking person is she?"

"A tall, bold-faced, dashing, dare-devil sort of a girl, with a snaky look in her eyes. She wears a pink hat with a white feather."

"Yes, I think I have seen some one like that, but she's not been around here long."

"When did you see her last?"

"If it's the same one you mean, I saw her go by here not ten minutes ago. She lives somewhere down the alley."

"Do you know the house?"

"I do not; but it can be found, no doubt. You called

T. S. Arthur

her Pinky."

"Yes. Her name is Pinky Swett."

"O-h! o-h!" ejaculated the shop-woman, lifting her eyebrows in a surprised way. "Why, that's the girl the police were after. They said she'd run off with somebody's child."

"Did they arrest her?" asked Mrs. Bray, repressing, as far as possible, all excitement.

"They took her off once or twice, I believe, but didn't make anything out of her. At any rate, the child was not found. It belonged, they said, to a rich up-town family that the girl was trying to black-mail. But I don't see how that could be."

"The child isn't about here?"

"Oh dear, no! If it was, it would have been found long before this, for the police are hunting around sharp. If it's all as they say, she's got it hid somewhere else."

While Mrs. Bray talked with the shop-woman, Pinky, who had made a hurried call at her room, only a hundred yards away, was going as fast as a street-car could take her to a distant part of the city. On leaving the car at the corner of a narrow, half-deserted street, in which the only sign of life was a child or two at play in the snow and a couple of goats lying on a cellar-door, she walked for half the distance of a block, and then turned into a court lined on both sides with small, ill-conditioned houses, not half of them tenanted. Snow and ice blocked the little road-way, except where a narrow path had been cut along close to the houses.

Without knocking, Pinky entered one of these poor tenements. As she pushed open the door, a woman who was crouching down before a small stove, on which something was cooking, started up with a look of surprise that changed to one of anxiety and fear the moment she recognized her visitor.

"Is Andy all right?" cried Pinky, alarm in her face.

The woman tried to stammer out something, but did not make herself understood. At this, Pinky, into whose eyes flashed a fierce light, caught her by the wrists in a grip that almost crushed the bones.

"Out with it! where is Andy?"

Still the frightened woman could not speak.

"If that child isn't here, I'll murder you!" said Pinky, now white with anger, tightening her grasp.

At this, with a desperate effort, the woman flung her off, and catching up a long wooden bench, raised it over her head.

"If there's to be any murder going on," she said, recovering her powers of speech, "I'll take the first hand! As for the troublesome brat, he's gone. Got out of the window and climbed down the spout. Wonder he wasn't killed. Did fall— I don't know how far—and must have hurt himself, for I heard a noise as if something heavy had dropped in the yard, but thought it was next door. Half an hour afterward, in going up stairs and opening the door of the room where I kept him locked in, I found it empty and the window open. That's the whole story. I ran out and looked everywhere, but he was off. And now, if the murder is to come, I'm going to be in first."

And she still kept the long wooden bench poised above

her head.

Pinky saw a dangerous look in the woman's eyes.

"Put that thing down," she cried, "and don't be a fool. Let me see;" and she darted past the woman and ran up stairs. She found the window of Andy's prison open and the print of his little fingers on the snow-covered sill outside, where he had held on before dropping to the ground, a distance of many feet. There was no doubt now in her mind as to the truth of the woman's story. The child had made his escape.

"Have you been into all the neighbors' houses?" asked Pinky as she came down hastily.

"Into some, but not all," she replied.

"How long is it since he got away?"

"More than two hours."

"And you've been sticking down here, instead of ransacking every hole and corner in the neighborhood. I can hardly keep my hands off of you."

The woman was on the alert. Pinky saw this, and did not attempt to put her threat into execution. After pouring out her wrath in a flood of angry invectives, she went out and began a thorough search of the neighborhood, going into every house for a distance of three or four blocks in all directions. But she could neither find the child nor get the smallest trace of him. He had dropped out of sight, so far as she was concerned, as completely as if he had fallen into the sea.

CHAPTER XXVI

DAY after day Mr. Dinneford waited for the woman who was to restore the child of Edith, but she did not come. Over a week elapsed, but she neither called nor sent him a sign or a word. He dared not speak about this to Edith. She was too weak in body and mind for any further suspense or strain.

Drew Hall had been nearly thrown down again by the events of that Christmas day. The hand of a little child was holding him fast to a better life; but when that hand was torn suddenly away from his grasp, he felt the pull of evil habits, the downward drift of old currents. His steps grew weak, his knees trembled. But God did not mean that he should be left alone. He had reached down to him through the hand of a little child, had lifted him up and led him into a way of safety; and now that this small hand, the soft, touch of which had gone to his heart and stirred him with old memories, sad and sweet and holy, had dropped away from him, and he seemed to be losing his hold of heaven, God sent him, in Mr. Dinneford, an angel with a stronger hand. There were old associations that held these men together. They had been early and attached friends, and this meeting, after many years of separation, under such strange circumstances, and with a common fear and anxiety at heart, could not but have the effect of arousing in the mind of Mr. Dinneford the deepest concern for the unhappy man. He saw the new peril into which he was thrown by the loss of Andy, and made it his first business to surround him with all possible good and strengthening influences. So the old memories awakened by the coming of Andy did not fade out and lose their power over the man. He had taken hold of the good past again, and still held to it with the tight grasp of one conscious of danger.

"We shall find the child—no fear of that," Mr. Dinneford would say to him over and over again, trying to comfort his own heart as well, as the days went by and no little Andy could be found. "The police have the girl under the sharpest surveillance, and she cannot baffle them much longer."

George Granger left the asylum with his friends, and dropped out of sight. He did not show himself in the old places nor renew old associations. He was too deeply hurt. The disaster had been too great for any attempt on his part at repairing the old dwelling-places of his life. His was not what we call a strong nature, but he was susceptible of very deep impressions. He was fine and sensitive, rather than strong. Rejected by his wife and family without a single interview with her or even an opportunity to assert his innocence, he felt the wrong so deeply that he could not get over it. His love for his wife had been profound and tender, and when it became known to him that she had accepted the appearances of guilt as conclusive, and broken with her own hands the tie that bound them, it was more than he had strength to bear, and a long time passed before he rallied from this hardest blow of all.

Edith knew that her father had seen Granger after securing his pardon, and she had learned from him only, particulars of the interview. Beyond this nothing came to her. She stilled her heart, aching with the old love that crowded all its chambers, and tried to be patient and submissive. It was very hard. But she was helpless. Sometimes, in the anguish and wild agitation of soul that seized her, she would resolve to put in a letter all she thought and felt, and have it conveyed to Granger; but fear and womanly delicacy drove her back from this. What hope had she that he would not reject her with hatred and scorn? It was a venture she dared not make, for she felt that such a rejection would kill her. But for her work among the destitute and the neglected, Edith would have shut herself up at home. Christian charity drew her forth daily, and in offices of kindness and mercy she found a peace and rest to which she would otherwise have been stranger.

She was on her way home one afternoon from a visit to the mission-school where she had first heard of the poor baby in Grubb's court. All that day thoughts of little Andy kept crowding into her mind. She could not push aside his image as she saw it on Christmas, when he sat among the children, his large eyes resting in such a wistful look upon her face. Her eyes often grew dim and her heart full as she looked upon that tender face, pictured for her as distinctly as if photographed to natural sight.

"Oh my baby, my baby!" came almost audibly from her lips, in a burst of irrepressible feeling, for ever since she had seen this child, the thought of him linked itself with that of her lost baby.

Up to this time her father had carefully concealed his interview with Mrs. Bray. He was in so much doubt as to the effect that woman's communication might produce while yet the child was missing that he deemed it best to maintain the strictest silence until it could be found.

Walking along with heart and thought where they dwelt for so large a part of her time, Edith, in turning a corner, came upon a woman who stopped at sight of her as if suddenly fastened to the ground—stopped only for an instant, like one surprised by an unexpected and unwelcome encounter, and then made a motion to pass on. But Edith, partly from memory and partly from intuition, recognized her nurse, and catching fast hold of her, said in a low imperative voice, while a look of wild excitement spread over her face,

"Where is my baby?"

The woman tried to shake her off, but Edith held her with a grasp that could not be broken.

"For Heaven's sake," exclaimed the woman "let go of me! This is the public street, and you'll have a crowd about us in a moment, and the police with them."

But Edith kept fast hold of her.

"First tell me where I can find my baby," she answered.

"Come along," said the woman, moving as she spoke in the direction Edith was going when they met. "If you want a row with the police, I don't."

Edith was close to her side, with her hand yet upon her and her voice in her ears.

"My baby! Quick! Say! Where can I find my baby?"

"What do I know of your baby? You are a fool, or mad!" answered the woman, trying to throw her off. "I don't know you."

"But I know you, Mrs. Bray," said Edith, speaking the name at a venture as the one she remembered hearing the servant give to her mother.

At this the woman's whole manner changed, and Edith saw that she was right—that this was, indeed, the accomplice of her mother.

"And now," she added, in voice grown calm and resolute, "I do not mean to let you escape until I get sure knowledge of my child. If you fly from me, I will follow and call for the police. If you have any of the instincts of a woman left, you will know that I am desperately in earnest. What is a street excitement or a temporary arrest by the police, or even a station-house exposure, to me, in comparison with the recovery of my child? Where is he?"

"I do not know," replied Mrs. Bray. "After seeing your father—"

"My father! When did you see him?" exclaimed Edith, betraying in her surprised voice the fact that Mr. Dinneford had kept so far, even from her, the secret of that brief interview to which she now referred.

"Oh, he hasn't told you! But it's no matter—he will do that in good time. After seeing your father, I made an effort to get possession of your child and restore him as I promised to do. But the woman who had him hidden somewhere managed to keep out of my way until this morning. And now she says he got off from her, climbed out of a second-story window and disappeared, no one knows where."

"This woman's name is Pinky Swett?" said Edith.

"Yes."

Mrs. Bray felt the hand that was still upon her arm shake as if from a violent chill.

"Do you believe what she says?—that the child has really escaped from her?"

"Yes."

"Where does she live?"

Mrs. Bray gave the true directions, and without hesitation.

"Is this child the one she stole from the Briar-street mission on Christmas day?" asked Edith.

"He is," answered Mrs. Bray.

"How shall I know he is mine? What proof is there that little Andy, as he is called, and my baby are the same?"

"I know him to be your child, for I have never lost sight of him," replied the woman, emphatically. "You may know him by his eyes and mouth and chin, for they are yours. Nobody can mistake the likeness. But there is another proof. When I nursed you, I saw on your arm, just above the elbow, a small raised mark of a red color, and noticed a similar one on the baby's arm. You will see it there whenever you find the child that Pinky Swett stole from the mission-house on Christmas day. Good-bye!"

And the woman, seeing that her companion was off of her guard, sprang away, and was out of sight in the crowd before Edith could rally herself and make an attempt to follow. How she got home she could hardly tell.

CHAPTER XXVII

FOR weeks the search for Andy was kept up with unremitting vigilance, but no word of him came to the anxious searchers. A few days after the meeting with Mrs. Bray, the police report mentioned the arrest of both Pinky Swett and Mrs. Bray, *alias* Hoyt, *alias* Jewett, charged with stealing a diamond ring of considerable value from a jewelry store. They were sent to prison, in default of bail, to await trial. Mr. Dinneford immediately went to the prison and had an interview with the two women, who could give him no information about Andy beyond what Mrs. Bray had already communicated in her hurried talk with Edith. Pinky could get no trace of him after he had escaped. Mr. Dinneford did not leave the two women until he had drawn from them a minute and circumstantial account of all they knew of Edith's child from the time it was cast adrift. When he left them, he had no doubt as to its identity with Andy. There was no missing link in the chain of evidence.

The new life that had opened to little Andy since the dreary night on which, like a stray kitten, he had crept into Andrew Hall's miserable hovel, had been very pleasant. To be loved and caressed was a strange and sweet experience. Poor little heart! It fluttered in wild terror, like a tiny bird in the talons of a hawk, when Pinky Swett swooped down and struck her foul talons into the frightened child and bore him off.

T. S. Arthur

"If you scream, I'll choke you to death!" she said, stooping to his ear, as she hurried him from the mission-house. Scared into silence, Andy did not cry out, and the arm that grasped and dragged him away was so strong that he felt resistance to be hopeless. Passing from Briar street, Pinky hurried on for a distance of a block, when she signaled a street-car. As she lifted Andy upon the platform, she gave him another whispered threat:

"Mind! if you cry, I'll kill you!"

There were but few persons in the car, and Pinky carried the child to the upper end and sat him down with his face turned forward to the window, so as to keep it as much out of observation as possible. He sat motionless, stunned with surprise and fear. Pinky kept her eyes upon him. His hands were laid across his breast and held against it tightly. They had not gone far before Pinky saw great tear-drops falling upon the little hands.

"Stop crying!" she whispered, close to his ear; "I won't have it! You're not going to be killed."

Andy tried to keep back the tears, but in spite of all he could do they kept blinding his eyes and falling over his hands.

"What's the matter with your little boy?" asked a sympathetic, motherly woman who had noticed the child's distress.

"Cross, that's all." Pinky threw out the sentence in at snappish, mind-your-own-business tone.

The motherly woman, who had leaned forward, a look of kindly interest on her face, drew back, chilled by this repulse, but kept her eyes upon the child, greatly to Pinky's annoyance. After riding for half a mile, Pinky got out and took another car. Andy was passive. He had ceased crying, and was endeavoring to get back some of the old spirit of brave endurance. He was beginning to feel like one who had awakened from a beautiful dream in which dear ideals had almost reached fruition, to the painful facts of a hard and suffering life, and was gathering up his patience and strength to meet them. He sat motionless by the side of Pinky, with his eyes cast down, his chin on his breast and his lips shut closely together.

Another ride of nearly half a mile, when Pinky left the car and struck away from the common thoroughfare into a narrow alley, down which she walked for a short distance, and then disappeared in one of the small houses. No one happened to observe her entrance. Through a narrow passage and stairway she reached a second-story room. Taking a key from her pocket, she unlocked the door and went in. There was a fire in a small stove, and the room was comfortable. Locking the door on the inside she said to Andy, in a voice changed and kinder,

"My! your hands are as red as beets. Go up to the stove and warm yourself."

Andy obeyed, spreading out his little hands, and catching the grateful warmth, every now and then looking up into Pinky's face, and trying with a shrewder insight than is usually given to a child of his age to read the character and purposes it half concealed and half made known.

"Now, Andy," said Pinky, in a mild but very decided way— "your name's Andy?"

"Yes, ma'am," answered the child, fixing his large, intelligent eyes on her face.

"Well, Andy, if you'll be a good and quiet boy, you needn't be afraid of anything—you won't get hurt. But if you make a fuss, I'll throw you at once right out of the window."

Pinky frowned and looked so wicked as she uttered the last sentence that Andy was frightened. It seemed as if a devouring beast glared at him out of her eyes. She saw the effect of her threat, and was satisfied.

The short afternoon soon passed away. The girl did not leave the room, nor talk with the child except in very low tones, so as not to attract the attention of any one in the house. As the day waned snow began to fall, and by the time night set in it was coming down thick and fast. As soon as it was fairly dark, Pinky wrapped a shawl about Andy, pinning it closely, so as to protect him from the cold, and quietly left the house. He made no resistance. A car was taken, in which they rode for a long distance, until they were on the outskirts of the city. The snow had already fallen to a depth of two or three inches, and the storm was increasing. When she left the car in that remote neighborhood, not a person was to be seen on the street. Catching Andy into her arms, Pinky ran with him for the distance of half a block, and then turned into a close alley with small houses on each side. At the lower end she stopped before one of these houses, and without knocking pushed open the door.

"Who's that?" cried a voice from an upper room, the stairway to which led up from the room below.

"It's me. Come down, and be quiet," answered Pinky, in a warning voice.

A woman, old and gray, with all the signs of a bad life on her wrinkled face, came hastily down stairs and confronted Pinky.

"What now? What's brought you here?" she demanded, in no friendly tones.

"There, there, Mother Peter! smooth down your feathers. I've got something for you to do, and it will pay," answered Pinky, who had shut the outside door and slipped the bolt.

At this, the manner of Mother Peter, as Pinky had called her, softened, and she said,

"What's up? What deviltry are you after now, you huzzy?"

Without replying to this, Pinky began shaking the snow from Andy and unwinding the shawl with which she had bound him up. After he was free from his outside wrappings, she said, looking toward the woman,

"Now, isn't he a nice little chap? Did you ever see such eyes?"

The worn face of the woman softened as she turned toward the beautiful child, but not with pity. To that feeling she had long been a stranger.

"I want you to keep him for a few days," said Pinky, speaking in the woman's ears. "I'll tell you more about it after he's in bed and asleep."

"He's to be kept shut up out of sight, mind," was Pinky's injunction, in the conference that followed. "Not a living soul in the neighborhood must know he's in the house, for the police will be sharp after him. I'll pay you five dollars a week, and put it down in advance. Give him plenty to eat, and be as good to him as you can, for you see it's a fat job, and I'll make it fatter for you if all comes out right."

The woman was not slow to promise all that Pinky demanded. The house in which she lived had three rooms, one below and two smaller ones above. From the room below a stove-pipe went up through the floor into a sheet-iron drum in the small back chamber, and kept it partially heated. It was arranged that Andy should be made a close prisoner in this room, and kept quiet by fear. It had only one window, looking out upon the yard, and there was no shed or porch over the door leading into the yard below upon which he could climb out and make his escape. In order to have things wholly secure the two women, after Andy was asleep, pasted paper over the panes of glass in the lower sash, so that no one could see his face at the window, and fastened the sash down by putting a nail into a gimlet-hole at the top.

"I guess thatt will fix him," said Pinky, in a tone of satisfaction. "All you've got to do now is to see that he doesn't make a noise."

On the next morning Andy was awake by day-dawn. At first he did not know where he was, but he kept very still, looking around the small room and trying to make out what it all meant. Soon it came to him, and a vague terror filled his heart. By his side lay the woman into whose hands Pinky had given him. She was fast asleep, and her face, as he gazed in fear upon it, was even more repulsive than it had looked on the night before. His first impulse, after comprehending his situation, was to escape if possible. Softly and silently he crept out of bed, and made his way to the door. It was fastened. He drew the bolt back, when it struck the guard with a sharp click. In an instant the old woman was sitting up in bed and glaring at him.

"You imp of Satan!" she cried, springing after him with a singular agility for one of her age, and catching him by the arm with a vice-like grip that bruised the tender flesh and left it marked for weeks, drew him back from the door and flung him upon the bed.

"Stay there till I tell you to get up," she added, with a cruel threat in her voice. "And mind you, there's to be no fooling with me."

The frightened child crept under the bed-clothes, and hid his face beneath them. Mother Peter did not lie down again, but commenced dressing herself, muttering and grumbling as she did so.

"Keep where you are till I come back," she said to Andy, with the same cruel threat in her voice. Going out, she bolted the door on the other side. It was nearly half an hour before the woman returned, bringing a plate containing two or three slices of bread and butter and a cup of milk.

"Now get up and dress yourself," was her sharply-spoken salutation to Andy as she came into the room. "And you're to be just as still as a mouse, mind. There's your breakfast." She set the plate on a table and went out, bolting, as before, the door on the other side. Andy did not see her again for over an hour. Left entirely alone in his prison, his restless spirit chafed for freedom. He moved about the apartment, examining everything it contained with the closest scrutiny, yet without making any noise, for the woman's threat, accompanied as it had been with such a wicked look, was not forgotten. He had seen in that look a cruel spirit of which he was afraid. Two or three times he thought he heard a step and a movement in the adjoining chamber, and waited, almost holding his breath, with his eyes upon the door, expecting every moment to see the scowling face of his jailer. But no hand touched the door.

Tired at last with everything in the room, he went to the

T. S. Arthur

window and sought to look out, as he had already done many times. He could not understand why this window, was so different from any he had ever seen, and puzzled over it in his weak, childish way. As he moved from pane to pane, trying to see through, he caught a glimpse of something outside, but it was gone in a moment. He stepped back, then came up quickly to the glass, all the dull quietude of manner leaving him. As he did so a glimpse of the outside world came again, and now he saw a little hole in the paper not larger than a pin's head. To scrape at this was a simple instinct. In a moment he saw it enlarging, as the paper peeled off from the glass. Scraping away with his finger-nail, the glass was soon cleared of paper for the space of an inch in diameter, and through this opening he stood gazing out upon the yards, below, and the houses that came up to them from a neighboring street. There was a woman in one of these yards, and she looked up toward the window where Andy stood, curiously.

"You imp of Satan!" were the terrible words that fell upon his ears at this juncture, and he felt himself caught up as by a vulture. He knew the cruel voice and the grip of the cruel hands that had already left their marks in his tender flesh. Mother Peter, her face red with passion and her eyes slowing like coals of fire, held him high in the air, and shook him with savage violence. She did not strike, but continued shaking him until the sudden heat of her passion had a little cooled.

"Didn't I tell you not to meddle with anything in this room?" and with another bruising grip of Andy's arms, she threw him roughly upon the floor.

The little hole in the paper was then repaired by pasting another piece of paper over it, after which Andy was left alone, but with a threat from Mother Peter that if he touched the window again she would beat the life out of him. She had no more trouble with him that day. Every half hour or so she would come up stairs noiselessly, and listen at the door, or break in upon the child suddenly and without warning. But she did not find him again at the window. The restlessness at first exhibited had died out, and he sat or lay upon the floor in a kind of dull, despairing stupor. So that day passed.

On the second day of Andy's imprisonment he distinctly heard the old woman go out at the street door and lock it after her. He listened for a long time, but could hear no sound in the house. A feeling of relief and a sense of safety came over him. He had not been so long in his prison alone without the minutest examination of every part, and it had not escaped his notice that the panes of glass in the upper sash of the window were not covered with paper, as were those below. But for the fear of one of Mother Peter's noiseless pouncings in upon him, he would long since have climbed upon the sill and taken a look through the upper sash. He waited now for full half an hour to be sure that his jailer had left the house, and then, climbing to the window-sill with the agility of a squirrel, held on to the edge of the lower sash and looked out through the clear glass above. Dreary and unsightly as was all that lay under his gaze, it was beautiful in the eyes of the child. His little heart swelled and glowed; he longed, as a prisoner, for freedom. As he stood there he saw that a nail held down the lower sash, which he had so often tried, but in vain, to lift. Putting his finger on this nail, he felt it move. It had been placed loosely in a gimlet-hole, and could be drawn out easily. For a little while he stood there, taking out and putting in the nail. While doing this he thought he heard a sound below, and instantly dropped noiselessly from the window. He had scarcely done so when the door of his room opened and Mother Peter came in. She looked at him sharply, and then retired without speaking.

T. S. Arthur

All the next day Andy listened after Mother Peter, waiting to hear her go out. But she did not leave the house until after he was asleep in the evening.

On the next day, after waiting until almost noon, the child's impatience of confinement grew so strong that he could no longer defer his meditated escape from the window, for ever since he had looked over the sash and discovered how it was fastened down, his mind had been running on this thing. He had noticed that Mother Peter's visits to his room were made after about equal intervals of time, and that after she gave him his dinner she did not come up stairs again for at least an hour. This had been brought, and he was again alone.

For nearly five minutes after the woman went out, he sat by the untasted food, his head bent toward the door, listening. Then he got up quietly, climbed upon the window-sill and pulled the nail out. Dropping back upon the floor noiselessly, he pushed his hands upward against the sash, and it rose easily. Like an animal held in unwilling confinement, he did not stop to think of any danger that might lie in the way of escape when opportunity for escape offered. The fear behind was worse than any imagined fear that could lie beyond. Pushing up the sash, Andy, without looking down from the window, threw himself across the sill and dropped his body over, supporting himself with his hands on the snow-encrusted ledge for a moment, and then letting himself fall to the ground, a distance of nearly ten feet. He felt his breath go as he swept through the air, and lost his senses for an instant or two.

Stunned by the fall, he did not rise for several minutes. Then he got up with a slow, heavy motion and looked about him anxiously. He was in a yard from which there was no egress except by way of the house. It was bitter cold, and he had on nothing but the clothing worn in the room from which he had just escaped. His head was bare.

The dread of being found here by Mother Peter soon lifted him above physical impediment or suffering. Through a hole in the fence he saw an alley-way; and by the aid of an old barrel that stood in the yard, he climbed to the top of the fence and let himself down on the other side, falling a few feet. A sharp pain was felt in one of his ankles as his feet touched the ground. He had sprained it in his leap from the window, and now felt the first pangs attendant on the injury.

Limping along, he followed the narrow alley-way, and in a little while came out upon a street some distance from the one in which Mother Peter lived. There were very few people abroad, and no one noticed or spoke to him as he went creeping along, every step sending a pain from the hurt ankle to his heart. Faint with suffering and chilled to numbness, Andy stumbled and fell as he tried, in crossing a street, to escape from a sleigh that turned a corner suddenly. It was too late for the driver to rein up his horse. One foot struck the child, throwing him out of the track of the sleigh. He was insensible when taken up, bleeding and apparently dead. A few people came out of the small houses in the neighborhood, attracted by the accident, but no one knew the child or offered to take him in.

There were two ladies in the sleigh, and both were greatly pained and troubled. After a hurried consultation, one of them reached out her hands for the child, and as she received and covered him with the buffalo-robe said something to the driver, who turned his horse's head and drove off at a rapid speed.

CHAPTER XXVIII

EVERY home for friendless children, every sin or poverty-blighted ward and almost every hovel, garret and cellar where evil and squalor shrunk from observation were searched for the missing child, but in vain. No trace of him could be found. The agony of suspense into which Edith's mind was brought was beginning to threaten her reason. It was only by the strongest effort at self-compulsion that she could keep herself to duty among the poor and suffering, and well for her it was that she did not fail here; it was all that held her to safe mooring.

One day, as she was on her way home from some visit of mercy, a lady who was passing in a carriage called to her from the window, at the same time ordering her driver to stop. The carriage drew up to the sidewalk.

"Come, get in," said the lady as she pushed open the carriage door. "I was thinking of you this very moment, and want to have some talk about our children's hospital. We must have you on our ladies' visiting committee."

Edith shook her head, saying, "It won't be possible, Mrs. Morton. I am overtaxed now, and must lessen, instead of increasing, my work."

"Never mind, about that now. Get in. I want to have some talk with you."

Edith, who knew the lady intimately, stepped into the carriage and took a seat by her side.

"I don't believe you have ever been to our hospital," said the lady as the carriage rolled on. "I'm going there now, and want to show you how admirably everything is conducted, and what a blessing it is to poor suffering children."

"It hurts me so to witness suffering in little children," returned Edith, "that it seems as if I couldn't bear it much longer. I see so much of it."

"The pain is not felt as deeply when we are trying to relieve that suffering," answered her friend. "I have come away from the hospital many times after spending an hour or two among the beds, reading and talking to the children, with an inward peace in my soul too deep for expression. I think that Christ draws very near to us while we are trying to do the work that he did when he took upon himself our nature in, the world and stood face to face visibly with men—nearer to us, it may be, than at any other time; and in his presence there is peace—peace that passeth understanding."

They were silent for a little while, Edith not replying. "We have now," resumed the lady, "nearly forty children under treatment—poor little things who, but for this charity, would have no tender care or intelligent ministration. Most of them would be lying in garrets or miserable little rooms, dirty and neglected, disease eating out their lives, and pain that medical skill now relieves, racking their poor worn bodies. I sat by the bed of a little girl yesterday who has been in the hospital over six months. She has hip disease. When she was brought here from one of the vilest places in the city, taken

T. S. Arthur

away from a drunken mother, she was the saddest-looking child I ever saw. Dirty, emaciated, covered with vermin and pitiable to behold, I could hardly help crying when I saw her brought in. Now, though still unable to leave her bed, she has as bright and happy a face as you ever saw. The care and tenderness received since she came to us have awakened a new life in her soul, and she exhibits a sweetness of temper beautiful to see. After I had read a little story for her yesterday, she put her arms about my neck and kissed me, saying, in her frank, impulsive way, 'Oh, Mrs. Morton, I do love you so!' I had a great reward. Never do I spend an hour among these children without thanking God that he put it into the hearts of a few men and women who could be touched with the sufferings of children to establish and sustain so good an institution."

The carriage stopped, and the driver swung open the door. They were at the children's hospital. Entering a spacious hall, the two ladies ascended to the second story, where the wards were located. There were two of these on opposite sides of the hall, one for boys and one for girls. Edith felt a heavy pressure on her bosom as they passed into the girls' ward. She was coming into the presence of disease and pain, of suffering and weariness, in the persons of little children.

There were twenty beds in the room. Everything was faultlessly clean, and the air fresh and pure. On most of these beds lay, or sat up, supported by pillows, sick or crippled children from two years of age up to fifteen or sixteen, while a few were playing about the room. Edith caught her breath and choked back a sob that came swiftly to her throat as she stood a few steps within the door and read in a few quick glances that passed from face to face the sorrowful records that pain had written upon them.

"Oh, there's Mrs. Morton!" cried a glad voice, and Edith saw a girl who was sitting up in one of the beds clap her hands joyfully.

"That's the little one I was telling you about," said the lady, and she crossed to the bed, Edith following. The child reached up her arms and put them about Mrs. Morton's neck, kissing her as she did so.

It took Edith some time to adjust herself to the scene before her. Mrs. Morton knew all the children, and had a word of cheer or sympathy for most of them as she passed from bed to bed through the ward. Gradually the first painful impressions wore off, and Edith felt herself drawn to the little patients, and before five minutes had passed her heart was full of a strong desire to do whatever lay in her power to help and comfort them. After spending half an hour with the girls, during which time Edith talked and read to a number of them, Mrs. Morton said,

"Now let us go into the boys' ward."

They crossed the hall together, and entered the room on the other side. Here, as in the opposite ward, Mrs. Morton was recognized as welcome visitor. Every face that happened to be turned to the door brightened at her entrance.

"There's a dear child in this ward," said Mrs. Morton as they stood for a moment in the door looking about the room. "He was picked up in the street about a week ago, hurt by a passing vehicle, and brought here. We have not been able to learn anything about him."

Edith's heart gave a sudden leap, but she held it down with all the self-control she could assume, trying to be calm.

"Where is he?" she asked, in a voice so altered from its

natural tone that Mrs. Morton turned and looked at her in surprise.

"Over in that corner," she answered, pointing down the room.

Edith started forward, Mrs. Morton at her side.

"Here he is," said the latter, pausing at a bed on which child with fair face, blue eyes and golden hair was lying. A single glance sent the blood back to Edith's heart. A faintness came over her; everything grew dark. She sat down to keep from falling.

As quickly as possible and by another strong effort of will she rallied herself.

"Yes," she said, in a faint undertone in which was no apparent interest, "he is a dear little fellow."

As she spoke she laid her hand softly on the child's head, but not in a way to bring any response. He looked at her curiously, and seemed half afraid.

Meanwhile, a child occupying a bed only a few feet off had started up quickly on seeing Edith, and now sat with his large brown eyes fixed eagerly upon her, his lips apart and his hands extended. But Edith did not notice him. Presently she got up from beside the bed and was turning away when the other child, with a kind of despairing look in his face, cried out,

"Lady, lady! oh, lady!"

The voice reached Edith's ears. She turned, and saw the face of Andy. Swift as a flash she was upon him, gathering him in her arms and crying out, in a wild passion of joy that could not be repressed,

"Oh, my baby! my baby! my boy! my boy! Bless God! thank God! oh, my baby!"

Startled by this sudden outcry, the resident physician and two nurses who were in the ward hurried down the room to see what it meant. Edith had the child hugged tightly to her bosom, and resisted all their efforts to remove him.

"My dear madam," said the doctor, "you will do him some harm if you don't take care."

"Hurt my baby? Oh no, no!" she answered, relaxing her hold and gazing down upon Andy as she let him fall away from her bosom. Then lifting her eyes to the physician, her face so flooded with love and inexpressible joy that it seemed like some heavenly transfiguration, she murmured, in a low voice full of the deepest tenderness,

"Oh no. I will not do my baby any harm."

"My dear, dear friend," said Mrs. Morton, recovering from the shock of her first surprise and fearing that Edith had suddenly lost her mind, "you cannot mean what you say;" and she reached down for the child and made a movement as if she were going to lift him away from her arms.

A look of angry resistance swept across Edith's pale face. There was a flash of defiance in her eyes.

"No, no! You must not touch him," she exclaimed; "I will die before giving him up. My baby!"

And now, breaking down from her intense excitement, she

T. S. Arthur

bent over the child again, weeping and sobbing. Waiting until this paroxysm had expended itself, Mrs. Morton, who had not failed to notice that Andy never turned his eyes for an instant away from Edith, nor resisted her strained clasp or wild caresses, but lay passive against her with a look of rest and peace in his face, said,

"How shall we know that he is your baby?"

At this Edith drew herself up, the light on her countenance fading out. Then catching at the child's arm, she pulled the loose sleeve that covered it above the elbow with hands that shook like aspens. Another cry of joy broke from her as she saw a small red mark standing out clear from the snowy skin. She kissed it over and over again, sobbing,

"My baby! Yes, thank God! my own long-lost baby!"

And still the child showed no excitement, but lay very quiet, looking at Edith whenever he could see her countenance, the peace and rest on his face as unchanging as if it were not really a living and mobile face, but one cut into this expression by the hands of an artist.

"How shall you know?" asked Edith, now remembering the question of Mrs. Morton. And she drew up her own sleeve and showed on one of her arms a mark as clearly defined and bright as that on the child's arm.

No one sought to hinder Edith as she rose to her feet holding Andy, after she had wrapped the bed-clothes about him.

"Come!" she spoke to her friend, and moved away with her precious burden.

"You must go with us," said Mrs. Morton to the physician.

They followed as Edith hurried down stairs, and entering the carriage after her, were driven away from the hospital.

T. S. Arthur

CHAPTER XXIX

ABOUT the same hour that Edith entered the boys' ward of the children's hospital, Mr. Dinneford met Granger face to face in the street. The latter tried to pass him, but Mr. Dinneford stopped, and taking his almost reluctant hand, said, as he grasped it tightly,

"George Granger!" in a voice that had in it a kind of helpless cry.

The young man did not answer, but stood looking at him in a surprised, uncertain way.

"George," said Mr. Dinneford, his utterance broken, "we want you!"

"For what?" asked Granger, whose hand still lay in that of Mr. Dinneford. He had tried to withdraw it at first, but now let it remain.

"To help us find your child."

"My child! What of my child?"

"Your child and Edith's," said Mr. Dinneford. "Come!" and he drew his arm within that of Granger, the two men moving away together. "It has been lost since the day of its birth—cast adrift through the same malign influence that cursed your life and Edith's. We are on its track, but baffled day by day. Oh, George, we want you, frightfully wronged as you have been at our hands—not Edith's. Oh no, George! Edith's heart has never turned from you for an instant, never doubted you, though in her weakness and despair she was driven to sign that fatal application for a divorce. If it were not for the fear of a scornful rejection, she would be reaching out her hands to you now and begging for the old sweet love, but such a rejection would kill her, and she dare not brave the risk."

Mr. Dinneford felt the young man's arm begin to tremble violently.

"We want you, George," he pursued. "Edith's heart is calling out for you, that she may lean it upon your heart, so that it break not in this great trial and suspense. Your lost baby is calling for you out of some garret or cellar or hovel where it lies concealed. Come, my son. The gulf that lies between the dreadful past and the blessed future can be leaped at a single bound if you choose to make it. We want you—Edith and I and your baby want you."

Mr. Dinneford, in his great excitement, was hurrying the young man along at a rapid speed, holding on to his arm at the same time, as if afraid he would pull it away and escape.

Granger made no response, but moved along passively, taking in every word that was said. A great light seemed to break upon his soul, a great mountain to be lifted off. He did not pause at the door from which, when he last stood there, he had been so cruelly rejected, but went in, almost holding his breath, bewildered, uncertain, but half realizing the truth of what was transpiring, like one in a dream.

T. S. Arthur

"Wait here," said Mr. Dinneford, and he left him in the parlor and ran up stairs to find Edith.

George Granger had scarcely time to recognize the objects around him, when a carriage stopped at the door, and in a moment afterward the bell rang violently.

The image that next met his eyes was that of Edith standing in the parlor door with a child all bundled up in bed-clothing held closely in her arms. Her face was trembling with excitement. He started forward on seeing her with an impulse of love and joy that he could not restrain. She saw him, and reading his soul in his eyes, moved to meet him.

"Oh, George, and you too!" she exclaimed. "My baby and my husband, all at once! It is too much. I cannot bear if all!"

Granger caught her in his arms as she threw herself upon him and laid the child against his breast.

"Yours and mine," she sobbed. "Yours and mine, George!" and she put up her face to his. Could he do less than cover it with kisses?

A few hours later, and a small group of very near friends witnessed a different scene from this. Not another tragedy as might well be feared, under the swift reactions that came upon Edith. No, no! She did not die from a excess of joy, but was filled with new life and strength. Two hands broken asunder so violently a few years ago were now clasped again, and the minister of God as he laid them together pronounced in trembling tones the marriage benediction.

This was the scene, and here we drop the curtain

Other books by this author

After A Shadow

After The Storm

Danger; or Wounded in the House of a Friend

Ten Nights in a Bar Room

The Allen House

The Hand But Not the Heart

The Two Wives

Trials and Confessions of a Housekeeper

True Riches

Woman's Trials

T. S. Arthur

Choose from Thousands of 1stWorldLibrary Classics By

A. M. Barnard
Ada Leverson
Adolphus William Ward
Aesop
Agatha Christie
Alexander Aaronsohn
Alexander Kielland
Alexandre Dumas
Alfred Gatty
Alfred Ollivant
Alice Duer Miller
Alice Turner Curtis
Alice Dunbar
Allen Chapman
Alleyne Ireland
Ambrose Bierce
Amelia E. Barr
Amory H. Bradford
Andrew Lang
Andrew McFarland Davis
Andy Adams
Angela Brazil
Anna Alice Chapin
Anna Sewell
Annie Besant
Annie Hamilton Donnell
Annie Payson Call
Annie Roe Carr
Annonaymous
Anton Chekhov
Archibald Lee Fletcher
Arnold Bennett
Arthur C. Benson
Arthur Conan Doyle
Arthur M. Winfield
Arthur Ransome
Arthur Schnitzler
Arthur Train
Atticus
B.H. Baden-Powell
B. M. Bower
B. C. Chatterjee
Baroness Emmuska Orczy
Baroness Orczy
Basil King
Bayard Taylor
Ben Macomber
Bertha Muzzy Bower
Bjornstjerne Bjornson

Booth Tarkington
Boyd Cable
Bram Stoker
C. Collodi
C. E. Orr
C. M. Ingleby
Carolyn Wells
Catherine Parr Traill
Charles A. Eastman
Charles Amory Beach
Charles Dickens
Charles Dudley Warner
Charles Farrar Browne
Charles Ives
Charles Kingsley
Charles Klein
Charles Hanson Towne
Charles Lathrop Pack
Charles Romyn Dake
Charles Whibley
Charles Willing Beale
Charlotte M. Braeme
Charlotte M. Yonge
Charlotte Perkins Stetson
Clair W. Hayes
Clarence Day Jr.
Clarence E. Mulford
Clemence Housman
Confucius
Coningsby Dawson
Cornelis DeWitt Wilcox
Cyril Burleigh
D. H. Lawrence
Daniel Defoe
David Garnett
Dinah Craik
Don Carlos Janes
Donald Keyhoe
Dorothy Kilner
Dougan Clark
Douglas Fairbanks
E. Nesbit
E. P. Roe
E. Phillips Oppenheim
E. S. Brooks
Earl Barnes
Edgar Rice Burroughs
Edith Van Dyne
Edith Wharton

Edward Everett Hale
Edward J. O'Biren
Edward S. Ellis
Edwin L. Arnold
Eleanor Atkins
Eleanor Hallowell Abbott
Eliot Gregory
Elizabeth Gaskell
Elizabeth McCracken
Elizabeth Von Arnim
Ellem Key
Emerson Hough
Emilie F. Carlen
Emily Bronte
Emily Dickinson
Enid Bagnold
Enilor Macartney Lane
Erasmus W. Jones
Ernie Howard Pie
Ethel May Dell
Ethel Turner
Ethel Watts Mumford
Eugene Sue
Eugenie Foa
Eugene Wood
Eustace Hale Ball
Evelyn Everett-green
Everard Cotes
F. H. Cheley
F. J. Cross
F. Marion Crawford
Fannie E. Newberry
Federick Austin Ogg
Ferdinand Ossendowski
Fergus Hume
Florence A. Kilpatrick
Fremont B. Deering
Francis Bacon
Francis Darwin
Frances Hodgson Burnett
Frances Parkinson Keyes
Frank Gee Patchin
Frank Harris
Frank Jewett Mather
Frank L. Packard
Frank V. Webster
Frederic Stewart Isham
Frederick Trevor Hill
Frederick Winslow Taylor

Friedrich Kerst	Hayden Carruth	James Branch Cabell
Friedrich Nietzsche	Helent Hunt Jackson	James DeMille
Fyodor Dostoyevsky	Helen Nicolay	James Joyce
G.A. Henty	Hendrik Conscience	James Lane Allen
G.K. Chesterton	Hendy David Thoreau	James Lane Allen
Gabrielle E. Jackson	Henri Barbusse	James Oliver Curwood
Garrett P. Serviss	Henrik Ibsen	James Oppenheim
Gaston Leroux	Henry Adams	James Otis
George A. Warren	Henry Ford	James R. Driscoll
George Ade	Henry Frost	Jane Abbott
Geroge Bernard Shaw	Henry James	Jane Austen
George Cary Eggleston	Henry Jones Ford	Jane L. Stewart
George Durston	Henry Seton Merriman	Janet Aldridge
George Ebers	Henry W Longfellow	Jens Peter Jacobsen
George Eliot	Herbert A. Giles	Jerome K. Jerome
George Gissing	Herbert Carter	Jessie Graham Flower
George MacDonald	Herbert N. Casson	John Buchan
George Meredith	Herman Hesse	John Burroughs
George Orwell	Hildegard G. Frey	John Cournos
George Sylvester Viereck	Homer	John F. Kennedy
George Tucker	Honore De Balzac	John Gay
George W. Cable	Horace B. Day	John Glasworthy
George Wharton James	Horace Walpole	John Habberton
Gertrude Atherton	Horatio Alger Jr.	John Joy Bell
Gordon Casserly	Howard Pyle	John Kendrick Bangs
Grace E. King	Howard R. Garis	John Milton
Grace Gallatin	Hugh Lofting	John Philip Sousa
Grace Greenwood	Hugh Walpole	John Taintor Foote
Grant Allen	Humphry Ward	Jonas Lauritz Idemil Lie
Guillermo A. Sherwell	Ian Maclaren	Jonathan Swift
Gulielma Zollinger	Inez Haynes Gillmore	Joseph A. Altsheler
Gustav Flaubert	Irving Bacheller	Joseph Carey
H. A. Cody	Isabel Cecilia Williams	Joseph Conrad
H. B. Irving	Isabel Hornibrook	Joseph E. Badger Jr
H. C. Bailey	Israel Abrahams	Joseph Hergesheimer
H. G. Wells	Ivan Turgenev	Joseph Jacobs
H. H. Munro	J. G.Austin	Jules Vernes
H. Irving Hancock	J. Henri Fabre	Julian Hawthrone
H. R. Naylor	J. M. Barrie	Julie A Lippmann
H. Rider Haggard	J. M. Walsh	Justin Huntly McCarthy
H. W. C. Davis	J. Macdonald Oxley	Kakuzo Okakura
Haldeman Julius	J. R. Miller	Karle Wilson Baker
Hall Caine	J. S. Fletcher	Kate Chopin
Hamilton Wright Mabie	J. S. Knowles	Kenneth Grahame
Hans Christian Andersen	J. Storer Clouston	Kenneth McGaffey
Harold Avery	J. W. Duffield	Kate Langley Bosher
Harold McGrath	Jack London	Kate Langley Bosher
Harriet Beecher Stowe	Jacob Abbott	Katherine Cecil Thurston
Harry Castlemon	James Allen	Katherine Stokes
Harry Coghill	James Andrews	L. A. Abbot
Harry Houidini	James Baldwin	L. T. Meade

L. Frank Baum
Latta Griswold
Laura Dent Crane
Laura Lee Hope
Laurence Housman
Lawrence Beasley
Leo Tolstoy
Leonid Andreyev
Lewis Carroll
Lewis Sperry Chafer
Lilian Bell
Lloyd Osbourne
Louis Hughes
Louis Joseph Vance
Louis Tracy
Louisa May Alcott
Lucy Fitch Perkins
Lucy Maud Montgomery
Luther Benson
Lydia Miller Middleton
Lyndon Orr
M. Corvus
M. H. Adams
Margaret E. Sangster
Margret Howth
Margaret Vandercook
Margaret W. Hungerford
Margret Penrose
Maria Edgeworth
Maria Thompson Daviess
Mariano Azuela
Marion Polk Angellotti
Mark Overton
Mark Twain
Mary Austin
Mary Catherine Crowley
Mary Cole
Mary Hastings Bradley
Mary Roberts Rinehart
Mary Rowlandson
M. Wollstonecraft Shelley
Maud Lindsay
Max Beerbohm
Myra Kelly
Nathaniel Hawthrone
Nicolo Machiavelli
O. F. Walton
Oscar Wilde
Owen Johnson
P.G. Wodehouse
Paul and Mabel Thorne

Paul G. Tomlinson
Paul Severing
Percy Brebner
Percy Keese Fitzhugh
Peter B. Kyne
Plato
Quincy Allen
R. Derby Holmes
R. L. Stevenson
R. S. Ball
Rabindranath Tagore
Rahul Alvares
Ralph Bonehill
Ralph Henry Barbour
Ralph Victor
Ralph Waldo Emmerson
Rene Descartes
Ray Cummings
Rex Beach
Rex E. Beach
Richard Harding Davis
Richard Jefferies
Richard Le Gallienne
Robert Barr
Robert Frost
Robert Gordon Anderson
Robert L. Drake
Robert Lansing
Robert Lynd
Robert Michael Ballantyne
Robert W. Chambers
Rosa Nouchette Carey
Rudyard Kipling
Saint Augustine
Samuel B. Allison
Samuel Hopkins Adams
Sarah Bernhardt
Sarah C. Hallowell
Selma Lagerlof
Sherwood Anderson
Sigmund Freud
Standish O'Grady
Stanley Weyman
Stella Benson
Stella M. Francis
Stephen Crane
Stewart Edward White
Stijn Streuvels
Swami Abhedananda
Swami Parmananda
T. S. Ackland

T. S. Arthur
The Princess Der Ling
Thomas A. Janvier
Thomas A Kempis
Thomas Anderton
Thomas Bailey Aldrich
Thomas Bulfinch
Thomas De Quincey
Thomas Dixon
Thomas H. Huxley
Thomas Hardy
Thomas More
Thornton W. Burgess
U. S. Grant
Upton Sinclair
Valentine Williams
Various Authors
Vaughan Kester
Victor Appleton
Victor G. Durham
Victoria Cross
Virginia Woolf
Wadsworth Camp
Walter Camp
Walter Scott
Washington Irving
Wilbur Lawton
Wilkie Collins
Willa Cather
Willard F. Baker
William Dean Howells
William le Queux
W. Makepeace Thackeray
William W. Walter
William Shakespeare
Winston Churchill
Yei Theodora Ozaki
Yogi Ramacharaka
Young E. Allison
Zane Grey